Chapter One

There was something not quite right about Santa Claus.

Anna didn't *see* it so much as *feel* it, a vague uneasiness that spread through her the moment he glanced in her direction. But it was there, and it was unmistakable, and she wondered for a moment if she should call security and have him checked out.

He stood in the middle of the crowded mall, between Anna's shop and a small dress boutique across the aisle, ringing his bell next to a Save the Children donation canister. Something in his eyes said he couldn't care less about the children, however, and for the brief moment he looked at Anna, she was pretty sure his interest lay somewhere else entirely.

Like the area just south of her neck and shoulders.

Anna was in the middle of helping a customer—a gentle old woman who wanted a peach-blossom body care set for her granddaughter—and did her best to ignore Santa's leer, chalking it up to typical

Neanderthal behavior. But Anna had her share of lascivious looks in the past, and this one seemed to go beyond the norm and straight into the realm of creepy.

Was this guy even authorized to be here?

He wasn't your typical holiday bell ringer. Most were retirees looking for something to do, but not this one.

He was about thirty years old, and there was a shady, wanted-poster quality to his demeanor that couldn't be disguised by the floppy hat and the fake white beard. Strip away the red suit and all the padding, and you'd probably find a common street thug underneath.

Maybe Anna wasn't being very charitable herself. Maybe he was just a poor unfortunate who was down on his luck and needed any job he could find. That wasn't unusual in this economy.

After what she'd been through over the past week, Anna would be the first to admit she wasn't in the greatest frame of mind. So maybe she should cut this guy a break.

Still, there was a sense of menace in his look that seemed to say he *wanted* something from her, and the kernel of dread doing somersaults through her stomach right now was not a feeling she could easily ignore.

Just go away, she felt like telling him. *Pack up your stuff and leave.*

And to her surprise, a few minutes later, he did.

ANNA HAD DOUBTS ABOUT coming back to work tonight. Thought it might be too soon. In fact, she didn't normally *work* at night, but with only three days left until Christmas, and a store overflowing with anxious last-minute shoppers, she didn't feel she had a choice.

Trudy had done a wonderful job of covering for her the past week, but it was time for Anna to swallow her grief and get on with her life. If not for herself, then for little Adam. He deserved a normal Christmas.

As normal as it could be, that is.

She also had other matters to consider. Anna's Body Essentials was *her* baby, and with her lease about to expire and her rental fee threatening to increase, she couldn't afford to sit at home obsessing over all the things she could have said or done that might have kept her brother, Owen, alive.

The sheriff's department psychologist had told her that it's typical for the family of suicides to wonder where they might have gone wrong.

"Owen took his life because he *wanted* to," he'd said somberly. "Not because anyone drove him to it. It's unlikely there's any way you could have stopped him, short of catching him in the act."

"My mother thinks that if we'd paid more attention, seen the signs..."

"The signs aren't always evident, Anna. Especially when you only see someone a couple times a week.

Owen probably felt it was his duty to put on a brave face, make everyone believe he was okay. Such behavior isn't atypical."

Anna had listened carefully, nodding politely, more stunned by this turn of events than the psychologist could ever possibly know, but she hadn't said what she was thinking at the time.

That she wasn't entirely convinced that Owen *had* committed suicide.

It just didn't make sense.

Admittedly, her brother had seemed agitated lately, and he hadn't been in the best frame of mind after losing his job. But he was one of the most happy-go-lucky people Anna had ever known, and even if he *was* depressed, she just couldn't believe he'd try to find the solution through a bullet to the head.

Not the Owen Sanford she knew.

She had no proof of this, of course. Just gut instinct. But one thing Anna had learned in her time on this planet was that her instincts were rarely wrong.

When she finally broke down and confessed this belief to the psychologist, however, she was treated as if she were a child with a vivid imagination, her ability to reason clouded by grief.

And who knows? Maybe that was true.

Maybe she hadn't known Owen as well as she thought she had.

AFTER SAYING GOOD-NIGHT to her last customer around 11:00 p.m., Anna closed up shop then spent another hour in her office, catching up on some of the bookkeeping she'd neglected for the past week. As she worked, her gaze drifted to a photo of her brother on the desktop, the one with that smile that always reminded her of their father.

She remembered how strong Owen had been when Daddy had his heart attack. How he had stepped up and become a man in the face of their tragedy, consoling their devastated mother and watching after an eleven-year-old sister who had handled her grief badly by withdrawing from the world, locked in her room, blasting Nirvana at all hours.

That girl was all grown up now, with a three-year-old son and a two-year-old divorce, doing her best to eke out a living as she coped with yet another family tragedy. And the sad irony was that the person she needed most right now was Owen.

Little Adam needed him, too. After the divorce, Owen had taken over as surrogate father, and she knew that his absence in her son's life was a hole about the size of Veterans Memorial Stadium.

A hole that might never be filled.

Anna felt tears in her eyes and knew that this was her cue. She couldn't pretend anymore. She was just going through the motions here and needed to get home.

Shutting down her computer, she grabbed her keys

and her purse and her jacket and let herself out the back door.

Then she navigated the wide hallway to the service elevator, still thinking about Owen and trying very hard not to cry.

THE UNDERGROUND PARKING lot was nearly empty at this hour.

There were maybe five cars total, most of them hidden by shadow. The maintenance down here was shoddy at best and half the fluorescent bulbs were either dead or on life support. It was the *employees* lot, after all, and who cared about the employees?

Anna was almost to her car, a gray Ford sedan, her footsteps reverberating against the cement walls, when she thought she saw a flicker of movement in the corner of her eye.

She paused, turned, found nothing there. But that didn't keep her heartbeat from kicking up a notch.

Was she alone?

Feeling the sudden need to move quickly, she continued on toward her car, fumbling for her keys as she went, pressing the remote to unlock it. A moment later she was at the door, about to open it, thinking she was just being silly and paranoid, when—

—wham—

—a pair of hands grabbed her from behind, pushing her back toward the aisle. Headlights came

alive in a dark corner and a battered green van shot toward her.

Anna tried to twist away. Saw that her attacker was none other than *Santa Claus,* still wearing that ridiculous hat and white beard—his face hard, his eyes as empty as the parking lot—and she knew immediately that she was in *very big trouble.*

"Where is it?" he hissed. "Where's the button?"

This surprised Anna. She had no earthly idea what he was talking about. She sputtered something unintelligible, the dread she'd felt earlier coming back like a blow to the belly.

She tried again to twist away, but he kept shoving her into the aisle.

"We know he gave it to you—*where is it?*"

He shoved her hard and she slammed against the side of the van, which was directly in front of them now. Reaching out, he gripped a handle, slid the door open then grabbed her again and pushed her toward the seats inside.

"Get in."

"Please," she cried, "I don't understand what you want from me."

"The hell you don't." Anna heard a soft *snick.* Santa had popped his switchblade. He pointed it at her throat. "Get in, sugar lips, or I'll cut you right—"

There was a roar behind them—a rumbling, beefy engine coming to life, filling the parking lot with the sound of a jet taking off.

They both turned and saw a large black motorcycle emerge from the shadows. It rocketed straight toward them and didn't slow down, the driver's face hidden by his helmet and visor.

Santa's eyes went wide and he grabbed Anna by her jacket and spun her around, pushing her directly into the bike's path.

Then he was scrambling into the van, shouting "Go! Go! Go!" as Anna stumbled forward and lost her footing, falling to her knees.

Pain shot through her as her kneecaps pounded into the asphalt. The bike roared straight for her, its lone headlight illuminating her terrified face. Then it quickly veered to the right, its driver laying the machine on its side as he struggled to maintain some kind of control.

The bike skidded into a cement post, crashing to an abrupt halt, but the rider had already jumped free and rolled to his feet. He pulled a gun from the small of his back as he started running toward the van.

The van peeled out, laying a long patch of rubber, the squeal so loud it pierced Anna's eardrums like feedback, as the man in the motorcycle helmet raised his gun.

But before he could fire, the van screeched around a corner and up the exit ramp, disappearing from sight.

The man in the helmet looked as if he might squeeze off a shot anyway, but then he lowered the

gun, tucked it under his leather jacket and turned toward Anna.

Seeing that she was still on her knees, he moved quickly and helped her to her feet.

"Are you all right?"

Anna nodded, wincing against the pain, and looked up at him as he reached for the visor and raised it.

She had expected to see a stranger, forever grateful that he had intervened, but to her utter astonishment the man looking back at her was someone she knew.

Intimately.

She hadn't seen him in four long years, but it was a face so achingly familiar that she suddenly felt her legs weaken, thinking for a moment that she might collapse again.

All at once her heart began to thump wildly against her chest and she couldn't quite breathe as shock began to overcome her.

He smiled at her then, a smile laced with a hint of melancholy, a subtle sadness reflected in his intense blue eyes—eyes that spoke of a history between them that would never be forgotten.

"How've you been, Anna?"

It was Brody Carpenter.

Owen's best friend.

The man she had once hoped to marry.

Chapter Two

Anna didn't know where even to begin.

After all these years she had pretty much given up on ever seeing Brody again. Had halfway convinced herself that he was either dead or living under an alias somewhere, never to be found.

Her life with him seemed to be part of some vague, half-imagined fantasy relegated to a part of her mind she rarely visited. Surely no more than once or twice a day.

Yet here he stood in front of her. Not an illusion, but a living, breathing human being who didn't look much different from how she remembered him. The same rugged jawline, the same hard, angular body. The wide shoulders. The strong hands. Towering over her as he always had.

She suddenly felt as if she'd been hurtled into the past—a feeling that was both exhilarating and unsettling. She couldn't decide whether to slap him across the face or throw her arms around him and hug him

as if he were a soldier who had just returned home from the war.

In the end, she did neither.

Brody Carpenter. A name that had sent shivers of pleasure through her ever since the day she first met him, nearly fifteen years ago. A name he had once promised to share with her.

Before he broke her heart.

Anna tried to speak, but she could barely put together a sentence. "What… What are you doing here?"

"Saving your life, I think. Those idiots looked like they meant business."

"I mean what are you doing in Cedarwood? We all thought you were—"

"Dead?"

She nodded. Then shook her head. "No. No, I never really thought that."

"I wouldn't blame you if you did," he said.

Anna stared at him. "It's just you disappeared so suddenly after the trial, and every time we tried to contact you, you'd either changed your number or moved on, and…"

She couldn't finish. The thought was too exhausting. Too painful. All the heartbreak she'd felt back then was bubbling up to the surface, compounding the grief she'd been battling ever since Owen died.

Then she realized that this was why Brody was here.

He'd heard about Owen.

Somehow word had gotten to him that his best friend since high school, the boy who had played wide receiver to his quarterback, had taken his own life.

But before she could ask him about this, a door near the service elevator boomed open.

“Hands! Show us your hands!”

Two security guards stood near the stairwell, out of breath, their weapons leveled directly at Brody.

He slowly raised his hands to show them empty. “Easy, boys. Take it easy.”

“Don’t move,” one of the guards warned.

Anna knew him. Barely out of his teens, he looked as nervous as a kid facing off against a gang of bullies, and she was afraid he might get stupid and actually pull the trigger.

“You okay, Ms. Sanford? We saw him grab you on the surveillance cameras. The sheriff’s on the way.”

“He’s not the one you’re after,” Anna said. “Put your guns down or somebody might get hurt.”

The kid considered this, glancing at Brody’s fallen motorcycle before returning his gaze to Anna. “You sure you’re okay?”

“Still in one piece, thanks to him.”

The guard spent a long moment evaluating the situation then finally holstered his gun. His partner followed suit.

Relieved, Anna released a long, shaky breath.

"Thank you," she said.

WHEN THE SHERIFF'S patrol car glided into the lot, the young guard crossed toward it, waving his hands to let the deputies know that everything was under control.

The car came to a stop in the middle of the aisle. As the deputies climbed out, one of them took a look at Brody, his eyes lighting up in surprise and delight.

"Carpenter? Is that you?"

"That's the rumor," Brody said then shook the deputy's hand. "Good to see you, Brett."

Anna wasn't surprised that they knew each other. Before dropping off the face of the earth, Brody Carpenter had been one of Cedarwood, Iowa's finest sheriff's deputies. A man destined for great things.

Until it all went seriously wrong.

"Man, we all figured you were dead," the deputy said. "Where the heck you been for the past four years?"

"It would probably take that long to explain," Brody told him.

"Can't say I blame you for disappearing like you did. Brass did everything they could to make an example of you. Scared the heck out of all of us."

Anna had no doubt that Brody still had a lot friends in the department, many of whom knew—just as she

had—that he'd gotten a raw deal. He'd been accused of destroying evidence against a local drug kingpin and taking a payoff for the effort.

The county undersheriff had forced him to resign long before the case against him had been fully evaluated, and despite his eventual acquittal, Anna knew that Brody had considered it a matter that should never have come to trial. There were people on the force who were working against him, he'd told her, trying to destroy the dream he'd carried with him since he was a boy.

And they had succeeded. Their cynicism and petty politics ultimately won, even if the prosecutor hadn't. Rather than reinstate Brody to a job that he more than deserved—a job he had earned and excelled at—his bosses had turned their backs on him. Proclaimed him guilty despite what the jury had decided.

He was a tarnished warrior, and Anna knew better than anyone that the entire ordeal had deeply wounded him. She'd felt his pain more than even *he* could know.

But that wasn't an excuse to run away. To abandon your friends and the woman you love. And as relieved as she was to see him, to know that he was safe, she wasn't sure she'd ever be able to forgive him.

Where *had* he been for the past four years?

And why hadn't *she* been with him?

As Brody and the deputy dredged up old memories, he glanced at her and she once again felt her

heart stutter, a feeling she'd never been able to control. His look was so full of regret that it took everything she had to keep from crying.

She wanted to punch him, kiss him, scream at him, make love to him, tell him to go back to wherever he came from and stay there—all at the same time.

She didn't need this now. Couldn't handle it. She was normally a strong woman, but at that moment the world seemed to be caving in on her—Owen, the attack, now Brody—and she began to wonder about her capacity to stay upright. She felt dizzy and her vision seemed to narrow.

"I have to sit down," she said suddenly, and before the words were fully out of her mouth, Brody took her by the arm, helping her to the asphalt as the others crowded around her to see if she was okay.

"I'm fine," she told them. "I'll be all right. I just feel a little faint."

As if this was the kick in the butt they needed, the deputies now got down to business, Brett pulling a notepad out of his back pocket and asking Brody to give him a run-through of the incident.

The other deputy took the two guards aside to question them, as well.

Anna listened as Brody explained that he'd seen her get off the elevator and head for her car, when a guy in a Santa suit popped up out of nowhere and

grabbed her. Then instinct kicked in and Brody did what had to be done.

"I just wish they hadn't gotten away," he said.

"Did you get a tag number?"

Brody shook his head. "I'm a little out of practice. And everything happened so fast."

"I'm curious," the deputy said. "Why were you even down here? Was Anna expecting you?"

Brody glanced at her again. He seemed a bit thrown by the question, but he recovered quickly.

"I was waiting for her. Hoping to get the chance to talk to her. About Owen."

"Owen?"

"My brother," Anna explained. "He died a few days ago."

"I'm sorry to hear that. My condolences." He looked from one to the other. "So this guy in the Santa Claus suit. Do either of you have any idea who he is?"

They both shook their heads. "Not a clue," Anna said. "But he seemed to want something from me. Kept asking me about a button."

"Button? What kind of button?"

"I have no idea. I don't know what he was talking about."

"What about the driver? Either of you get a look at him?"

Again they shook their heads.

"Well, we'll take a gander at the surveillance foot-

age. Hopefully we'll find something useful, but with this lousy lighting down here, I'm not counting on it." He turned to Anna. "Can you think of anyone who would want to harm you?"

Anna didn't have to think. The answer was a resounding *no.* Her life was wrapped up in the shop and Adam, and her potential to make enemies was, at best, slim. She had absolutely no idea why Santa had grabbed her.

She remembered the creepy leer he'd given her as he rang that bell outside her shop, but she never thought it would come to this.

She suddenly wondered if he'd been stalking her. And that put a whole new spin on things.

She'd been scared before, but now she was petrified.

What if he came back?

She told them about the earlier encounter, and the deputy assured her that they'd be speaking to mall management to find out if anyone could identify the guy.

"I'd like to be in on that," Brody said. "Get a look at the surveillance footage myself."

The deputy hesitated. "I'm sure we'll have video for you, but you're a witness, Brody—you know we can't let you get involved in the investigation. Besides, it isn't really up to me. I'm just the responding deputy."

"But you'll keep us apprised?"

Us? Anna thought. Was there suddenly an *us* now?

The presumption annoyed her. Did Brody think that he could show up out of the blue and immediately resume where they'd left off?

There *was* no us as far as she was concerned. Despite her mixed emotions, she at least knew that much. And at that moment she realized just how angry with him she really was. Even if he *had* saved her life.

Her light-headedness abruptly gone, she pushed herself off the asphalt and stood. As Brody moved to help her, she shifted away from him.

"I'm fine," she said curtly, and she could see by his reaction that he was both startled and hurt.

But she didn't care. His hurt couldn't possibly compare to what she'd gone through after he left.

The deputy, sensing the tension between them, said, "I think that's enough questions from me, but we got a call on the way in that a detective is already headed to the scene. I'm sure he'll have a few of his own."

As if on cue, a sleek white sedan turned a corner and rolled down the aisle toward them.

"Speak of the devil."

As the sedan drew closer, Anna saw the driver and thought for a moment that her head might just explode.

Could this night get any more complicated?

Whatever gods were conspiring against her, they

must have been mightily amused. She couldn't quite believe who had been dispatched to the scene, and she was convinced that it was no accident.

Despite its size, Cedarwood, Iowa, was starting to feel like a very small town.

The sedan came to a stop, then the engine shut down and two plainclothes sheriff's detectives climbed out, the driver buttoning his suit coat as he sauntered toward them, a look of concern on his face.

"You all right, babe?"

Hail, hail, the gang's all here, Anna thought.

It was her ex-husband, Frank.

Chapter Three

When the two detectives stepped out of the cruiser, Brody felt his whole body go stiff. The last thing he needed right now was an encounter with Frank Matson.

While he'd known that coming back to Cedarwood would dredge up a lot of old emotions and hostilities, he hadn't expected it all to happen in one night. He marveled at how cruel fate could sometimes be, and he knew that Anna was probably feeling it, too.

Matson's concentration centered on her, genuine concern in his eyes. "You all right, babe?"

It took him a moment to finally look at Brody, and when he did, the world seemed to stop for a moment as the reality of what he'd just walked into began to sink in.

"Carpenter?"

"The one and only," Brody said. "How you been, Frank?"

Matson's concern abruptly vanished, replaced by a hardness that betrayed his utter contempt for Brody.

They had been rivals since high school—rivals for Anna's heart, to be precise—and Brody had a hard time reconciling the fact that Anna had not only been married to the man but given birth to his child.

But then a lot had happened in his absence.

And whose fault was that?

Matson frowned at him. "What are you doing here, Carpenter? Are you part of this?"

"Meaning what?"

Matson moved in close. "Meaning if you've done anything to hurt Anna..."

Brody didn't back away. "You see any cuffs on me?"

"Oh, for God's sakes," Anna said. "Both of you, stop it. You don't see each other in years and you just pick up where you left off?"

Matson backed down first. "Sorry, babe, you're right."

"Quit calling me that."

He threw his hands up. "All right, all right. You're upset, I understand. But I hear over the radio that someone at the mall has been attacked and the name Sanford comes up, you might understand why *I'm* a little upset, too. Did they hurt you?"

"No. Thanks to Brody."

Matson shifted his gaze again. "Your knight in shining armor. I guess things never really change."

Brody felt heat rising in his chest. "Look, Frank, I've got no beef with you. Do we need to make an

unpleasant situation even worse? If you care about Anna—"

"If *I* care about her?" His eyebrows went up. "I'm the one who picked up the pieces when you left her behind, hotshot. And I don't know if you remember, but I supported you. Told the undersheriff that Internal Affairs had the wrong guy." He shook his head in disgust. "That support stopped the minute you ran out on Anna."

Brody said nothing. There wasn't much he *could* say. Matson was right. He could try to explain that he'd been in a strange place at the time, that he hadn't been thinking straight and just needed to get away from Cedarwood and all the whispers. People thinking he was dirty and had just gotten lucky.

But Matson had never been the kind of guy who would understand such things. He had one switch: on and off. And if you didn't conform to his narrow view of the world, you were the object of his derision.

And maybe Brody deserved that.

"Look," he said. "I don't want to argue with you."

"Of course you don't. Things get too hot for Brody Carpenter, he'll hop on his little motor scooter and run for the—"

"*Stop!*" Anna said.

She turned away, moving across the aisle toward her car, and Matson immediately followed her, stopping her before she reached it. Brody watched as he

took her aside, trying to console her, calm her down. He could plainly see that Matson still cared for her.

Brody didn't know what had gone wrong between them, but it was clear that Frank wasn't over it yet. Not by a long shot.

Who could blame him? Anna wasn't the type of woman you get over.

Brody never had.

But he was the outsider here. The intruder. And despite their differences, he could see that she was in good hands with Matson. Maybe he should just back off and let the department do what it did best.

For now, at least.

Moving to his Harley, he lifted it off the asphalt and checked it for damage—some scrapes and dings. He'd pulled it out of storage three days ago and was surprised to discover how much he'd missed riding it.

He approached his old buddy Brett, who was huddled in conversation with Frank's partner, Joe Wilson. Wilson's contempt for him seemed even deeper than Frank's.

"Why are you here, Carpenter?"

"Just doing a friend a favor. You think I can cut out now? I already gave Brett my statement."

Wilson narrowed his eyes at him. "Guards tell us you used a piece tonight. You still got a carry permit?"

Brody nodded. "I'm up-to-date. Not sure why I kept renewing it, but I did."

"Yeah, well you better believe we'll be checking into that. You staying some place we can reach you?"

"The Motor Court Inn. On Sycamore."

"Get out of here," Wilson said. "Can't stand the sight of you anyway."

Brody let the comment pass. He nodded to Brett then climbed on his bike and started it up. The thunderous roar filled the parking lot, getting Anna and Matson's attention. Anna looked at him expectantly.

Their gazes connected, but Brody couldn't read her as he used to.

She was still as beautiful as ever, and he'd been a fool to leave her behind. A selfish, unthinking fool. Seeing her like this only drove that point home. There were no words, no deeds, that could make up for what he'd done to her. No path to redemption.

He deserved her scorn. Matson's, too.

Grabbing the throttle, he gave them a nod then roared out of the parking lot. That look in Anna's eyes just about broke his aching heart.

FRANK INSISTED ON taking her home.

Anna was too keyed up to resist, so she gave him the keys to her car and let him drive as Joe Wilson followed in the cruiser.

They were silent for most of the ride, Anna running the night's events through her head over and over again, still vacillating between elation and anger over Brody's sudden reappearance.

As she had watched him ride away tonight, she had wondered if another handful of years would pass before she'd see him again.

She remembered how Brody had hesitated when the deputy asked why he was in the parking lot. He'd mentioned Owen, but Anna got the feeling that there was more to it than that. As if there was a specific purpose for his presence there.

But *what,* exactly?

Owen's funeral had come and gone, and there was nothing anyone could do to bring him back. So why was Brody here?

To torture her?

If so, he was succeeding admirably, and as grateful as she was that he'd saved her life, she'd be in a much better place emotionally if her rescuer had turned out to be a kindhearted stranger.

Frank finally broke the silence. "You okay?"

Anna closed her eyes, almost smiled. An involuntary reaction to an impossible situation. There was no humor behind it at all. "I swear if somebody asks me that one more time tonight, I may scream."

"I'm concerned about you—is that so bad?"

"If you were concerned about me, you'd do what I asked you to do."

He looked at her. "You mean Owen?"

She nodded.

"Come on, babe, we've been over this how many times? I know it's hard, but sooner or later you're going to have to accept the simple fact that your brother killed himself. And the sooner you do, the faster you'll heal."

"I can see you're really broken up about it."

Frank frowned. "Don't do that. You know I liked Owen. The point is, if I thought there was even a shred of evidence that he was the victim of foul play…"

"You'd what?" Anna asked. "Make a notation in a report and file it away somewhere?"

"That isn't fair."

"I'm tired of being fair. And I'm tired of people telling me I'm crazy. Owen would never hurt himself. He wouldn't do that to me, or Mom, or to Adam."

Frank sighed. "I'm not trying to be an insensitive jerk here, Anna, but do you know how many times I've heard people say that? I must do death notifications for a dozen suicides every year, and I can't tell you how many of them end with some family member saying exactly what you just said."

"Fine. But were any of those family members attacked by a guy in a parking lot?"

Frank frowned again. "What's that got to do with it?"

"The guy wanted something from me, Frank."

"Yeah. The same thing every guy since junior high has wanted."

"No. I told you what he said about the button."

"Right. Complete and utter nonsense."

"Is it?"

Frank took his gaze from the road and stared at her. "Isn't it? You think you know what he was talking about?"

Anna shook her head. "I don't have a clue. But that wasn't all of it. He also said, '*I know he gave it to you.*'"

"Meaning what?"

Anna was silent for a moment. This was something that had been quietly working at the periphery of her mind ever since Santa had said it.

"What if this button is something that he thinks Owen gave me? Something that Owen himself was killed for?"

Frank was looking at the road again, but she could see by the subtle hardening of his jaw that he wasn't buying this at all.

Then he said, "Anna, I think you need to consider talking to the sheriff's psychologist again."

"Don't shut me out, Frank. That's the last thing I need right now."

"I'm not shutting you out. I'm trying to help you."

"By telling me I'm certifiable?"

Frank sighed and nudged the wheel, pulling up to the curb in front of Anna's house.

Then he turned to her. "That's not what I'm saying, and you know it. Let's pretend for a moment that you're right about this button thing. Did Owen ever mention it to you?"

Anna thought about it, shook her head.

"Did he ever give you something to keep? To hide for him?"

"No," Anna said. "Nothing."

"You're sure about that?"

"As sure as I can be."

Frank took his hands off the wheel, put one on her shoulder. It was meant to be a gesture of support and reassurance, but Anna was long past being reassured by his touch. If she ever had been.

"Look, babe, I know this whole thing has been tough for you, but you've gotta get your head on straight about your brother. Even if I thought there was foul play, I don't have the authority to reopen his case."

"Why am I not surprised?" She pulled away from him and opened her door. The cold December air filled the car as she held out a hand, palm up. "I'll take my keys now."

Frank ignored the request. "What I *can* do," he said, "is catch the punks who attacked you tonight. And if this button business has anything to do with Owen at all—and I'm not saying it does—I'll try to

convince the brass that we need to take another look at his suicide."

This was the first sliver of hope Anna had gotten out of him, and her anger suddenly dissolved. "Is that a promise?"

"Cross my heart and hope to die."

She managed a smile. Genuine this time. "Thank you, Frank."

He shrugged. "You'll always be my girl."

It was a phrase he'd used over and over again during their marriage. One that had turned out to be decidedly untrue, but she didn't feel the need to remind him of that. No point in stirring that particular fire.

He took her keys from the ignition and handed them to her. "I don't think it's anything to worry about, but I'll have a unit patrol the area, to make sure you guys are safe."

She nodded her thanks and was about to climb out when she had a sudden thought. "Adam's asleep, but I bet he'd be happy to wake up long enough to say good-night. You want to come up for a minute?"

Frank's expression darkened. "It's late and I need to get home. Maybe some other time."

Then they were out of the car, Frank moving to his cruiser to join Joe. She watched them drive away, wondering how much more emotional turmoil she could go through before she collapsed under the weight of it all.

Collapsing wasn't an option, however. She needed to be strong for Adam. To follow up on her promise to herself and make this as normal a Christmas as she possibly could.

So far that wasn't working out too well.

Maybe life would look a little brighter tomorrow.

MOM WAS ASLEEP ON THE sofa, the TV tuned to a shopping channel. The woman on-screen was hawking a bath and body set that Anna sold for nearly twice the price in her shop. Between the internet and these discount shows, it was a wonder she could make a living at all. Maybe she should join the modern age, open a website and throw customer service out the window.

Anna took off her jacket and hung it on the coat stand. Grabbing a blanket from the pile next to the armchair, she laid it over her mother then gently kissed her forehead. She didn't want to wake her. Mom had been having a rough time of it, too, and sleep was therapeutic.

After turning off the TV, she went upstairs to check in on Adam. His night-light was on, and he was curled up into a tight little ball atop his bed, hugging the toy sheriff's car that Owen had given him for his third birthday.

The sight almost broke Anna's heart.

She moved to the bed, carefully pried it from his

arms and set it next to him on the pillow. Pulling the blankets up around him, she tucked him in, kissed his cheek and thought about how blessed she was to have him.

He was her life. Her reason to be strong. When he smiled, she smiled. When he laughed, she laughed. And when he cried…

Helping him heal was more important than anything else right now.

She placed her palm against his narrow chest, feeling it rise and fall, hoping that his dreams were good ones. She was about to turn back to the door when she heard a car outside and went to the window, staring down at the street below.

As Frank had promised, a sheriff's patrol unit approached, slowing as it reached the house. The deputy shone a light across the yard before picking up speed and moving on.

But as it rolled away, Anna's gaze was drawn to a nearby street lamp and the pool of light beneath it.

There was a familiar-looking black motorcycle parked there. A Harley.

As the patrol car rounded the corner, the shadows behind the bike began to shift, and Anna once again felt her heart kick up as all the emotions she'd been battling tonight renewed their relentless attack on her.

Then Brody Carpenter stepped into the light and looked up toward the window.

Chapter Four

She was out the door and crossing toward him before she could even think. She'd forgotten her jacket, and the night air bit into her. She hugged herself to keep from shivering.

"What are you doing out here, Brody?"

He gestured to the porch behind her. "You left your door hanging open. Not a good idea."

"What do you want from me?"

"Same as that patrol unit," he said. "To make sure you're safe."

"Is that why you were at the mall tonight?"

He nodded. "More or less."

"So why *now?* You didn't seem to care much four years ago."

She could see that the words hit home, but she didn't regret them. Rational or not, the resentment she felt outweighed any gratitude she had for what he'd done tonight.

"I'm not here to ask for forgiveness," he said.

"Africa's away, all right."

"It didn't start there. That's just where I wound up."

"So where did you go?"

"My first stop was New York. I figured I could get lost in the crowd there, be as anonymous as possible. Nobody looking at me as if I were a disappointment."

Anna frowned. "Is that what you thought? That I considered you a disappointment?"

"No, not you. But a lot of people in Cedarwood did. People I once considered friends."

"You were *acquitted,* Brody. Everyone knew that."

The kettle started to boil. Anna turned off the burner then poured hot water into two cups and dunked a tea bag into each.

"Maybe so," Brody said, "but it sure didn't feel that way. My career was finished, I couldn't get work and I just didn't want to be a burden to anyone. Especially you. So I wound up in New York. And after a few months there, I ran into an old college friend who set me up overseas. In London."

Anna carried the cups to the table, a renewed look of surprise on her face. "London? What did you do there?"

"Bodyguard work, mostly."

"For who?"

"I had a lot of clients. Actors, businessmen, politicians. You ever heard of Clive Banks?"

She nodded. "The movie star."

"I worked for him on and off for a couple years. Premiere parties, public appearances, that kind of thing."

Anna sipped her tea. "I'd already given up on you by then. I was desperate to talk to you, and Owen had been trying to find you for months, but…"

She let the words trail and Brody once again felt guilt overcoming him. "I guess that's when Frank stepped in?"

"Can you blame him? He'd always had a thing for me. Ever since freshman year."

"Believe me, I know. And you?"

She hesitated. "Finish your story."

Brody finally took a sip of his own tea, its welcome warmth radiating through his body. "Between gigs with Banks, I started doing work for a British MP. One day I was sent to do the advance security for a humanitarian trip to a refugee camp in Chad, and when I got there, I was pretty devastated by what I saw."

The disenfranchised families, the hungry children. The desperation in their eyes.

"I guess I felt a kind of kinship with the people there. Their lives uprooted by genocide. My own problems were so pale in comparison, it wasn't even funny." He took another sip. "So I quit the security

gig right then and there. Joined in the effort to pull refugees out of Darfur and smuggle them across the border. And that's what I'd just finished doing when Owen's message came."

"When was this?"

"Less than a week ago."

"He was already dead by then."

Brody nodded. "I didn't know that at the time, but yeah, the message probably passed through several different hands before it got to me. A Red Cross worker had tried to deliver it earlier, but I was in Darfur. I took the first flight home, but by the time I got here Owen was already gone."

"So what was the message? What did he say?"

"Why don't I show you?"

Reaching into his shirt pocket, Brody pulled out a small slip of paper. He had folded and unfolded it so many times in the past few days that it was threatening to fall apart.

"It's brief and to the point," he said, "but it's the reason I'm here."

He handed it to Anna and she pulled it open, staring down at the words that had been written by a stranger's hand, dictated over a static-filled phone line from several thousand miles away.

Brody knew those words by heart:

Trouble. Too late for me.
Protect Anna.
Owen

ANNA SUCKED IN A BREATH.

These words only confirmed what she had suspected all along: Owen *hadn't* committed suicide. He'd been in trouble and someone had murdered him and staged the whole thing to make it look as if he'd shot himself in his own bed.

She had been right to question the official findings, and this note was proof of that.

Her scalp prickled and something toxic blossomed in her stomach, spreading through her bloodstream, making her whole body go numb.

"My God," she said. "We have to show this to Frank."

Brody shook his head. "Consider the source. He's never thought much of me and he'll probably think I'm running some kind of scam."

"Well, I don't. And he'll listen to me."

"Oh? Has he so far?"

The question gave Anna pause.

"You knew Owen better than anyone," Brody said, "and I can't believe this is the first time you've considered he didn't take his own life. You must have mentioned it to Frank."

She nodded. "He thinks my doubts are all part of the grieving process, but this should convince him he's wrong."

"Come on, Anna, you know how he is. He'll take one look at that thing and either call foul or claim it's some kind of suicide note."

Anna looked at the worn sheet of paper again.

Trouble.

Too late for me.

If you read these words with the preconceived notion that Owen had killed himself, then yes, Brody was right. But there were other things to consider, as well.

"What about the men who attacked me?" she asked. "I told Frank I thought they had something to do with Owen."

"And I have no doubt that they did. But I'd lay odds that if you show Frank that note, it'll only convince him he's right." Brody paused. "Worse yet, he may try to stop us from finding out what really happened."

Anna's heart froze in her chest.

Had he really just said what she thought he had?

"What are you telling me?"

"I may be a little rusty, but I still know my way around an investigation, and I still know how to follow my instincts."

"Then you'll look into Owen's death?"

"My first priority is protecting you. Just like your brother asked me to. So you've got a bodyguard whether you want one or not."

"I don't care about me," she said. "What about Owen?"

Brody looked directly at her now, his expression dark, his gaze unwavering, and she knew he wasn't

playing games, wasn't making idle conversation or halfhearted promises.

He was deadly serious. And anyone listening to him should pay very close attention.

"As far as I'm concerned," he said, "the best friend I ever had was brutally murdered in his own home. And I'm not about to let those punks get away with it."

Chapter Five

Anna had offered to put him up in Owen's room, but Brody wasn't about to let himself be confined.

He wasn't here for a sleepover.

His mission was to protect and defend, and if Anna's attackers were to track her here and show up in the middle of the night, he needed to be ready for them. He didn't expect another attempt so soon, but it didn't hurt to be prepared.

After telling Anna to get her mother safely into her own room, Brody took one of the kitchen chairs to the upstairs hallway and stationed himself near a window overlooking the street.

It was past two in the morning when they finally said good-night, and the sky seemed darker somehow, as if a storm might be coming. Cedarwood had thankfully been free of snow since Brody had arrived, but he had to wonder if it would soon be falling, or if the turbulence in the air was a signal of another kind of storm altogether.

Brody decided to allow himself to doze, but noth-

ing more than that. Catnaps would keep him fresh and alert. The tea would help, too, but before they'd left the kitchen, Anna had surprised him by preparing a thermos full of coffee for him.

It was a ritual she had performed at least a hundred times in the past, back when they had lived together in their small apartment downtown. Brody would be heading out on night patrol and Anna would stand by the doorway, holding the thermos out to him.

"Come back to me in one piece," she'd say then pull him into an embrace, kissing him, pressing her body against his as if to remind him what he'd be coming home to.

Not that he'd ever needed a reminder.

This time, however, there was no embrace. No press of the body. She had filled the thermos and set it on the kitchen table without comment, not quite willing to look him in the eye—as if she, too, remembered those nights but wasn't sure she really wanted to.

Brody's regret was a festering wound in his gut. He knew it did him no good to obsess over the past, but if there was one thing he could change, one course of action he could go back to and revise…

Leaving her was his greatest mistake.

As he settled into the chair, the sheriff's patrol car did another drive-by. If it were up to him, the deputy would be sitting at the curb all night, but the

department was undoubtedly stretched thin. This was the best they could do.

He watched the car pass then sat back, looking toward the long hallway in front of him—the bathroom at the far end, the carpeted stairs to the left, the closed bedroom doors on the right.

The Sanford family home hadn't changed much over the years. He'd been up here many times as a teenager. First with Owen, the two of them reading comic books and playing video games, talking about girls at school. Then later with Anna, sneaking into her room late at night. A time that played in an endless loop in his mind: the anxious moments, the quiet kisses, the feverish exploration of each other's body. The feeling that they could never get enough.

Could never *give* enough.

Brody looked at Anna's bedroom door and saw light seeping out from the crack beneath it.

Still awake.

He couldn't help wondering what she was thinking as she lay in bed. About Owen, no doubt. About the men who had attacked her.

About him?

No matter how he tried, he couldn't keep from imagining himself throwing that door open and crossing toward her, tearing at his clothes as he moved, then pulling her off the bed and into his arms.

Feeling her lips pressed against his.

Her warm flesh…

He knew it was a pipe dream. Nothing more. But something ached inside him, a deep carnal desire that was difficult to ignore. It took everything he had to stay seated in that chair.

He had returned to Cedarwood three days ago and had been watching Anna from a distance ever since. He had told himself that he was merely fulfilling Owen's last wish, had come here only as a favor to his fallen friend.

But he knew that he was really here for Anna.

While he was gone, he'd kept tabs on her. Knew that she had married Frank and they'd had a son. He'd be the first to admit that he'd envied his old rival, had been torn apart knowing that Frank was sharing Anna's bed and raising her child. When word of the divorce finally reached him, he'd been saddened for her but overjoyed for himself, even though he knew he'd never take advantage of the situation. Returning home was not an option at the time. He had no desire to exploit Anna's loss, and there was too much pain involved for everyone concerned. Too much history.

But Owen's note had changed everything. Had given him an excuse to come home again.

Trouble. Too late for me.

Protect Anna.

That was his mantra now. Protecting Anna.

And finding the men who sent her brother to an early grave.

HE STRETCHED AT REGULAR intervals, but after a while, he realized he couldn't sit any longer. Too much nervous energy. He could blame the coffee, but he didn't think that was it.

He went downstairs and checked windows and doors as he turned the events of the night over and over in his mind, thinking about what he'd seen and heard as he sat on his Harley in the shadows of the mall's underground parking lot—

—Anna walking to her car.

—Santa Claus grabbing her.

—Her startled yelp as he pushed her toward the van, his voice echoing—

"The button. Where's the button?"

Santa had seemed desperate for an answer, and Brody wanted one, too.

What exactly *was* this button?

The only thing that came to mind were the buttons on a shirt, or a campaign souvenir, or maybe the power switch on a piece of electronic equipment. Or if you really wanted to stretch it: the protective knob on the end of a fencing foil—how was that for an obscure bit of knowledge?

Yet none of these fit.

"I know he gave it to you. Where is it?"

The *he* being Owen, of course. A point that Brody and Anna had agreed on when they rehashed the event.

Who else could it be? And if these creeps had known Owen well enough to make such an accusation, then Brody could only conclude that his friend had somehow gotten himself involved in some very bad business.

Trouble.

Too late for me.

But *why* was it too late? What had Owen done? What did he know that had pitted him against these men?

Had he stolen from them? Was this button a rare artifact of some kind? An antique that was valuable enough to kill for? Enough to make grabbing Anna seem like a reasonable way to obtain it?

And if this were true, and if Owen had passed it on to her, then why didn't Anna know this? Why was she completely clueless about it?

Brody had met Owen when they were juniors in high school. Brody's family had recently moved from another district, and he and Owen had become fast friends when they both tried out for the varsity football team.

After practice most days, they would grab sodas from a nearby Frostee's then hike across the street

to the comic book store to stock up on the latest releases.

But Brody's interest in comic books disappeared the moment he met Anna. She was sixteen years old and had just returned from a semester abroad, part of a student-exchange program.

Brody could remember that moment with exquisite clarity. He was sitting on Owen's bedroom floor, poring over the latest issue of X-Men, when the door flew open and Anna stood framed in the doorway.

"Hey, Owen, guess who's…"

The words caught in her throat, and Brody knew she was surprised to see a strange boy sitting on her brother's floor. Owen had gone to the bathroom, so it was just Brody and Anna, staring at each other awkwardly.

But Brody immediately liked what he saw.

Anna was not only flawless in just about every way, but she had startling blue eyes that seemed to see things that most girls her age couldn't. Maybe it was the trip to Europe, but she carried herself with a kind of feminine sophistication that Brody wasn't used to, and he instantly fell in love.

As he thought about that moment, he couldn't quite fathom how he had managed to screw things up with her. He also realized that his mind was starting to drift. He needed to focus on the crime now, focus on that button.

What had his friend gotten himself into?

HE WAS BACK IN THE CHAIR and dozing by 6:00 a.m. A sound awoke him and he opened his eyes to see a small boy standing less than a yard away, dressed in footed pajamas dotted with multicolored dinosaurs. He had a toy sheriff's car tucked under an arm.

"Who're you?" the boy asked.

He looked just like Anna. Same intelligent blue eyes. And his voice had an underlying maturity that Brody doubted he himself could have mustered at that age. He sounded like a little adult.

"I'm a friend of your mom's," Brody said. "You must be Adam."

"Uh-huh. Were you sleeping out here?"

"Yeah, I guess I was."

"Why?"

Brody debated how to answer this. "I'm on Santa watch. Just in case he comes early this year."

Not strictly a lie.

"Santa comes on Christmas Eve," Adam said. "He leaves me presents and eats all our cookies. He's big and fat and likes chocolate chips. Do you like chocolate chips?"

Brody smiled. "Love 'em. Especially in pancakes."

The boy's eyes lit up. "Pancakes?"

"Yep," Brody said. "They used to be your mom's favorite. She never made them for you?"

Adam shook his head. "Unh-uh." He scrunched

his face up, as if remembering something, then said, "You ride a motorcycle."

Brody was surprised. "That's right. How did you know?"

"Uncle Owen showed me your picture. He had it in his wallet."

Brody felt the stab of grief. He knew exactly the photograph Adam was talking about. It was a shot of him and Owen down in Nuevo Laredo, after a long weekend of barhopping to celebrate Owen's new job with Northboard Industries. Anna had been scheduled to join them, but she had caught a cold just before the trip and had insisted they go without her.

They had both been wiped out when the photo was taken, not looking forward to the twenty-hour ride back to Cedarwood. And it was shortly after their return that Brody's troubles with the department began.

"My daddy drives a sheriff's car," Adam said, as if somehow picking up on Brody's thoughts. "Uncle Owen says he's one of the best deputies ever."

Brody assumed that Owen was being charitable when he'd said that. Owen had never thought much of Frank, and Brody knew the marriage to Anna must have been a tough pill for his friend to swallow. Frank *was* a good deputy, but Brody couldn't imagine Owen ever admitting that out loud. Maybe it was easier to say it to a three-year-old child.

Whatever the case, this boy was about the cutest thing Brody had ever seen, and he felt an instant warmth toward the little guy.

Frank must be very proud, he thought.

Brody got to his feet. "So you've never had chocolate chip pancakes, huh?"

Adam shook his head.

"Well, you don't know what you've been missing, my friend. What d'you say we go down to the kitchen and see if we can whip us up a batch?"

"Really?"

"I'll even let you pour in the chips."

A slow smile crept into Adam's face, reaching all the way up to his eyes, and at that moment Brody knew that he had made a friend forever.

He stood up, patted the boy's head. "Let's get to it."

ANNA AWOKE THAT MORNING to the sound of Adam's laughter. His familiar high-pitched trill floated up from downstairs, muffled but clearly identifiable behind her bedroom door.

It was a sound she hadn't heard in over a week.

Climbing out of bed, she pulled her robe on then padded to her door and opened it. Brody's chair was empty, and she thought she heard *his* laugh, too, coming from the kitchen.

What was going on?

When Anna got downstairs, her mother, Sylvia,

was sitting on the sofa, already dressed for the day, a sour, intolerant look on her face.

"When did *he* come back?"

"Mom, please, don't start."

"I can't believe you let that man in this house. After everything he put you through, you take him back with open arms?"

"It's not like that," Anna assured her. "He's here because of Owen. He heard what happened and he wants to help."

"Help himself right into those pants of yours."

"Oh, for God's sakes, Mom, nothing happened. We're long past all that."

"Are you?" Her mother looked skeptical. "I know how you feel about him, young lady. You've been carrying a torch since you were a teenager. Even after he deserted you. Even during that preposterous charade you and Frank called a—"

"*Enough,* Mother." Anna felt her face growing hot. "I know you're hurting about Owen, but that doesn't give you the right to be so cruel."

Sylvia caught herself, looked stricken, as if she'd suddenly realized the venom in her words. She brought a hand to her mouth as tears filled her eyes. "Oh my God, Anna. I'm so sorry."

Anna calmed herself. "It's okay, Mom. We're all on edge. But let's try to pull it together for Adam, all right? He needs us."

They both listened for a moment to Adam's

giggles. Then Anna said, "It sounds like he's feeling better. Maybe we should take our cue from him."

Sylvia nodded and wiped her tears with her shirt sleeve. "It's just so hard, hon. I miss your brother so much."

"I know you do. So do I."

She squeezed her mother's shoulder, forced a smile and finally got one in return.

Her smile disappeared, however, when she went to the kitchen and saw what Brody and Adam were up to. Brody stood at the table, stirring batter in a mixing bowl as Adam poured in a bag of chocolate chips.

They were making pancakes.

Brody's famous chocolate chip pancakes.

As they worked, there was a natural camaraderie between them, both smiling broadly, obviously enjoying this time together. A few of the chips spilled onto the table and Brody snatched one up, popping it into Adam's mouth.

"Good for the soul," he said, and Adam giggled.

Despite what Anna had just told her mother, this scene was simply too much to bear, and tears flooded her own eyes. She was suddenly awash in memories—memories of the life she had once dreamed of but had never come to pass.

A life with Brody.

She started to turn away. He looked up and saw her crying, his face reflecting surprise and concern.

"Anna?"

Then she was out the door and crossing toward the stairs, not wanting him to see her like this. She knew she was being ridiculous, that reality rarely matched the hopes and desires people often wrap themselves in, but she couldn't help herself. With sudden, gut-wrenching clarity, she realized that she would *never* have that dream.

Brody caught up to her on the stairs, grabbing her sleeve. "Anna? What's wrong?"

"What *isn't* wrong?" she cried, yanking her arm free, unable to keep the sarcasm at bay. "I'm happy you went out into the world and found yourself, Brody. I'm happy you were able to help people who needed it. But what about me? *I* needed you, too, and you were nowhere to be found."

She continued up the stairs, but Brody reached out and grabbed her sleeve again, stopping her.

"Anna, listen to me, please."

She turned. "I don't want to have this conversation. Let go."

"Not until you listen," he said. "I need you to listen."

She gave in. Didn't move. Just stood there, sniffing back her tears. Waiting.

"I can talk from now until forever," Brody continued, "but nothing I say will ever make up for what I did to you. I know that." He tried to clear the hoarseness that had overtaken his voice. "You don't know

how many times I wanted to pick up the phone and beg for your forgiveness. To tell you how sorry I was. But I knew that wouldn't erase what I'd done."

"You could have tried," she said.

"Maybe. But I was so full of poison after the trial. Had become something I didn't want to be, and the last thing I wanted was to drag you down with me." He shook his head. "I was too stupid to realize that you were exactly what I needed. And by the time I finally *did,* it was too late."

Anna was silent. She could plainly see the regret in his eyes, but that didn't ease her pain, and Brody seemed to sense this.

"Saying I'm sorry will never be enough," he told her. "I know that. And I don't ever expect you to forgive me, but I'm not here for forgiveness. I'm here because Owen wanted me to be, and I'm hoping we can both put the past behind us and do what needs to be done to find his killers."

Anna said nothing. She knew he was right.

She looked at her mother, who still sat on the sofa, a fresh set of tears glistening. Anna knew that while she might not approve of Brody, she wanted an answer to her son's death just as much as they did.

This was a time for strength, not weakness. There were things Anna and Brody needed to talk about, yes. Things that needed to be said and understood—but now wasn't the time for it. The past was a distrac-

tion, and they had to focus their energy in another direction.

So despite the conflict still raging inside her, Anna nodded. “For Owen, then. But where do we start?”

“Same place I’d start any investigation,” he said. “At the crime scene.”

Chapter Six

Anna hadn't been to Owen's condo since before he died. She still had to pack up his things and either donate or move them to storage and possibly put the place up for sale, but she just didn't have the will to deal with it yet.

Frank had given her the number of a crime scene cleaning service, but she'd put off calling them and was starting to regret it. She had no idea what she and Brody might be walking into.

The condo was located in the center of town, a tall, modern tower of cement and glass that was well beyond Anna's budget. Until recently, Owen had worked in research and development for Northboard Industries, a weapons manufacturer with several lucrative government contracts, so money hadn't been an issue for him, and his choice of dwelling reflected that.

They rode there on Brody's Harley, Anna wearing her old helmet and doing her best to keep her memories at bay. She hadn't been on the back of a

motorcycle since he left, and she was surprised to discover that she felt right at home, riding with her body pressed against his, her arms wrapped around his waist, the winter wind chafing her skin. She felt the familiar ripple of abs beneath her palms and would be lying if she'd told anyone it wasn't affecting her.

There had always been an undeniable chemistry between her and Brody, both mental and physical. That didn't mean she was planning to act on it—far from it—but she was well aware of its existence, and the feel of his body didn't exactly repulse her.

She had brought Owen's keys with her, but it turned out they didn't need them. When they stepped off the elevator, they both instinctively froze.

Down the hall, the crime scene tape had been pulled aside and Owen's door was ajar. It was open no more than a crack but was clearly visible from where they stood.

Anna glanced at Brody. "A break-in?"

"That would be my guess," he whispered then held up a hand, warning her back as he drew his gun from his waistband. "Stay here."

She watched him step toward the doorway, his body tense but fluid, moving with the assurance of a man who had done this kind of thing many times before. As he reached the end of the hall, he brought the gun up then nudged the door open with his foot and disappeared inside.

Anna waited. Felt a vague sense of panic rising.

What if Santa Claus and his van-driving partner were in there?

Her stomach tightened as she started running different scenarios and their possible outcomes through her mind—most of them bad. She half expected to hear gunshots and wondered how she should react if she did.

Should she flee?

Try to find building security?

Or try to help Brody somehow?

Her fears were put to rest when he stepped into the hall again and gestured to her.

"It's clear," he said. "But somebody's definitely been here."

Releasing a breath, Anna entered behind him. Owen's condo had always been immaculate, with sleek, postmodern furniture arranged in a way that gave the place a sense of spaciousness despite its relatively small size. Her brother had been something of a clean freak, and the condo usually reflected that—but not so much now. Now it was a mess. Furniture overturned. Stuffing ripped out of the sofa and chairs. Framed artwork and photographs torn from the walls and scattered on the floor. Drawers yanked open and emptied.

Completely trashed.

"Okay," Anna said, "that's it. We need to call Frank. He needs to see this."

"Don't waste your time," Brody told her. "He'll

just blame it on vandals. And we need to take a look around."

"For what?"

"The same thing the people who trashed this apartment were looking for. The button. I'm guessing they did this before they came after you, which means they didn't find it."

"And you think *we* can? We don't even know what it is."

"But if we get lucky and we can figure it out, we might be able to trace it back to its origin. And the more we know, the more likely we are to find the people who did this."

"That's a lot of *ifs,*" Anna said.

"There are always a lot of *ifs* in a murder investigation. Doesn't mean we can't try." He gestured to the room. "You stay in here and I'll take the bedroom. Work a grid, look through everything. If anything jumps out at you, let me know."

"Like what?"

"A receipt, a key to a safe-deposit box. Or anything that might lead us to the identity of Santa Claus. A name, a photograph, a note. Something tangible."

"What about fingerprints? Won't we contaminate the scene?"

"Trust me, the people who did this didn't leave any prints. And yours are probably all over the place anyway. It's not like you've never been here before."

Anna nodded. That made sense.

Brody crossed toward the bedroom and stopped in the doorway. "And do yourself a favor and don't come in here. You won't like what you see."

Anna considered the weight of these words, unwanted images flashing through her mind:

Owen's bed.

Blood on the pillow. The headboard. The wall.

She didn't think the truth could be any worse than what she imagined, but she had no desire to see it and she nodded again. "Don't worry, I'll stay out here."

IT TOOK THEM NEARLY an hour to do the job.

Brody knew that finding the button or anything useful was a crapshoot, but he worked methodically anyway, scouring the bedroom section by section, going through the clothes scattered on the floor, checking beneath the mattress and under the bed, running his hands along the surfaces of the furniture, looking for indentations or holes or possible hidden compartments.

It wasn't until he reached the other side of the room—where Owen kept a desk—that he found two things of interest.

If Owen had a computer, it was gone. The drawers had all been yanked out, books and papers and office supplies scattered everywhere. But as he worked the grid, Brody found a crumpled sheet of paper and carefully flattened it out.

A bank receipt dated two weeks before Owen's death.

A five-thousand-dollar withdrawal.

This didn't necessarily mean anything on its own, but a moment later, Brody found a rectangular pad with cardboard backing lying facedown on the carpet. He flipped it over to discover that it was a desk calendar, Owen's daily notations scribbled in the numbered squares.

On the very same day as the bank withdrawal, Owen had written a time and address in blue ink.

A meeting of some kind?

Brody's initial feeling was that the withdrawal was a coincidence and that Owen was merely going in to interview for a new job. But the address was located in an area Brody knew quite well from his days as a patrol deputy—and was notoriously dangerous.

So what had Owen been up to? Why had he gone there?

A possible payoff? A purchase of some kind?

Drugs?

No, drugs didn't make any sense. Owen had been something of a health nut since high school, had always eaten right and taken good care of himself. He barely drank alcohol and he'd never picked up a cigarette in his life, so the idea that he'd go to the South Side looking for narcotics, or even a bag of weed, just didn't compute.

So why *had* he gone there?

Getting to his feet, Brody crossed to the doorway and stepped into the living room. Anna was sitting on the floor, surrounded by a pile of photographs that had been dumped from a drawer. She had one of the photos in hand and a cell phone to her ear.

"A couple hours early should do it," she said into the phone. "Thanks again, Trudy."

As she hung up, Brody glanced at the photo in her hands. It was a shot of Owen, Adam and her mother, all wearing broad smiles. Adam couldn't have been more than a year old in the photograph, and the sight of him touched something in Brody's heart. He felt it the moment he saw the boy's smile. Remembered how oddly adultlike Adam had seemed when he'd encountered him in the upstairs hallway.

Pulling himself from the distraction, Brody looked at Anna, nodding to the phone.

"What was that about?"

"Work problems," she said. "Did you find anything?"

"Maybe. Can you think of anyone your brother might know on the South Side? Any reason he'd go there?"

Anna considered the question and shook her head. "No. Why?"

He already knew the answer, but he had to ask anyway. "What about drugs? Do you know if he started taking them?"

Anna frowned. “No, of course he didn’t. Owen wouldn’t go near that stuff.”

“I didn’t think so, but according to his calendar, he had a meeting with someone in a very bad neighborhood. The same day he withdrew five grand from his bank account.”

“You think it’s significant?”

“Anything that raises questions right now is significant. Whether it’ll pan out is anyone’s guess, but I think we need to go there.”

“Now?”

Brody nodded.

“Then you might have to go alone. One of my employees called in sick and I have to cover for her at the mall.”

“You can’t get someone else to do it?”

Anna shook her head. “Mom’s watching Adam, and my other girl, Trudy, can’t get in until later this afternoon, so it’s either go to work or stay closed, and I can’t afford to do that. I’ll be there most of the day.”

“Well, I’m not about to leave you alone,” Brody said. “Especially at the mall.”

“You’ll be bored to death.”

Brody showed her a smile. “I can tell you’ve never worked as a bodyguard before.”

Chapter Seven

There was nothing even remotely boring about bodyguard work. Brody had gotten some training during his days as a sheriff's cadet, but he'd really honed his skills on the job over the past few years and knew that the nature of the profession didn't allow you to be bored.

It was all in the eyes. They were constantly moving, constantly evaluating, always aware, always seeing what others paid little attention to.

He looked for anomalies. Signs of agitation. Checking faces, hands, unusual bulges in clothing. People wearing sunglasses when the weather or lighting didn't warrant it. Hiding their eyes.

Hiding their fear.

Fear was always a factor in crime, and very few people knew how to disguise it. A bodyguard was trained to recognize that fear, to notice that faint trickle of sweat rolling down a forehead on a winter night. The stiffness of a walk that would normally

be fluid. A subtle hesitation in both movement and attitude.

It was impossible to be bored when both your eyes and your mind were working overtime, taking in everything while focusing on a single objective:

Protecting your client.

Trying to practice your trade in a mall, however, wasn't easy. Especially a mall three days before Christmas, overrun by last-minute shoppers, most of them in a hurry and anxious and irritated.

Then there were the hundreds of bags and boxes and purses of all sizes. Hands reaching into them, pulling out wallets, keys, cell phones, shopping lists.

You could never let your guard down.

Brody sat on a bench outside Anna's Body Essentials, carefully assessing each new customer who entered, not allowing himself to assume that they were harmless or that they'd be foolish to try to grab Anna in her own store.

He'd seen a lot of foolishness in his time.

Another important discipline for a bodyguard was the ability to stay focused while still allowing for the inevitable: a wandering mind. You had to learn to give in to that parallel line of thought that kept you sane while never letting it distract you from the objective.

As Brody looked around him at all the Christmas decor—the winking lights, the giant tree in

the middle of the mall, the red and green bows, the wreaths—he was struck by the stark contrast between Cedarwood Mall and the refugee camp in Chad.

Last Christmas Eve, he'd been stuck in a tent, sharing a can of peaches by candlelight with a Red Cross worker, an attractive French woman named Sophie.

Brody was human and had not been a monk after he left Cedarwood. He had shared a bed or two, moments of intimacy that had never really gone anywhere, with women he had cared for, but never fulfilled him the way Anna had.

After he learned of her marriage to Frank, he seemed to be on some kind of quest to find her in another woman. And when that woman was ultimately unable to *be* Anna, he pulled away. Always a gentle release, but not something he was proud of.

That Christmas Eve, however, was anything but gentle. As he and Sophie made love, he'd gotten lost in the fantasy and called her Anna, putting an abrupt end to the moment.

The night had quickly gone downhill from there.

After that, Brody gave up women entirely. A yearlong drought that only fueled his desire every time he looked at Anna now. He knew it wasn't meant to be, but that didn't keep him from wanting her.

HE WAS ABOUT FOUR HOURS into his watch when he was approached by two mall security guards. Unlike last night's duo, they were both big and hard and wore

their uniforms well. There was an air of ex-military about them. Not the kind of guys you'd want to get into a scuffle with.

"Brody Carpenter?" the bigger of the two asked.

"That's right," Brody said then gestured. "You're blocking my view."

The two guards exchanged a glance then stepped aside slightly so that Brody could see Anna from where he was sitting. She was at the cash register now, ringing up a sale for a teenage girl.

"We'd like you to come with us."

"Am I breaking some kind of law? Have I been sitting here too long?"

"Frankly, sir, you could sit here until closing and I wouldn't really care. I'm just following orders."

"Whose orders?"

Now the second one spoke up, and he didn't seem amused by all the questions. "Let's go."

"Let me guess. Deputy Frank Matson?"

"All I know is they had badges. Now are you going to cooperate or do we need to get rough?"

Brody knew these guys were just doing their job, but he wasn't about to leave Anna alone. "I'm sure you both heard what happened to Ms. Sanford last night. So if you think I'm going to walk away from her right now, I'm afraid you're mistaken."

"That's why they sent two of us," the bigger one said. "Stokes here is gonna take your post."

Brody looked at the second guard. "I assume you know what you're doing?"

Stokes seemed annoyed. "Don't you worry, she'll be safe with me."

That was the problem, wasn't it? Brody couldn't help but worry. But Stokes looked like a guy who could handle himself, so he reluctantly got to his feet.

"Do me a favor," he said, "and take a position inside the shop."

The bigger one gestured to Stokes, and Stokes moved across the aisle and stationed himself just inside the entrance.

Brody turned to the partner. "Lead the way."

THEY WENT DOWN SOME stairs and took a long hallway to what looked like an employee break room. There was a refrigerator in the corner, a snack machine next to it, a bulletin board full of government notices and work-related memos, and several table-and-chair sets scattered throughout.

Frank Matson and Joe Wilson stood near one of the tables, looking exactly like what they were: a couple of plainclothes detectives who had seen it all and done quite a bit of it themselves.

When Brody entered, Frank gestured to a chair.

Brody crossed toward them and sat. "What can I do for you, Frank?"

"That's a loaded question," Matson said. He sank

into his own chair and leaned forward. "There're a lot of things you can do for me. The real question is, will you do them?"

"I'm a reasonable man."

"That you are, Carpenter. For all your faults, that's one thing I can say about you. With a couple of notable exceptions, you've always kept a level head."

"So I repeat," Brody said. "What can I do for you?"

Frank took a moment, as if he were trying to find a way to phrase his next sentence, but Brody already knew what was coming before he spoke. "I'll keep it simple. I want you out of here. Go back to wherever it is you came from and stay there."

"Why?"

"Because I know what kind of effect you have on Anna. She's been through enough these past few days. She doesn't need you dredging up all your ancient history."

"This doesn't have anything to do with history, Frank. It's all about the here and now."

"Who do you think you're kidding?"

Brody reached into his shirt pocket and pulled out Owen's note. "Anna wanted me to show this to you, but I told her it was a waste of time. Let's see who was right."

Frank took the note and unfolded it, reading Owen's words.

Then he looked up. "What is this?"

"A message from Owen."

Frank read it again then shrugged and handed it to Wilson. "So it's proof he committed suicide."

"That's what I told Anna you'd say, but that's not the way I see it. I think the trouble Owen was in got him killed and the attack on Anna last night confirms it."

Now Joe Wilson moved forward, getting into Brody's face. "What kind of scam are you running, Carpenter?"

"I don't know what you're talking about."

"I think it's pretty convenient you were in that parking garage when Anna was attacked."

"I was just doing what Owen asked me to."

Wilson waved the note in Brody's face. "And we're supposed to believe this just because you scribbled a few words on a piece of paper?"

"Not my handwriting, Joe. So don't even start."

"You know what I think?" Wilson said. "Maybe you had something to do with that attack last night. Maybe you been pal'in around with the wrong element. Like the guy in the Santa suit."

Brody smiled at him. "You never were much of a critical thinker, were you, Joe?"

Suddenly Wilson kicked out, knocking the chair out from under Brody. Brody fell back, slamming against the linoleum, and Wilson stepped over him,

grabbing him by the shirt. "Tell us who they are, Carpenter."

Brody didn't resist. He knew he was being baited and didn't want to give them any reason to arrest him and haul him in. He just lay there, not moving.

"Like I said—I don't know what you're talking about."

"You're dirty, and we all know it." Wilson tightened his grip. "You gonna tell me you aren't part of—"

"Enough," Frank said suddenly. "Get off him, Joe."

Wilson looked up at his partner in surprise. "Come on, Frank, you know he's—"

"I said get off him."

Wilson scowled then released the shirt. He reluctantly stepped away as Frank helped Brody to his feet.

"I didn't want that to happen," Frank said. "You okay?"

Brody knew that this was *exactly* what Frank had wanted to happen. There was nothing spontaneous about it. The two had rehearsed the moment before Brody had walked into the room.

Nothing like a little intimidation to get a suspect to cooperate.

Or to scare him away.

And Brody knew that's what he was. A suspect. Not because of any evidence against him, but simply

because Frank still cared about Anna and couldn't bear the thought that Brody was back in her life.

But there was nothing Frank could do about that, was there? And he knew it.

"Joe's never been the model of restraint," Brody said, "but I'll forgive him his transgressions. Are you two done with me now? I need to get back to work."

Frank frowned. "Think about what I said, Brody."

"About leaving town? Sorry to disappoint you, but Anna needs me right now."

"She needed you before and that didn't stop you."

Brody shook his head, smiled. "Now why did I know you'd go there?"

"She's my wife, Carpenter."

"*Ex*-wife, Frank. She doesn't share your name anymore and you've had a couple of years to get used to that fact. Why prolong your misery?"

The two men locked gazes, Brody knowing that Frank's anger was brimming, his brain working overtime, looking for an excuse to either arrest him or force him to leave town. There was no way Frank could do that, however, without upsetting Anna. And that wasn't an option for him.

Brody didn't really blame the guy. The heart wants what it wants.

But he had a job to do. "Are we done?"

Frank finally backed down. "Go on," he said with a dismissive flick of the hand. "Get out of here."

Brody stared at him for a moment then turned and walked out the door.

Chapter Eight

"Where did you disappear to?"

Anna had seen the two security guards approach Brody and watched one of them escort him away. She tried asking the one left behind about it, but the guard simply said, "I've been told to keep an eye on you."

Now her shift was over and she and Brody rode the elevator to the parking garage.

"Your ex-husband's feeling insecure," he said. "He wants me to leave town."

"Frank was here? At the mall?"

Brody nodded. "He's afraid I'll steal you way from him."

"Is that supposed to be a joke?"

"He's still in love with you, Anna. He and Wilson tried to cover it all by accusing me of being behind the attack last night, but that's about what it boiled down to. He thinks I'm some kind of threat to your relationship."

"Relationship?" Anna felt her hackles rise. She

reached into her purse and pulled out her cell phone. "I can't believe this. If anything, Frank should be thanking you for—"

Brody put a hand over hers. "Don't. You'll only aggravate him, and we can't afford any interference right now."

She thought about this then nodded and put the phone away. "I take it you didn't tell him about the money Owen withdrew? Or the address on his calendar?"

Brody shook his head. "He's already made up his mind about your brother."

"So instead of trying to do what's right, he wastes time harassing you."

"That pretty much sums it up," Brody said.

He looked at her as if he wanted to say something more but couldn't quite bring himself to do it. Then he plunged forward anyway. "Not that it's any of my business, but why did you two break up?"

Anna's stomach tightened. Such conversations were always a source of anxiety for her. She felt guilty about her failed marriage, even though the problems underlying the divorce had been mutual.

Frank's continued affection for her was obvious. Whenever she was around him, she got the feeling that he was waiting for her to respond to his cues, to fall into his arms and beg him for another try. But she knew that would never happen.

There was a time when she had fooled herself

into believing that she loved him, too, but it had become clear after only a year of marriage that she was simply going through the motions. Neither of them could give what the other needed, and a lifetime of banal pleasantries and passionless sex was not the future Anna had envisioned for herself.

It wasn't fair to Frank. Or her. Or Adam.

"You're right," she said to Brody. "It isn't any of your business."

And in that moment, she realized the depth of her fury toward Brody. If he hadn't left her, she never would have taken up with Frank, and there wouldn't *be* a failed marriage to fret over.

But she couldn't let that fury consume her now. What was the point? He was trying to help her.

And that counted for something, didn't it?

THE AREA AROUND FIRST Avenue and Pike was not one of Cedarwood's finer neighborhoods. At the edge of the industrial center of the city, it boasted more liquor stores and tattoo parlors in six square blocks than most people saw in a lifetime, and the women prowling the streets in spandex and short shorts were not charity workers looking for a donation.

Anna had come down this way only once, on a dare back in high school, and had been scared half to death by the experience. It was the last time she let peer pressure get the better of her.

Brody took a turn on Worthington, past a small,

boarded-up chapel that looked as if it hadn't seen business in over a decade. At the far end of the street was a grouping of old factory buildings, perched on the edge of the industrial section but long ago abandoned by anything having to do with industry.

Most of them were boarded up like the chapel, but one looked as if it might have some life to it, and Anna wasn't surprised when Brody came to a stop out front.

"Definitely not a job interview," he said.

A feeling of trepidation overcame Anna. "I can't even imagine why Owen would come here."

"There's only one way to find out."

The entrance to the building was along the left side. The door had been secured by a chain and padlock, but the padlock hung open and they were inside in only a matter of seconds.

What they found were the remnants of an old garment factory. Battered industrial sewing machines were laid out in two rows, covered with a thick film of dust. Spools of faded fabric were stacked in a corner alongside a cluster of rusty file cabinets. The only light filtered in through broken windows that hung high along the walls.

"Are you sure you got the address right?" Anna asked.

"I'm sure," Brody said, then he gestured to a set of steps across the room that led up to an enclosed office with an open doorway. A broom was leaning

against the wall at the bottom, and the steps looked as if they'd recently been swept, a minimal bit of housekeeping by squatters.

They moved past the rows of sewing machines, then Brody cupped a hand next to his mouth and called up the stairs. "Hello? Is anyone home?"

No answer.

"Wait here," he said to Anna then moved cautiously up toward the doorway, his palm resting against the butt of the pistol in his waistband.

A moment later, he was peering inside. "Hello?"

He stood there a moment, scanning the room, then he relaxed and gestured for Anna to join him. She moved up the steps, that feeling of trepidation still percolating in the pit of her stomach.

It threatened to boil over when she stepped into the doorway.

The room beyond had been ransacked, just like Owen's condo, which pretty much confirmed that they were on the right track.

There was a cluttered workbench along one side of the room holding a computer and a bunch of electronic gear that Anna couldn't identify if her life depended on it. The floor was littered with more equipment and overturned drawers—the plastic, rectangular kind that her father used to have in their garage, full of screws and washers and other workshop doodads.

The doodads here, however, all seemed to be elec-

tronic. Transistors, circuit boards, switch components and other parts that were beyond Anna's vocabulary or comprehension. The person who occupied this space was obviously an electronics geek.

Brody flipped a switch on the wall and fluorescent lights came to life overhead.

"Looks like he managed to tap into the city's electrical grid. There's probably a functioning warehouse nearby whose owners are wondering why their energy bill is so high."

"So what is this place for?" Anna asked.

"I'm not sure. But he's working off the radar, so it's probably not entirely legal."

Brody crossed to the computer on the workbench and studied it. One side of the case had been removed, exposing the various components inside. To Anna, it was nothing more than a jumble of multicolored wires and circuitry, but Brody seemed to know what he was looking at.

"Hard drive is missing," he said, then he looked around at the rest of the mess, and spotted something of interest.

He moved to one of the plastic drawers on the floor and picked it up. A piece of masking tape above the handle had the word TAGS written across it in black marker.

Getting down on his haunches, he looked around the floor, running his fingers through the debris, but he didn't seem to be finding what he was looking for.

Then his gaze abruptly shifted to a leg of the workbench. Crossing to it, he bent down, pinched something between his fingers and held it up for Anna to see.

"I think I may have figured out what we're looking for."

It was a tiny, flat disk, about the size and thickness of a dime.

"The button? Is that it?"

"Hard to say, but I'd like to get a closer look at this thing."

"I don't understand," Anna said. "What is it?"

"I could be mistaken, but have you ever heard of an RFID tag?"

"RFID?"

"Radio frequency identification."

Anna shook her head.

"What about Owen?" Brody asked. "He ever mention anything about security devices?"

"Not a word. Why?"

"If I've got this thing figured right, Owen paid a visit to this guy with five thousand dollars in cash in his pocket. And like you said, he wasn't buying drugs."

Brody showed her the disk again. "He was buying one of these. And the simple fact that the drawer marked 'tags' is the only one that's completely empty leads me to believe that whoever trashed this place thought the same thing. Only they missed one."

"I still don't understand," Anna said. "How could that thing be worth five thousand dollars?"

"It may be worth a lot more than that." Brody pocketed the disk before taking Anna by the elbow. "Right now I think we'd better head out. It's getting late and we've spent enough time in this godforsaken neighborhood. It's not safe here after dark."

Anna didn't argue.

Her uneasiness hadn't waned, and the sooner they got out of here, the better she'd feel.

Brody flicked off the fluorescents and they moved together down the steps, Anna noting that the light from the windows was nearly gone now, the sewing machines little more than dark silhouettes in the dim room below. Someone could be hiding down there and they'd never know it.

As they reached the bottom of the steps, Brody tensed and moved in front of her, bringing his gun out again. A precautionary measure, she was sure, but a welcome one.

They continued past the sewing machines, Brody carrying himself like a man who was ready for just about anything. They reached the exit door without incident, however. No bogeymen jumped out of the darkness.

Anna let out small sigh of relief as they stepped outside, feeling her uneasiness dissipate as they moved around the building to Brody's bike.

But just as they pulled their helmets on and were

about to climb aboard, she heard the roar of an engine as a pair of headlights came to life—

—and a familiar green van headed straight for them.

Chapter Nine

Brody was in motion before he even saw the gun.

He pushed Anna to the ground as the guy in the passenger seat stuck an arm out his window and the weapon flashed. A bullet rocketed past Brody's head, gouging the wall behind him.

Shielding Anna, he brought his own gun up, returning fire.

Once. Twice. Three times—in quick succession.

The first shot clipped a side mirror, the second one went wild and the third punched through the windshield, hitting the driver in the center of his chest.

He slammed back against his seat then slumped forward, his foot falling heavily onto the accelerator.

The passenger—whom Brody assumed was Santa Claus—grabbed hold of the wheel, sheer panic on his face. But it was too late. The van shot forward and swerved sharply, the momentum tipping it onto its side.

It crashed down and slid toward an adjacent fac-

tory building, the scrape of metal against blacktop assaulting their ears. It smashed into the side of the building, knocking a hole through it, the impact rupturing the van's gas tank. Suddenly flames erupted, filling the air with thick, oily smoke.

Trapped, the thug formerly known as Santa crawled across the dead driver and tried to climb out his window, but something was holding him back.

"Help me!" he squealed. "Help!"

Quickly checking to make sure Anna wasn't hit, Brody sprang toward the van, the flames growing higher with every step he took. He leaped onto the vehicle, scrambled to the thug and yanked his arms.

"I'm stuck," the man screamed. "Pull harder!"

Brody doubled his efforts. "What are you people after? Who sent you?"

But the thug kept screaming, too blinded by panic to respond.

"Who sent you?"

The thug begged Brody for help, and Brody tugged at him with all his might, but the guy wouldn't budge.

"Brody!" Anna called from somewhere behind him, and he turned, realizing the flames had grown perilously high.

Smoke filled his lungs and he coughed, expelling as much of it as he possibly could, but he didn't let go

of the thug's arms, trying desperately to shake him loose.

Then he felt Anna's hands on his waist, her fingers slipping into the belt loops of his jeans, tugging him back toward the blacktop.

"It's too late!" she shouted. "You can't do anything!"

Brody knew she was right, but he tried again anyway. He yanked with everything he had but it wasn't enough. As the flames grew even higher, threatening to consume him, Brody released the thug's arms and stumbled back as Anna dragged him away from the burning vehicle.

They were several yards clear when he felt a rumble under his feet and the gas tank finally exploded, sending up a ball of fire and smoke, the impact knocking Brody and Anna to the ground, abruptly cutting off the thug's tortured squeal.

They lay there, Anna wrapping her arms around him protectively as they watched the blackened shell of the van shudder and burn.

"Oh, my God," Anna murmured. "Oh, my God."

Then Brody turned to her and said, "I think it's finally time to call Frank."

THEY TOOK THEM BACK to the sheriff's office and put them in separate interrogation rooms.

Brody had been expecting this. It was the way

investigations worked. You were guilty until proved innocent, no matter what the courts might say. He also knew that despite being known to the deputies, he and Anna would be regarded with suspicion until the details of the incident had been discussed, analyzed and regurgitated. Again and again.

Brody was paired off with Joe Wilson, who sat him in a chair in the tiny room then left him to stew there for close to an hour before questioning him.

It was a technique that was supposed to wear a suspect down, but Brody had used it so many times himself in the old days that its effect on him was zilch. He leaned back in the chair and thought about that squealing thug trapped in the van, wishing he could have pried the guy loose before it had exploded.

Brody had seen enough death and torture overseas to have developed a strong aversion to it, and despite what Santa had tried to do to Anna, the fool hadn't deserved the fate he'd suffered. It also would have been nice to question the guy and hopefully gain some insight into Owen's death.

Did this mean the search for the killers was done? Were these guys the brains behind the crime, or had they simply been following orders?

Brody was banking on the latter. The two hadn't struck him as mental giants.

Identifying their bodies, however, would take time, patience and a certain amount of forensics skill. And if there were no dental records on file, and the van

turned out to be stolen—which seemed likely—the department might never know who the two men were.

Which meant the investigation into Owen's death literally hit a wall before it had really gotten started.

Brody was thinking about what his next move might be when the door to the interrogation room flew open and Joe Wilson stepped inside.

"You should have taken our advice and left town, Carpenter."

Brody stared at him. He was really sick of Wilson's condescending tone. "No offense, Joe, but it'll have to snow in Bermuda before I ever take advice from you."

"See what that attitude's gotten you? Now you're looking straight down the barrel of a double-homicide rap."

"It was self-defense and you know it."

"Yeah? Where's your proof?"

"Come on, Joe. Just ask your partner's ex-wife. She'll corroborate. It was the same vehicle used in the attack against her and the same two guys. They shot first, and I did my job."

Wilson snorted. "Your job? I don't know if you noticed, hotshot, but you're not a deputy anymore."

"Thanks for the reminder," Brody said. He knew it was another attempt to get him riled up, make him do something he'd regret, but he didn't take the bait.

"Besides," Wilson continued, "all I saw at the crime scene was a burnt-out shell and two crispy critters. Nothing there that necessarily connects them to the attack on Anna."

"You're kidding me, right?"

"Videotape from the garage is pretty fuzzy, Carpenter. We got nothing on the driver and the other one was hiding behind that Santa suit. So we could be talking about two completely different guys. And for all I know, you're the one who shot first."

Brody was silent for a moment as he tamped down the heat rising in his chest. Then, in measured tones, he said, "Is this really the game you want to play?"

"To be honest? No. But those two goons are the least of your worries."

"What do you mean?"

Wilson pulled a manila folder out from under his arm and dropped it on the table. "Take a look."

Brody slid it toward him and opened it. Inside were autopsy photos. Shots of a guy in his mid-forties who looked as if he'd spent way too much time in the bathtub. His skin was bone-white, almost blue, and flaking off his body.

"We pulled this guy out of the river yesterday," Wilson said. "Take a guess what he did for a living."

"No idea." Brody had never seen the guy before.

"He was an electronics whiz who lived and worked in that garment factory you broke into." He paused.

"But you already knew that, didn't you?" He showed Brody a broad, self-satisfied grin that did little to hide the sneer behind it. "And that makes body number three, my friend. Looks like you just hit the trifecta."

ANNA WASN'T SURPRISED when Frank walked into the interrogation room.

He'd let her stew in here for a while, and that alone irritated her. But either he was oblivious or just didn't care. He seemed to be struggling with his own irritation.

He pulled a chair out and sat. "What the heck were you thinking, Anna?"

"What do you mean?"

"Going to the South Side? Getting involved in a shootout, for God's sakes?"

Anna sighed. "It's not as if we planned it. Those guys came out of nowhere. Just like last night."

"And if you weren't out there running around with that fool Carpenter…"

"What's the matter, Frank? Are you upset because he's doing what *you* won't do?"

Frank said nothing for a moment, clearly trying to put his irritation in check. He studied her patiently. "Carpenter's a loose cannon, Anna. He's interfering with an ongoing investigation—and so are you."

"What investigation? All you ever seem to do is

ask questions and file reports. Brody showed you the note he got from Owen and—"

"Have you told him the truth?"

The question stopped her. "About what?"

"Have you told him why you were so anxious to get hold of him in the months after he left?"

All the fight went out of Anna. Those months had been foremost in her mind lately, but she'd obscured them with thoughts of Owen. And she supposed her anger had prevented her from telling Brody what she'd wanted so desperately to tell him almost four years ago.

"Not yet," she said. "I've been working up to it."

This was a lie. She'd known she'd have to spill all of her secrets eventually, but she hadn't even tried at this point. The emotional price was just too heavy for her right now.

"Don't," Frank said suddenly.

"What?"

"Don't tell him. He's the one who ran out on you, and there's no reason he has to know."

"Come on, Frank, that wouldn't be fair. Sooner or later I'll have to."

"Why? So he can run away again?"

The thought made her heart heavy. "You don't know that's what he'd do."

"Don't I? I'm a simple man, Anna. When I look at the world, I like to strip it down to its essence. I do the same thing when I look at people. People like

Brody. When it came down to it, he took the coward's way out and left town, and I'll be damned if I'll let him do that to you again."

Anna frowned at him. "He's not a coward, Frank. That much I know."

Frank was quiet then reached across the table and took her hands in his. The move was unexpected, but she didn't pull away.

"Maybe you're right," he said. "Maybe I'm just being selfish. I tend to get that way when I want something."

"And what would that be?"

"You, babe. It's always been you. You know that." He ran his thumb along her knuckles. "We never quite took the way I hoped we would, and I know I wasn't much of a father to Adam. But maybe we can try again."

"Frank, don't..."

"My apartment seems so empty without the two of you. I keep thinking that if you give me a chance, maybe we can get it right this time." He paused. "In fact, I know we can."

Anna gently pulled her hands away. She might not love Frank, but she did care for him, and she had no desire to hurt him any more than necessary.

"You had your chance to get it right last night," she said softly. "But you wouldn't even take half a minute to come in and say good-night to Adam. Why would anything be different now?"

His expression sagged. It obviously hadn't even occurred to him that he'd made a mistake last night.

She thought about Brody and Adam making chocolate chip pancakes and could not even imagine such a scene with Frank in the lead. His interest in Adam had been perfunctory at best. A means to an end for him. A promise that had remained unfulfilled.

The problem hadn't been that he wasn't much of a father. It was that he hadn't even *tried* to be a father at all.

"I'm sorry, Frank. I know you mean well, but I just can't be what you want me to be. I've moved on, and so should you."

Frank did a slow burn. She could see that despite her attempt to be gentle, it hadn't worked.

His humiliation was clear.

She was about to say something, a conciliatory gesture to help ease his pain, when there was a sharp knock on the door and Joe Wilson stuck his head inside.

Frank didn't look pleased. "What do you want?"

"Carpenter's a wash. I can't get anything out of him. I say we just book the creep and throw him in a—"

"Cut him loose," Frank snapped.

"What?"

He looked at Anna, and she knew that he was doing this for her. He got to his feet. "We're cutting them both loose and calling it self-defense."

"But what about—?"

"We've got no evidence to connect either of them to the electronics guy, and unless and until we do, they walk. You got me?"

Wilson pulled back slightly, jarred by Frank's abruptness, but he didn't argue.

"Sure," he said. "Consider it done."

Frank turned to Anna. Softened.

"You be careful out there, babe. And tell that boyfriend of yours, if he gets you hurt, he'll have to answer to me."

Then he pulled the door open, pushed past Wilson and left the room.

Chapter Ten

It was long past dark by the time they got to Anna's house.

She had called ahead to her mother, and after a series of disapproving sighs, Mom finally agreed to have dinner waiting for them.

Sylvia Sanford and Brody once had a terrific relationship. She'd known how much both Owen and Anna had loved him, and the feeling had carried over to her. She'd welcomed Brody as a second son.

During high school, Brody's own parents—who both worked for an airline—had traveled a lot, often leaving the seventeen-year-old at home to fend for himself. Brody had no siblings to spend time with, so he'd been lonely inside that big house, and Sylvia often invited him over for dinner.

This was long after Dad died, and Anna remembered that once the plates were cleared, Mom would always bring out the cards and give the three of them a hopeful look, wanting to play a game of Hearts.

All Anna and Brody wanted to do was spend time

alone, but Brody always obliged Sylvia, sometimes even insisting on a second round when the first was done.

When they got older and Brody graduated from the Cedarwood Sheriff's Academy, Mom was in the very front row, smiling and clapping as he received his badge. And when Brody had asked for her daughter's hand in marriage, Sylvia cried.

"I wish Walt could be here," she'd said then pulled him into her arms and hugged him for a full minute.

Anna had watched them from the top of the stairs, unable to keep from crying herself.

During the "crazy days"—as Mom often called them—when Brody's life was ripped apart by finger-pointing and relentless hounding by Internal Affairs investigators, Mom had been one of his staunchest supporters.

So when Brody had disappeared in the wake of it all, after telling Anna that he "needed to get away for a while," it had been Mom who defended him. She'd told Anna and Owen that he would be back, to give him the space he needed to heal.

That space, however, had stretched much wider and longer than any of them had expected. After months of no contact, after the wedding date came and went and they finally realized that Brody wasn't coming back after all—not anytime soon at least—Mom finally broke down.

She felt betrayed, she'd told Anna.

Bewildered and betrayed.

Brody was, she'd said at the time, dead to her. And after this pronouncement they all began to wonder if perhaps he really *was* dead. Nobody knew where he'd gone. Owen had had no luck contacting him. And that dull ache they felt in his absence eventually grew more tolerable.

Adam's birth and Anna's marriage to Frank had helped, of course, but like Owen, Sylvia had never particularly liked Frank and his presence in their lives was no substitute for the real thing.

Bottom line, despite the betrayal, the broken trust, they all still loved Brody, and he was never very far from their hearts and minds.

They had learned, however, that the line that separated love and hate was a very thin one indeed.

ANNA KNEW THAT HER mother's fury was at least equal to her own. So getting her to agree to serve dinner to Brody tonight had been a minor miracle.

When they got home she remained stoic but civil, even sat down at the table with them. And to Anna's surprise, she had cooked Brody's favorite—meat loaf with mashed potatoes and gravy—which led Anna to wonder just how angry her mother really was.

Maybe the protests had all been for show. Now that the initial shock of his return had been absorbed, perhaps in the wake of their tragedy, Brody's staunchest supporter was willing to forgive—if not completely forget.

Anna's father, who was one of the most well-read men she'd ever known, had once said something to her that she'd always remember. She must have been ten years old at the time, and she had just caught her best friend stealing money out of the piggy bank in her room. The betrayal had been devastating, and she remembered crying in her father's arms, telling him how much she now hated the girl. Her father, who had been fond of quoting poets and writers and famous politicians, suggested Anna find a place in her heart to forgive her friend.

When Anna balked, her father shook his head and said, "Without forgiveness, sweetie, there's no future." Then he'd tucked her into bed, kissed her forehead and promised her that the sooner she learned to forgive, the faster she'd heal.

Many years later, Anna found those words—or words very similar—in a book of quotations boxed in the attic, attributed to the Reverend Desmond Tutu.

Without forgiveness there is no future.

Seeing them again only reinforced the sentiment behind them, and Anna now wondered if she should take heed.

Maybe the good reverend—and her father—were on to something.

THE CONVERSATION AT dinner was stiff but cordial. They stuck to small talk, mostly because they were all too raw to talk about anything else.

After a while they began to loosen up, lapsing into reminiscences about their younger years—before the "crazy days" came upon them—when Brody and Owen were playing football at Cedarwood High and Anna was on the cheerleading squad.

There was a kind of sweet melancholy to the moment, punctuated by knowing glances, and the elephant in the room was the empty chair across the table.

After a while, Mom finally gave in and nodded to that chair, a broken smile on her face.

Her voice wavered as she spoke. "He missed you so much, Brody. We all did."

Brody nodded absently then spent a long moment staring at the food on his plate.

When he finally looked up again, he said, "This may be a bit hard for you to swallow, but the Sanford family was the best thing that ever happened to me." He sighed. "I can't believe I threw it all away."

Without hesitating, Sylvia said, "Neither can we."

And suddenly they were all laughing, her words so unexpected yet so true, they found themselves doubled over. It was, Anna thought, a cleansing of the soul. A regeneration of the spirit. A brief but welcome return to what they'd once been.

As the moment subsided, a small voice said, "Why are you guys laughing?" and they turned to

find Adam standing at the foot of the stairs, only half awake and rubbing his eyes.

Brody took one look at him, broke into a wide smile and patted his lap. "Come here, tiger."

To Anna's surprise, Adam didn't hesitate. He scooted across the room, climbed into Brody's lap and snuggled against him as if it were the most natural thing in the world.

Anna felt a hitch in her throat.

She glanced at her mother and Mom had that knowing look in her eye, the one that told her it was time for some housekeeping. The world wouldn't be right until Anna had swept all the corners and dusted all the windowsills.

But Anna wasn't sure she was up to it just yet. She had to wait for the right moment.

"I'm hungry," Adam said, his eyes on all the food.

Sylvia frowned at him. "You already had your dinner, young man. You're supposed to be asleep."

"How come you guys get to stay up?"

"That's a good question," Brody said, ruffling Adam's hair. "After the day we've had, we should all probably go straight to bed."

Adam looked up at him. "Are you gonna sleep in the chair again?"

Another good question, Anna thought. Now that Santa and his partner were dead, was it still necessary

for Brody to keep vigil, or was the threat against her gone?

They didn't know exactly what the two thugs had wanted from her and why, or what Owen's involvement with them had been, and they certainly didn't know if there were other bad guys in the picture.

So was she safe now?

She definitely felt safer with Brody around, but until they had more answers, she doubted she'd be able to completely relax.

Before they left the sheriff's office, Frank had made noises about continuing to investigate. He'd even reluctantly agreed that the events of the day may cast new light on Owen's suicide, but Anna knew from hard experience that Frank's word could never be completely relied upon.

"I think," Sylvia said to her grandson, "that we can probably find a spare bed. Maybe Uncle Owen's old room." She turned to Brody. "Would that be all right with you?"

The offer was not an insignificant one. Mom had just extended the ultimate olive branch, and the look on Brody's face told Anna that he was both humbled and grateful.

"More than all right," he said softly. "I'd be honored."

UNLIKE MANY PARENTS after their children leave the nest, Sylvia had not turned her son's room into a

study or TV room or sewing den. She'd kept it pretty much the same as Brody remembered it, complete with posters on the wall, gaming console, TV atop the battered oak desk and the stack of comics piled knee-high in one corner.

Brody went to the stack, pulled an X-Men off the top and leafed through it, once again remembering the day he'd first met Anna and how she had taken his breath away the moment he saw her.

As if by magic, she appeared in the doorway carrying fresh sheets and blankets. Laying them atop the desk chair, she crossed to the bed and began stripping away the linen.

Brody dropped the comic book back on the stack and moved to help her. "You get the rug bunny squared away?"

"He's all bundled up with his sheriff's car in his arms. I swear he's practically attached to that thing."

Brody smiled. "I've gotta give you credit, kiddo. You and Frank really did something special there."

Anna smiled wistfully. "Me and Frank."

She looked as if she wanted to say something more then stopped herself. Her eyes clouded for a few brief seconds, then she seemed to shake away whatever it was that was bothering her. Brody knew her and Frank's relationship was none of his business. He wasn't sure why he'd even asked her before. He didn't really *want* to know about it.

Bundling the soiled sheets, Anna dropped them to the floor then reached past Brody for the fresh ones.

Heat radiated off her skin, and the close proximity of her body was just too much to resist.

He impulsively caught her waist in his arms, turning her toward him, looking into the face he'd cherished since he was seventeen.

She was startled by the move, but she didn't seem to mind. They stood there, saying nothing, the air between them charged with electricity. Brody considered that he might be risking a slap to the face, but he didn't care. He pulled her close, pressed his lips to hers—and they didn't tighten, didn't resist.

She seemed to need this as much as he did.

The kiss felt so familiar, so right, that he realized it was as unique to her as a fingerprint of a wanted man. No woman he had kissed before or since felt the same. The softness of her lips, the scent of her breath, the feel of her tongue against his…

They were all distinctly Anna.

His Anna.

"Mommy?"

They abruptly broke away from each other. Adam stood in the doorway, once again rubbing his eyes. He didn't seem to have noticed what they were up to.

"I can't sleep," he said.

Embarrassed, Anna involuntarily fluffed her hair

and straightened her clothes then started toward her son. “I’ll read you a story.”

Brody caught her arm.

“No,” he said. “Let me do it.” He looked at Adam. “Would that be okay with you, champ?”

The boy’s face lit up. “Yeah! Can we read X-Men?”

“I don’t see why not.”

Grabbing the comic book from atop the stack, he slipped past Anna—their gazes connecting—and followed Adam to his room.

Several minutes later, Anna appeared in Adam’s doorway and said good-night. Brody saw the faraway look in her eyes and knew that the moment between them had passed. She’d had time to think about what just happened and decided it was a mistake.

At least that’s what he thought he saw. He wasn’t a mind reader.

Maybe she was just sad.

There was a lot of that going around these days.

Chapter Eleven

The men in the sedan had been watching the house for over two hours.

They'd seen lights go on and off, first downstairs, then upstairs, and they knew they were witnessing the routine of a household getting ready for bed.

"None of this makes any sense," the passenger said. "We should've done this days ago."

"We shouldn't be having to do this at all," the driver told him. "If Chercover and Sakey had done their jobs, we'd have that button by now."

"And what makes you think she's got it?"

"Because I saw it in the pipsqueak's eyes."

"Whose eyes? Sanford's?"

The driver nodded. "He wasn't cooperating. It didn't seem to even faze him that I was about to put a bullet in him, like he'd made his peace with God or something. But right before I pulled the trigger, I asked him if he'd given it to her and he kept shaking his head, telling me 'no, no'—but I could see in his eyes he was lying."

"And that's what you're going on? His *eyes?*"

"Trust me," the driver said. "She's got it and she knows it, and it's hidden somewhere in that house."

"It better be. It's almost Christmas Eve—and you know what that means."

"We'll make it. Don't you worry."

"Tell that to Chercover and Sakey."

"Chercover and Sakey were cowboys. Tearing up Sanford's apartment, tossing Caldwell in the river, making that ridiculous play in the parking lot. All that trouble and they wound up dead. I told them we needed to finesse this thing, but they wouldn't listen."

"Like you finessed it with Sanford?"

The driver said nothing. Just turned and looked at the other man.

The passenger held his hands up. "I'm just sayin'. If you'd let *me* have a crack at him, I would've gotten him to talk."

The driver shook his head. "Not without consequences. If he'd had any suspicious marks on his body, that would've opened up a whole new kettle of worms. And we can't afford that."

"Yeah? What do we do when they figure out who Chercover and Sakey really are?"

"It'll be long past party time by then," the driver said, "and we'll be very rich men."

"So you keep tellin' me."

"You don't believe me? I've already got a buyer

lined up ready to drop two mil on those schematics. If I can find another bidder, we can name our price."

"Not if we don't get that button." He gestured toward the house. "And I don't relish stumbling around in the dark, looking for a needle in a haystack. Especially when I'm not sure the needle's even *in* the haystack."

"Trust me, it's there."

"So's the scooter boy. How do you plan on dealing with *him?*"

"I don't. If we're careful, he won't even know we're there. None of them will."

"You sound pretty confident," the passenger said. "You sure these gizmos you got us will work?"

"They'll work. The tech demoed them for me. All we have to do is wait for the beep."

"Sounds like voodoo to me."

The driver shook his head again. "Simple electronics. We kill the lights, go in, snatch the prize and we're gone."

"And if scooter boy wakes up?"

The driver smiled. "We put him right back to sleep."

IT WAS THE THOUGHT of her kiss that kept him awake.

He could still taste her on his tongue. Feel her lips. The hunger in them.

Her scent lingered in the room, an intoxicating mix of cologne and sweat and pheromones.

He had tried closing his eyes, putting her from his mind, but after a full hour of sleeplessness, he finally gave up.

He kept seeing the look on her face as she stood in Adam's doorway. The sadness. The regret.

He knew she was conflicted. Knew that she wanted him, but she wasn't quite sure she was willing to go there again. To make that commitment.

Why should she? He hadn't proved to be all that reliable.

But he was older now, and he'd learned that there were a lot more important things in the world than his own battered ego. He'd spent the past few years kicking himself for his selfish, unthinking behavior toward Anna, and he knew full well that her last memory of him was of a man walking out the door, never to return.

How could he possibly erase that?

As much as Brody liked to tell himself that Anna was the same woman he remembered, the reality was that she had moved on. She had a different life now.

A business to run. A son to raise.

Frank's son.

The thought tore at him. If he had played things right, he would have been making chocolate chip cookies with his *own* boy. He and Anna would have

created the family that he'd never really known. The family he'd never really *thought* about until he was welcomed into the Sanford home when he was barely a man himself.

It didn't really bother him that Adam was another man's son. Blood or no blood, he had taken to the boy right away. Felt an easy camaraderie with him. But while he sensed that Frank wasn't in the picture much, Brody had no doubt that if he were to stay in Anna's life, Frank would feel that old tug of rivalry, and things would get complicated very fast.

He wasn't sure he was willing to be the cause of that kind of friction. He'd already done enough to this family.

Yet as he lay there in Owen's bed, he couldn't stop thinking about that kiss. It had stirred something that had been dormant inside him for far too long.

He wanted Anna. Badly. So badly that he could hardly contain himself.

He didn't *want* to contain himself.

Impulsively, he got to his feet and went to the door. He didn't quite know what he was doing, what his plan was, his desire clouding all rational thought. Last night he had resisted the urge to go straight into Anna's room, but this was a different night now and he could no longer resist.

He opened Owen's door and stepped into the hallway. Anna's room was the last one on the right,

and he could see light coming from the crack at the bottom of her door.

Still awake.

He stopped thinking then. Didn't hesitate. Didn't evaluate. Didn't weigh his options and consider a course of action. Instead, he reacted. Simply aimed himself toward that light and moved. And when he reached the door, he grabbed the knob and pushed inside—

—and there was Anna, sitting on the edge of the bed as if she'd been waiting for him, wearing nothing but an unbuttoned shirt, one of his old uniform shirts from his early days on the force—the one she'd often be wearing when she handed him that thermos full of coffee at the door.

She looked like something from a fever dream, and Brody felt as if he had somehow stepped out of his own body and was observing this moment from another plane of existence.

Then her voice snapped him back to reality. She spoke softly, the underlying sadness still there.

"Why are you here, Brody? Why did you come back? What do you want from me?"

"I just want to make it right," he said.

"You can't. This will never work. I hate you too much. I'll never forgive you."

He nodded. "I know."

Then he went to her and pulled her into his arms.

A few moments later he was inside her—inside her body and her mind.

And he wanted to stay there.

Forever.

He just hoped she'd let him.

BRODY CAME AWAKE WHEN he heard the noise.

It was a subtle sound—nothing that would alarm the average Joe lying in an upstairs bedroom next to the woman he loved. Not a crash or the tinkling of broken glass or a stumbling thump or the creak of wood on the stairs.

But then Brody wasn't your average Joe. Just as he'd been trained to use his eyes, he had also learned to rely on his ears to alert him to signs of danger, and what he heard may have been subtle, but it was there.

A faint rustling. Nothing more.

Outside Anna's window.

It could have been the wind, but he knew it wasn't. A scurrying rodent, perhaps, but this particular rodent undoubtedly stood on two legs. There were bushes on this side of the house, and he knew that someone would have to squeeze past them to get to the electrical panel in the wall below the window.

A moment later the soft creak of a rusty hinge told him the panel door was being opened. There was a soft *thump,* then the digital clock on the side of the bed went blank.

Brody flew out of bed, grabbed his pants from the floor and yanked them on. Leaning toward Anna, he cupped his hand over her mouth and shook her awake.

She opened her eyes with a start, sucking in a quick breath. Brody put a finger to his lips, telling her to be quiet, then leaned in close and whispered in her ear.

"Get Adam and Sylvia and bring them in here. Move as quietly and as quickly as possible and hide in your closet."

He sensed that she wanted to say something, so he kept his hand cupped over her mouth.

"Someone's here," he told her. "You need to keep Adam safe."

She nodded, and he took his hand away. She got out of bed, her naked body silhouetted against the light from the window. Grabbing a robe from the closet, she pulled it on, wordlessly, then crossed to the door.

Brody snatched his gun off the nightstand and waited in the hallway as Anna moved silently to Sylvia's room then on to Adam's and brought them back. Adam was fast asleep on her shoulder, Sylvia blinking in fear and bewilderment as she followed her daughter into the bedroom.

After the three had squeezed into the closet and shut themselves inside, Brody closed the bedroom

door then crept down the hall to the top of the stairs.

He waited.

Listened.

The house was silent.

Almost eerily so.

Then he heard it: the faint *snick* of a dead bolt lock.

The door at the side of the house.

Whoever this guy was, he was good. Not many people could pick a lock that fast.

And his presence here meant only one thing.

Just as Brody had suspected, the two guys in the van were not the last of it. And whomever they'd left behind still thought that Anna had the button. Or that it was somewhere inside this house.

And maybe that was true.

Or maybe it was right here in Brody's pocket. The RFID tag he'd found in the garment factory.

What the hell was on this thing?

He quietly flicked the safety off his gun and raised it, stepping sideways down the stairs. By the time he got to the bottom, he'd heard the door open and close—barely a whisper—followed by two pairs of shoes, thumping quietly on the polished wooden floor.

Not one man, but two.

If they split up, as he fully expected them to, Brody would be at a distinct disadvantage. His *only*

advantage, he thought, was that they didn't yet know he was awake.

But even if he took one of them down, the other would still be roaming freely, and that just wouldn't stand.

He couldn't let either of them get up those stairs.

Not with Anna and her family up there.

Circling backwards he stepped into the shadows next to the stairway, where a tall Christmas tree stood, adorned with handmade ornaments, its lights dormant for the night.

He decided it was best to go on the defensive and wait these guys out. And just as he had expected, he heard their footfalls move in opposite directions, one heading toward the family room and kitchen, while the other came toward the carpeted steps.

A moment later, a dark silhouette emerged from a hallway and moved in his direction. Stepping deeper into the shadows, Brody waited as the man approached.

Only his eyes were visible through a ski mask, nothing more than two black dots in the wan moonlight filtering through the living room window.

The guy didn't seem to be in a hurry, one of his arms extended, holding a dark object in front of him.

Certainly not a flashlight.

A gun?

A knife?

It didn't look like either, but Brody couldn't be sure in this light. He'd have to be very careful when he took him down.

The man stopped for a moment, turning in his tracks, keeping the object extended in front of him. Then he continued toward the stairs.

When the man's foot hit the first step, Brody emerged from the shadows, circled around behind him and pressed the muzzle of his gun into the small of his back.

The guy froze.

"Two steps backwards," Brody whispered. "Very slowly."

The guy did as he was told. But as his foot came down to the floor, he shifted suddenly, feinting to Brody's left, then quickly moved to the right, bringing an elbow back, straight toward Brody's chest.

Anticipating the move, Brody stepped away and spun him around, grabbing hold of the wrist that held the weapon—or whatever it was—and driving the arm upward.

The man grunted and swung out again with his free arm, connecting with Brody's shoulder. Brody absorbed the impact and stumbled back, but it hadn't been enough to knock him down.

He started to bring his gun up again, but the guy charged, slamming him against the wall. The blow dazed him and the gun flew out of his hand and

straight into a nearby table lamp. The lamp crashed to the floor, shattering against the wood.

A split second later, he heard running footsteps in the hall and knew the second guy was on his way and likely to be armed. Twisting away from his attacker, he swung out hard, slamming his forearm into the side of the man's head. The guy grunted and fell to one knee, but before Brody could move in for another blow—

—the second one emerged from the hallway—also wearing a ski mask—the black ugly silhouette of a gun in his hand.

As the gun came up, Brody dove.

The weapon flashed, once, twice, three times, narrowly missing Brody as he hit the floor and rolled behind the couch.

Three more shots were fired, punching the sofa cushions. Then, without a word spoken between them, the two thugs turned tail and ran, the hallway echoing the sound of their retreat.

Jumping to his feet, Brody found his own gun amidst the lamp debris, snatched it up and barreled toward the front door. Throwing it open, he ran out onto the lawn just in time to see the two men running down the street, jumping into a dark sedan.

As the engine roared to life, Brody sprinted toward the sidewalk, raising the gun.

But he didn't fire.

This was a family neighborhood, and despite the

hour, he had no intention of adding any of his own bullets to the chaos.

Instead, he watched the sedan burn a long patch of rubber as it tore down the street and disappeared. And he knew this wasn't the last he'd see of these guys.

Chapter Twelve

When the closet door opened, Anna nearly shot Brody's head off.

Once they'd closed themselves inside, she had handed Adam off to her mom and quickly searched the closet shelf for the shoe box containing her dad's old pistol and loaded magazine.

Anna fumbled in darkness, trying to snap the clip in place. Her father never had a chance to teach her how to shoot, but she knew he'd kept the gun for their protection. Years after he died she dug it out of the attic, but had never taken it out of the box until now.

The silence that followed the gunshots downstairs was excruciating. She had no idea what had happened and could only think the worst.

Had Brody been shot?

Was he dead?

The thought sent such a violent wave of horror through her that it took everything she had to keep

from throwing the closet door open and crying out to him or running down to see if he was alive.

But she remained still, only the sound of her rapid breathing filling the silence.

Adam had miraculously slept through it all, but Mom looked as terrified as Anna felt. When they heard the door to the bedroom open and knew that someone was in the room, Anna tried to remain calm, but her knees began to buckle.

She brought the pistol up, her hands trembling uncontrollably, not knowing what to expect.

Could she pull the trigger if she had to?

Did she have that kind of courage?

If it meant protecting Adam, then yes, she would do what had to be done. But she didn't relish the thought of killing someone, no matter how heinous he might be.

A moment later, the closet door flew open and Anna came very close to squeezing off a shot. It took her a split second to realize that it was Brody standing there, but in that tiny moment of time, she almost put a bullet between his eyes.

He jumped back at the sight of the pistol. "Woah. Where'd you get that thing?"

Anna lowered it and fell into Brody's arms. "Oh my God, you're alive. Are you all right?"

He pulled her close, running his hands along her back. "My pride's a little bruised, but I'll survive. Unfortunately, the bad guys got away."

He stepped back now, letting them out of the closet, and gestured to the pistol. "You'd better put that where it belongs. There's been enough shooting around here for one night."

She nodded and immediately found the box and put the pistol away.

"Is it safe to take Adam to bed?" Sylvia asked.

Brody nodded. "They won't be coming back any-time soon."

As Mom carried Adam back to his room, Brody pulled out his cell phone and dialed. "This is Brody Carpenter. I need you to get Deputy Matson out of bed and over to his ex-wife's place right away. There's been an attack on her house." He looked at Anna. "There's no way Frank can ignore this thing now."

Anna only hoped he was right.

TWENTY MINUTES LATER, it seemed as if half the sheriff's deputies in Cedarwood County were inside Anna's house. Add the ballistics team to the mix, which was busy digging slugs out of the wall, and there was barely enough room to move.

It took Frank and Joe Wilson a while to show up. They both came in looking rumpled and only half awake, Frank studying the scene somberly—the broken lamp, the holes in the wall, the ruined sofa cushions. Then he approached Anna and Brody, who were sitting at the dining room table.

He gave Brody a look of mild disgust, then turned to Anna. "Can I speak to you in private, please?"

"You can talk in front of Brody," she said.

"I'd rather not. We need to interview you separately."

Anna glanced at Brody and he nodded, patting her hand. The gesture didn't get past Frank. He scowled at them then crossed into the kitchen, taking a seat at the table inside.

Anna didn't immediately follow. "Talk about déjà vu…"

"Go on," Brody told her. "It's standard procedure. Just answer his questions. We want him on our side."

Anna nodded, knowing Brody was right. But only a few hours ago she had been sitting in an interrogation room across from Frank and the situation hadn't been pleasant. She couldn't generate much excitement over the idea of a repeat performance. Especially so soon. Especially if it involved another "let's get back together" proposal.

Heaving a sigh, she got to her feet, crossed to the kitchen and stood in the doorway. "Well?"

"Have a seat," Frank said.

"I'd rather stand, thank you."

Frank waved dismissively. "Have it your way. But I just want you to know that the undersheriff has approved putting a couple of deputies at the doors.

Front and side." He paused. "And we're reopening Owen's case."

Anna was surprised. Brody had said this was bound to happen, considering tonight's turn of events, but she hadn't quite believed it.

"You're serious?"

"I don't joke about an investigation. You know that as well as anyone."

Anna sat at the table now, reaching across to take his hands in hers. "Thank you, Frank. Thank you."

He pulled his hands away. All business. "We still don't have IDs on the two guys in the van, but once we do, we're hoping we can find some kind of connection to Owen."

"Owen would never have anything to do with those creeps."

"Maybe it wasn't voluntary. Whatever the case, it looks like they wanted this button thing and their partners must be convinced Owen passed it on to you."

"I told you all this two nights ago."

"You still claiming you don't know what it is?"

Anna frowned at him. "Claiming?"

"Come on, Anna. You and Owen were like two peas in a pod. If he was in trouble, I can't imagine he wouldn't share something like that with you. Which is why you kept insisting it wasn't suicide."

Anna stiffened. "What are you saying, Frank? That I'm lying to you?"

"Maybe you just have some sort of misguided loyalty to Owen and think you need to cover for him. If he was involved in a crime—"

"Stop," Anna told him. "Don't even go there."

"It's just one theory of many, and I have to try them all. Are you sure Owen didn't give you something? Something to keep for him?"

"I already told you. No."

"A gift, maybe. Something you've forgotten about."

"How many times do I have to say this, Frank? He didn't give me anything. He didn't share any dark secrets, and I have no idea why he was killed. That's why I came to you. And that's why Brody's here."

The mention of Brody's name didn't make Frank happy. She could see that. While she was grateful that he was reopening Owen's case, she got the feeling that he was doing it grudgingly. That he wasn't completely convinced that Owen had been murdered. He was going through the motions because he'd been ordered to.

She had intended to tell him about the disk Brody found in the garment factory, but now she wondered if she should even bother. Frank would only insist that Brody give it to him, and she had a feeling that's the last they'd hear of it. That it would go into a plastic bag and be stuck in a box somewhere, never to be seen again.

Before dinner last night, Brody had called an

electronics guy he knew who had offered to see if he could help them figure out if the disk had any significance.

Would Frank do the same if it were in his possession?

Somehow she doubted it.

So basically what he was offering her was lip service and nothing more. Something he had always excelled at.

"Tell me what happened tonight," he said. "Start from the beginning."

She thought about it then told him, skipping over Brody's visit to her bed and picking up the story again at the point where Brody woke her up and told her to get Adam and her mother into the closet.

"Did he explain what was going on?"

"He just said someone was here. In the house."

"And how did he know this?"

"I don't know. He didn't say. I guess he heard a sound and reacted."

"Did you hear it, too?"

She shook her head. "I was fast asleep."

"So then you don't actually know if someone was in the house. You just took his word for it."

Anna looked at him, puzzled. She didn't like this line of questioning. "What are you getting at, Frank?"

He ignored her. "Where were you when the shots were fired?"

"Upstairs, in my closet, along with Mom and Adam."

"So nobody actually saw these so-called intruders fire at Brody."

"So-called?"

She just stared at him, not quite believing her ears. Was he serious about this? Did he think Brody had staged the whole thing?

Frank sighed and leaned back in his chair. "Look, Anna, I know you care about this guy, but I don't like what's shaping up here."

"Quit being cryptic, Frank. Get to the point."

"All right," he said. "When Joe and I had our little chat with Brody at the mall, Brody showed me a note he said he got from Owen."

"Right," Anna said. "So?"

"So if Owen managed somehow to locate Brody out in the middle of nowhere, who's to say they weren't in contact earlier?"

"Owen would have told me."

"Maybe, maybe not." Frank got to his feet and crossed to the stove. Grabbing the kettle, he went to the sink and filled it with water.

Although he was quite familiar with this kitchen, Anna thought he was being a bit presumptuous just helping himself like that.

He put the kettle on the burner and lit it. "What if I'm right? What if they were in contact earlier? What if Brody knows more than he's letting on? Maybe

Owen told him all about this button thing and he came here looking for it himself."

Anna was speechless. Even if she'd known how to react to this ridiculous notion, she wouldn't dignify it with a response.

Frank seemed to sense her frame of mind. He pulled the chair out again and sat.

"Just think about it," he said. "Brody shows up in town all of a sudden, just happens to be in the right place at the right time when you're attacked. So then he insinuates himself into your life, tries to get close to you again, because he's thinking the same thing those guys in the van were thinking. That you know where the button is."

"You're really stretching it, Frank. I know you don't like Brody, but do you even hear what you're saying?"

Frank shrugged. "He knows how to play you, babe. He always did. He gets you all gooey-eyed, you'll do just about anything for him."

Anna shook her head in disgust. "You're jealous. You always were."

He leaned toward her. "This doesn't have anything to do with me. I'm looking at this thing purely as a cop, and I don't like what I see. I thought the guy was clean back when the big storm came down, but maybe I was wrong. Maybe he was dirty then and he's dirty—"

Anna swung out, slapping Frank across the face.

Frank recoiled, bringing a hand to his cheek, anger filling his eyes.

"You just assaulted a sheriff's deputy," he said, barely able to control his fury.

No one else in the house seemed to notice what she'd done. Anna glanced at Brody, but he'd left the dining table and was talking to his deputy friend, Brett.

"I just slapped my idiot ex-husband who seems to think he's king of the world," she said. "And if you try even one more time to tell me that Brody had something to do with Owen's murder, it'll be a lot more than a slap."

"He's really got you snowed, doesn't he? What did he do? Tell you he loves you? That he's always loved you?" Frank shook his head. "He's just trying to get close to you again, so you'll give him what he wants."

"You have no idea what you're talking about."

Frank was about to bark a response when he paused, looking into Anna's eyes, seeing something there.

She had no idea what.

Then he said, "You slept with him, didn't you?"

Surprised by the question, Anna averted her gaze, felt her head prickle. She knew she was blushing. As wonderful as it was to be in Brody's arms again, she didn't quite know how she felt about it. Hadn't had time to evaluate and reflect.

The one thing she *did* know, however, was that Brody had nothing to do with these attacks, or with Owen's murder. That made about as much sense as the suicide.

"Well?" Frank asked. "You did, didn't you? You slept with him."

"That's none of your business," she said tersely then got to her feet. "You're way off base here, Frank, and I think you *know* that, but you're just trying to get a rise out of me. Your little bit of revenge for not wanting to get back with you."

"I just want to get to the truth."

"You want the truth?" Anna said. "I think it's *you* who's trying to take advantage of this situation. Which is nothing new. You came to me after Brody left, when I was vulnerable and needed someone, and you took advantage of *that* situation to fulfill some fantasy you'd had since high school."

"Now wait just a minute..."

"The truth is, Frank, you were a terrible husband, a terrible father to Adam, and as hard as I tried, I just never loved you." She could feel her legs trembling and her chest felt constricted. "If you think that's going to change now, you're crazy. So why don't you do us all a huge favor and just *leave me alone*."

She left him there and headed for the doorway, hearing the sharp, high whistle of the tea kettle behind her.

Chapter Thirteen

The guy's name was Coffey.

Brody had met him in a criminology class at Cedarwood Community College, back when he was studying up for the detective's exam that would finally put him in the homicide division—the job Brody had been aiming for ever since he joined the department.

This was just a few months before Brody's entire career took a nosedive, and he hadn't really known Coffey all that well, but they'd bonded pretty fast and had even caught a few cold ones together after class.

When the accusations about bribes had started flying, Coffey had called Brody up and offered him his support. Said if Brody ever needed someone to vouch for him, he'd be all too happy to do it.

"You're a stand-up, guy," he'd said over the phone. "And the only way I can figure this is that somebody set you up. So watch your back, amigo."

Coffey wasn't a sheriff's deputy, but he was a true

genius when it came to anything involving transistors and wired or wireless components. He'd spent time working for the Cedarwood district attorney's office in their electronic surveillance department.

Brody didn't know what Coffey was up to these days, but when he'd tried the old cell number, his friend answered and seemed genuinely pleased to hear from him after all these years.

"Hey, hey, amigo. There's a voice I never thought I'd hear again."

"I don't think you're alone on that count. How you been, man?"

"Life is good, ever since I quit doing government work. I came into some money, so I opened up a chain of electronics stores that pretty much run themselves."

"Glad to hear it."

"Yeah, I can't complain. You in town long? Want to catch a beer or two?"

Brody cleared his throat. "Actually," he said, "I'm hoping you can help me with something. Your area of expertise."

"Oh? What's up?"

Brody told him about the RFID tag he'd found in the garment factory and asked if Coffey would be willing to take a look at it.

Coffey didn't hesitate. "For you? No problem."

"Thanks, man."

They made arrangements to meet the next after-

noon at Coffey's place, and when Brody and Anna got there—feeling a little worn out after their ordeal with the thugs and the investigation that followed—they found a place that looked very much like a cleaner, neater version of the garment factory workshop.

A row of shelves and a long workbench dominated one side of the room, parts and equipment crowding most of the real estate. Coffey sat on a rollaway stool, hovering over a swing-arm magnifying lamp, staring intently at the minuscule speck of an electronic chip he'd caught between a pair of tweezers.

"I think it's blown," he said to Brody as they stepped inside the room. "Things are too darn fragile."

He stood up then and went to Brody, pulling him into a bear hug. "Good to see you, amigo. You're bigger than I remember. You been working out?"

Brody smiled. "I guess you could say that."

He introduced Anna and as they shook hands, Anna said, "I think we may've met briefly at a party a couple years ago. You were still working for the D.A., then."

Coffey studied her, then he grinned and nodded as the memory came back to him. "That's right. You're Frank Matson's wife."

"That was then, this is now," she said, and Coffey gave them a look that said he understood.

He gestured to Brody. "So where's this RFID tag you want to show me?"

Brody pulled the disk out of his pocket and handed it to him. Coffey held it up, giving it the once-over.

"Looks generic," he said. "Where'd you find it?"

"Place that looks a lot like this one, only in a much rougher neighborhood and with hacked electricity. I'm pretty sure he was working off the grid."

"You find any more?"

"No, but there was a drawer marked 'tags', and I have a feeling it once held a bunch of them."

Coffey nodded. "They're blanks. Ten to one this guy was making clones."

"Clones?" Anna asked. "Clones of what?"

"Radio-controlled security tags."

Anna frowned. "Brody mentioned that before. Security for what?"

Coffey went to his workbench and started rifling through the clutter.

"You ever have a job where the only way to get inside was through an electronically controlled door? There's no key, but there's a small box on the wall that you wave a card in front of?" He found what he was looking for and held it up. It was a blank credit card. No identifying marks. "One of these," he said.

Anna nodded. "I have one in my purse. I use it to get into the mall after hours."

Coffey held up the disk now. "This is essentially the same thing. A radio frequency identity tag—or

button as it's called in the biz. They're usually inserted inside key chains, so that all you have to do is wave your keys in front of the lock to gain entry."

"It's not just limited to key chains," Brody said. "Wristwatches, cell phones, compacts, you name it."

"So I assume it has some kind of special code in it?" Anna asked.

"Right," Coffey said. "They're coded with a unique ID that not only corresponds with the lock but stores the identity of the user and records the date and time of his or her entry." He held up the disk again. "Now, since you say this came out of a drawer that was probably full of these things, I'm guessing it's blank. But since you say this guy in the lab was working off the grid, I've got a feeling he was making clones, which is a very lucrative business."

"So he was making clones of existing ID cards?"

Coffey nodded. "He'd have to spoof the ID itself, but it can be done. And if one of these things falls into the wrong hands, you've got the potential for some major larceny. Whatever lock it corresponds to has just been rendered useless."

Brody gestured to the disk. "Can you check that thing, see if there's anything on it?"

"I can try."

He moved to his bench, played around for a moment with some of the gear there then waved

the button under it and shook his head. "Like I said—blank."

So it obviously wasn't the button they were looking for. Brody had hoped they'd get lucky, but he hadn't really been counting on it.

"If I wanted one of these clones made, how much would it cost me?"

Coffey frowned at him. "Sorry, amigo. You got the wrong guy. I'm not interested in going to prison."

"Relax, man, it's a hypothetical."

Coffey thought about it a moment, then said, "I guess if you want a sure thing—somebody who really knows what he's doing—you'd probably have to pay a few grand to get one."

Brody considered the withdrawal Owen had made shortly before visiting the garment factory. Five thousand dollars.

Had he been buying a clone?

And if so, why?

What lock was he trying to circumvent and how did Santa Claus and the other thugs figure into the equation?

Brody knew the clone must exist, otherwise people wouldn't be getting killed over it.

So where was it?

Somewhere in Anna's house?

In Owen's apartment?

Finding something so small in either place could be tough, if not impossible.

Unless you had assistance.

Brody thought back to the two thugs he'd tangled with that morning. Before he'd approached the one heading for the stairs, he'd noticed that the guy was carrying something that, at the time, he'd thought might be a weapon.

But what if it wasn't a weapon at all?

"If one of these tags was lost somewhere in my house," he said to Coffey, "is there a device I could use to home in on it? Make the search a little easier?"

"Sure," Coffey said. He crossed to a metal cabinet and opened the doors, revealing even more electronic gear stashed on its shelves. He rifled around for a moment and came back with a gray, rectangular device that was slightly larger than your average cell phone.

"This is a modified RFID reader," Coffey told them. "It's set to pick up any transmitter frequency within a three-foot range."

"How does it work?" Anna asked.

"You get close enough to your target and you'll know it." He flipped a switch on the side of the unit and extended his arm, moving toward the credit card tag on his workbench. As he got close, the device emitted a steady, high-pitched beep.

"Nice," Brody said. "You think we could borrow that?"

Coffey tossed the unit to Brody and it stopped

beeping. "Be my guest, amigo. Just make sure you turn it off when you're not using it. I don't know how long the battery will last." Then he grinned. "Oh, and don't get me in trouble."

Brody flicked the unit off and dropped it into his coat pocket.

"Wouldn't dream of it," he said.

Chapter Fourteen

When they got to Owen's place, they discovered that Frank hadn't been lying about reopening the case. The crime scene unit was parked out front, and several deputies were going in and out of the building.

"Bad timing," Brody told Anna. "They'll never let us into that apartment."

"So what do we do now?"

"Wait them out." He shifted his gaze to the sky. It was gray with clouds and threatening to burst. "It looks like a storm is coming, and I sure don't feel like waiting out here. I could use something hot to drink."

"We could go to the mall. Trudy's covering for me, but it wouldn't hurt to check in."

"Right before Christmas Eve? No thanks. I've had enough chaos for one day."

"Then where?"

Brody thought about it a moment. "How about Marlene's? Are they still in business?"

Anna's heart stuttered.

In the old days, Marlene's Diner had been one of their favorite haunts. They'd had their first date there, when, after months of endless flirting, Brody had finally mustered up the courage to ask her out.

The food at Marlene's was only passable and the Cokes were watered down, but none of this had registered that first awkward night, when all Anna could do was stare across the table at Brody while trying hard to pretend she wasn't madly in love with him. Admitting something like that was far too risky for a girl her age, especially when she wasn't sure how Brody had felt.

She knew by the end of the night.

As they lay in the darkness of her bedroom, in the afterglow of their first time together, Anna's heart pounding, her legs weak and trembling, her entire body still tingling with pleasure, she had known, with great certainty, that Brody was the boy—the man—she would be with forever.

Funny how things change.

MARLENE'S HADN'T CHANGED much, however. Anna hadn't been here in years, and it may have been a little worn around the edges, but it had the same red patent-leather booths, checkered tables and surly, disinterested waitresses.

They found their usual spot near the jukebox, both going to it automatically. Although the "forever" that Anna had dreamt of never materialized,

the familiarity of the place took her back to those simpler days, when all she wanted was time alone with Brody.

After the waitress brought their coffee, he said, "I think we need to talk about what happened last night."

Anna was surprised. Brody had always been a doer, not a talker. A creature of impulse. And last night had certainly been an impulsive move for both of them—the product of nearly four years of pent-up desire that ended with the same pounding heart, the same weak and trembling legs, the same tingling of pleasure she got whenever she was with Brody.

But with everything that had happened since, she still hadn't had time to process the moment, and she wasn't sure she was ready to talk about it.

"Can't we just leave it alone?" she said. "Enjoy it for what it was?"

"What *was* it?"

Anna thought about this, shrugged. "Two old friends trying to comfort each other?"

Brody looked wounded. "Is that all it meant to you?"

"To be honest, Brody, I'm not sure. I'd be lying to you if I said I didn't want it. Or that I wish it hadn't happened. But we aren't kids anymore. We have different lives now." She sighed. "I still love you, you know. That'll probably never change. But I

have complications in my life. There's Adam to think about and…"

She stopped herself.

Should she tell him the truth?

Could she?

"And what?" he asked.

Don't, Frank had said. *Don't tell him.*

Anna shook her head. She'd waited a long time for this moment, had tried desperately to contact Brody so that she could share the news, but now that the moment was finally here, now that they were sitting face-to-face, she couldn't bring herself to say it—just as she couldn't say it last night, when she lay in his arms.

This had nothing to do with what Frank had told her. Despite his overtures of late, she'd written him off long ago and his opinion had never been less important to her.

Still, she hesitated. Brody had a right to the truth—she knew that. But what she *didn't* know was where he'd be a week from now. Or a year.

Would he still be in Cedarwood?

Was this something she could count on?

The emotions swirling around them were too raw, too volatile to be introducing something new and unexpected into the mix, and her instincts told her that now just wasn't the time to broach the subject.

But if not now, when?

"Anna?"

"Nothing," she said. "It can wait."

Brody furrowed his brow at her. "What's going on? I keep feeling like you want to tell me something but you're holding back."

"It can wait," she said again then sipped her coffee in silence.

BY THE TIME THEY GOT back to Owen's apartment building, it was raining. Not hard, but Brody knew that they were only a thunderclap away from an all-out downpour.

The good news was that the deputies and CSI wagon were gone. Not really a surprise, he supposed, since there wasn't a whole lot of evidence to gather and the scene had been thoroughly contaminated, especially a week after the crime had taken place.

In fact, coming here again may well have been a waste of *their* time, but Brody believed in being thorough, and if that RFID tag was somewhere in Owen's condo, they had to find it.

He didn't expect the bodies in the van to be identified anytime soon, and that button—and the information encoded on it—was the only thing that might lead them to the truth.

After checking to make sure there weren't any stray deputies lingering, they made their way up to the fourteenth-floor hallway and saw a fresh new criss-cross of yellow crime scene tape blocking Owen's door.

Brody pulled it aside and turned to Anna. Ever since they'd left Marlene's she'd seemed subdued and preoccupied. He knew there were a number of things weighing on her mind right now, and he had decided to give her space.

He'd certainly taken enough of his own.

More than enough.

"Key?" he said.

She came out of her fog then dug around in her purse until she found one. Reaching past him, she unlocked the door and pushed it open.

Brody took the modified RFID reader from his pocket, switched it on then stepped into the living room, feeling Anna right behind him.

The place didn't look any different. Some of the clutter had been moved, and Brody was sure that the photographs Anna had found and any significant records or paperwork would have been bagged and tagged. But only a trained eye would know that anyone had been here since he and Anna had left the place yesterday.

He kept his arm extended and moved about the room, working his way past the sofa and chairs, the coffee table, the credenza against one wall, stepping gingerly around the contents of the drawers that had been dumped on the floor.

Nothing. The RFID reader remained silent.

They moved to the kitchen. The cabinets hung open and boxes of cereal, bags of flour and sugar

and canned goods were scattered across the linoleum, along with pots and pans and drawers full of utensils.

Brody waved the device past all of them, crouching to get low to the floor.

Still nothing. The reader didn't beep.

They crossed to the bedroom. As it had yesterday, the door hung open, and Brody knew that Anna wouldn't like what was waiting for them inside, so he repeated his warning.

"You might want to hold back."

But she shook her head this time. "No. I want to see. I want to know exactly what they did to him."

They stepped past the threshold, and as Anna stood near the doorway, taking it all in with a look of complete horror on her face, Brody moved about the room, arm extended.

The sheets had been stripped off the bed, but there was still a deep crimson stain on the mattress and blood splatter on the headboard, painting a vivid picture of the violence that had taken place in the room.

There were a couple of trajectory markers, complete with string and flags, and Brody knew that the crime scene techs were trying to establish whether the gunshot wound had been self-inflicted.

In his opinion they should have done this the first time around, and he blamed Frank for not following through.

"You gonna be okay?" he asked Anna.

She had a dazed look in her eyes, but she nodded. "I think so."

He went back to his task, but still the RFID reader picked up nothing.

As he reached the clutter left by the ransacking of Owen's desk, he discovered something he'd missed before—probably because it hadn't held much significance at the time.

It was a pink, rectangular sheet of paper. The duplicate layer of a form that had apparently been filled out and submitted. The header at the top read NORTHBOARD INDUSTRIES, followed by a list of checkboxes, indicating the items that were returned upon Owen's separation from the company.

Anna had told Brody that Owen had been laid off shortly before his death, and his depression over the loss of his job had contributed to the idea that he had taken his own life.

All of the boxes had been checked off, and Owen's signature was scribbled across the line at the bottom, along with the date of submission. Nothing unusual here, but one of the listed items caught Brody's attention.

"Look at this," he said to Anna.

She tore her gaze away from the bed and crossed to him. He handed her the sheet of paper.

She took a quick glance. "What about it?"

"Item number three," he said.

She scanned the list slowly this time, her expression changing as it registered. "A key card."

Brody nodded. "Which would open just about any secure room in the Northboard building. I seem to remember that Owen had a pretty high clearance rating."

"He was one of their top engineers. But what are you trying to say?"

"Look at the date under his signature."

She did. "So?"

"He turned that key card in a few days after he withdrew the five grand and met with the guy at the garment factory. Ten to one the technology behind that card was RFID."

Anna's expression grew heated. This wasn't the reaction Brody had expected. "So you think that's what he was trying to have cloned? Is that what you're getting at?"

"It only makes sense."

"But why?"

"Come on, Anna, I think it's pretty obvious. Northboard is one of the premier weapons manufacturers in the United States, with more government contracts than either of us can count. There's a lot of information in that building, locked behind very secure doors, and access to that information would be worth a heckuva lot of money to interested parties."

"So let me understand this," Anna said, and he could see that the heat was rising. "You're telling

me that Owen got his key card cloned because he planned on selling that access."

"I'm afraid that's what it looks like."

"You're saying my brother was a criminal."

"He'd just been laid off from his job," Brody said. "These are tough times, and he had a mortgage to pay, a pretty high one from the looks of this place. And even with his skills as an engineer, there was no guarantee he'd get a new job anytime soon."

Anna shook her head in disgust. "I can't believe I'm hearing this."

"What do you want me to do? Sugarcoat it?"

"I want you to listen to yourself. Owen was your best friend, for God's sakes. You know better than anyone that he wasn't some petty crook. He was a good man."

"Desperate times lead to desperate measures, Anna. And who knows, maybe he was coerced. The guys he was dealing with weren't playing patty-cake. Maybe after he got the card cloned, he had second thoughts. His conscience kicked in and he tried to back out on the deal, and he got himself killed because of it."

Anna's face was full of fury now. "I can't believe you're blaming him. You sound just like Frank."

"I'm a trained investigator. I have to call it like I see—"

"Owen stood *by you,* Brody. When people were saying the same kinds of things about you, he told

them they were out of their minds. That you'd never take a bribe."

Brody sighed. "I know that, Anna. I couldn't have asked for a better friend. But we have to look at this thing logically. We can't discard the obvious because we cared about the guy."

"And why should I listen to you?"

"I'm just trying to get to the truth here."

"The truth?" Anna cried. "You want the truth? You're the guy who couldn't be honest enough to tell me you weren't coming back after you left. You're the guy who ran away when things got tough, because there weren't enough people like Owen around to support you." She tossed the pink slip at him now, her anger at its boiling point. "And you're the guy who abandoned his pregnant girlfriend when she needed him most."

There was a sudden stillness to the air as Brody just stared at her.

Pregnant?

Anna had been *pregnant?*

Then the realization came down on him like a crumbling brick wall. "Are you telling me that Adam..." He could barely get the words out. "...that Adam is mine?"

"I hate you," Anna said suddenly then turned and ran for the door.

Chapter Fifteen

By the time he got downstairs, the rain was coming down hard and Anna was already climbing into a cab.

Brody raced after it, calling out to her, but it was too late. The car pulled away from the curb, throwing up a wide splash of rainwater in its wake.

Brody crossed to his Harley, his mind full of regret and guilt—but most of all, joy.

Adam was his son.

Their son.

His and Anna's.

It killed Brody that he hadn't known that Anna was pregnant when he left. If he had, he'd never have dreamed of going anywhere.

He could only believe that she hadn't known, either. That the revelation had come in the month or so after he was gone, when he was impossible to get hold of. He could only imagine how she must have felt, holding this news and wanting so desperately to share it with him.

The thought made him heartsick. Ashamed. Angry at himself for being such a damned fool.

As he climbed aboard and kicked the bike's engine to life, he thought about the instant connection he'd had with Adam, that feeling of warmth and affection as they'd spoken in the upstairs hallway. That bonding of blood between man and boy.

He thought about chocolate chip pancakes and pulling the boy into his lap at the dinner table and reading X-Men to him later on that night. All that time he had believed Adam was another man's child—yet it didn't matter to him. The kinship between them was unmistakable. Maybe if he had taken a moment to do the math, he would have realized the obvious truth.

That Adam was his son.

His *son.*

The idea of this seemed so surreal to Brody that he couldn't quite wrap his head around it. As he pulled onto the road, he tried to picture the boy's face in his mind.

Did he see himself there?

Did Adam look like *him?*

He remembered finding Anna in those young eyes, and he realized that must have been part of what had drawn him to Adam in the first place. That, and the way the boy had carried himself with a kind of quiet confidence, the understated maturity that had

always been part of Anna's DNA, and so lacking in his own.

All he wanted right now was to get to Anna's house, to see her and Adam, to do whatever it took to convince her to let him back into her life, to let him be a father to their son—even if she couldn't completely allow him into her own heart.

They could take it slow. Or fast. It didn't matter to Brody, as long as she gave him a second chance. Let him *prove* to her that he had grown, that his selfishness was a thing of the past and would never again keep them apart.

When it came down to it, Brody was tired of being alone. His long, self-imposed exile had made him realize that. And he could think of no better way to remedy the feeling than to get to know his blood. His boy.

His Adam.

HE WAS ABOUT TEN MILES AWAY from the house when he realized he was being followed.

The rain was coming down in sheets, and he had made the mistake of allowing himself to be distracted. Didn't notice the headlights behind him until it was almost too late.

He'd had to flip his visor up to keep the rain from obscuring his view, but he was riding against the wind and the drops came straight at his face, cold as ice, pummeling him without mercy.

The mirrors mounted on his handlebars were wet and blurred, but he could still see those headlights, turning when he turned, speeding up when he goosed the throttle and slowing down again when he eased off.

He couldn't see the driver's face or even make out the model of the car, but he had no doubt that it was following him.

And he wasn't entirely sure the driver cared if he knew this.

One of the thugs from last night.

Who else could it be?

Turning a corner, he found himself on a long, lonely straightaway bordered by a stone wall on one side and a grassy, overgrown field on the other. With the rain coming down so hard, however, the field looked more like swampland—something out of a gothic horror flick set in Florida or Louisiana.

He was traveling at a fairly decent clip, about half-way along the stretch of road—only a couple of miles now from Anna's house—

—when the car behind him made its move.

Without warning, the car swooped in directly behind him, getting a little too close for comfort.

Brody goosed the throttle and roared ahead, but the car rolled in close again, nearly kissing his rear tire.

Brody veered to the left and the headlights veered with him. He hammered the throttle now, shooting

forward in a burst of speed, but the car didn't hesitate this time, keeping a steady, relentless pace behind him.

Brody knew they had to be doing at least ninety now, and the car wasn't breaking a sweat. Keeping up this kind of speed in the rain was a recipe for disaster, but he couldn't seem to shake this maniac off his tail.

He veered to the left and the car went with him. Then, as if it had just been dosed by a shot of adrenaline, it sprang forward with a roar and rammed into the back of his bike.

Bumper met tire, the hit rattling through Brody's bones. The Harley lurched and swerved, the force of the blow ripping him from the handlebars. He hurtled sideways, flipped once and landed in a puddle of mud at the side of the road, the back of his helmet slamming against the ground.

Somewhere at the periphery of his brain he heard his bike crashing as the car's brakes squeaked, bringing it to a skidding halt. Gears shifted and it went into reverse, pulling up alongside him.

A car door opened and closed, followed by footsteps, as a dark figure moved through the pouring rain toward Brody.

He squinted up at it—a man by the size of him—but his vision was blurred, and darkness was rapidly crowding in on him, threatening to take him away.

The man hovered over him a moment, as if he'd

felled an animal and was checking the extent of the damage. Then he turned and hustled back to his vehicle.

As the engine revved and the car tore down the street, Brody struggled to remain conscious. The rain cleared for a brief moment, allowing him a final, unfettered glimpse at the vehicle as darkness finally overcame him.

He was certain he'd seen that car before.

It belonged to Frank Matson.

Chapter Sixteen

He didn't know how much time had passed.

It could have been hours or minutes. There was no real way to tell. He never wore a watch, and when he reached into his pocket for his cell phone, he found that the impact had crushed it.

So all he knew was that he'd been out cold and now he was awake and his head felt as if it had been worked over by a jackhammer.

On steroids.

Considering the speed he'd been traveling, he figured it was a miracle he was alive. The mud and grass had softened the blow some, but moving didn't come without a cost.

Was anything broken?

He didn't think so.

But he knew that he was battered and bruised, and getting to his feet would not be an easy task. Shifting his weight to his left side, he put an arm out and pushed himself upright, staring out at the street.

There were no cars around. The stretch of road was

as vacant as a high school parking lot on a summer night, and he didn't expect anyone to be coming by anytime soon. Not in this weather.

The rain had subsided some but not quite enough, and from his vantage point here in the mud, he saw his overturned bike across the street, lying in the gutter, rainwater rushing past it. He couldn't tell the extent of the damage.

Had that really been Frank's car behind him?

He didn't know for sure.

The car had been similar, no doubt about it, but maybe he was projecting his own prejudice onto the situation. He'd never cared for the guy, but he'd never really thought of him as a violent man.

What reason would Frank have to try to kill him?

Because of Anna?

Out of jealousy?

That didn't seem likely. Yet here he lay, and the only decent glimpse of the car he'd managed to get had conjured up visions of Frank Matson behind the wheel. That didn't make it true, but he couldn't shake the feeling and something told him he could well be right.

Shifting his weight again, he rested both hands against the ground and climbed to his feet, wobbling slightly as his head began to spin.

The helmet had surely prevented his brain from winding up like his cell phone, but the pounding in

his skull and the hollow light-headedness told him that some damage had been done.

He stood there a moment, the world swirling around him, and tried to maintain his balance.

His bike was only a few yards away, yet traveling that distance seemed like an insurmountable task. Pulling the thing upright and driving it away—even if he was lucky enough to find it still functioning—was not something he relished.

But what choice did he have?

Something in his gut told him that he needed to get moving. Whoever had mowed him down had obviously been following Anna and him, which meant she could be in danger.

Grave danger.

He needed to get to her house.

Praying for the world to stop spinning, he took a tentative step forward, his shoe sucking mud as he moved. He felt weak and helpless, like an invalid who had just fallen out of bed and was trying to figure a way to crawl back in.

Get a grip, Brody. You've been hurt before, so just shake it off and move.

Right, he thought.

Easier said than done.

Headlights appeared at the far end of the street, coming from the direction his attacker had gone. As they approached, Brody wondered for a moment if it was the same guy, checking to make sure the job

was done. But as they drew closer, he realized it was a pickup truck.

The truck slowed and the driver rolled his window down. He was an elderly man with a deeply lined face and a kind of cornfield vibe to him.

"You okay, fella?"

It took Brody a moment to form a sentence. "Yeah…I think so."

The driver glanced across at Brody's bike. "Looks like you took a pretty bad spill there."

Brody nodded, and the effort made his brain slosh loosely inside his skull, sending a wave of nausea through him.

"The rain…" he managed. "I lost control."

The driver set his brake and put the truck in Park, then he climbed out and crossed to where Brody was standing. "I think I need to get you to a hospital."

"No," Brody said. "Just help me with my bike. I have to get home."

The driver glanced at the Harley again. "That thing ain't goin' nowhere anytime soon. And neither are you, from the looks of you."

"I'll be fine," Brody insisted, and he was already starting to feel a little better. His head wasn't pounding so hard, and the nausea had passed.

Now if only he could get the world to stop spinning.

"You're one of them stubborn fellas, aren't you? I've had a coupla farmhands like you. Think you're

big and invulnerable, and you're too darn stupid to know when to lie down."

"No choice," Brody said.

"Man's always got a choice. But you're free to make the wrong one, whether I like it or not. Tell me where you wanna go and I'll take you there."

"I don't want to trouble you."

"Don't you worry about that," the driver told him. "I could use a little trouble in my life." He gestured to the truck. "Come on, let's get you in."

Putting an arm around Brody, the driver escorted him to the passenger side, pulled open the door and helped him into the cab.

Sitting down was the remedy Brody needed and he started to feel even better now, the world around him finally leveling off.

He felt his strength returning. A slow but steady recharging of the batteries.

The driver climbed in next to him and released the brake. "You sure you won't change your mind? Cedarwood General's only a few miles from here."

"I'm invulnerable, remember? Don't worry, I'll be fine."

The driver grinned. "Okay, Superman, where we headed?"

THE DRIVER DROPPED BRODY off a little more than a block from Anna's house. If his instincts were

right and Anna was in danger, there was no point in announcing his arrival.

His only source of comfort was that Frank had posted a couple of deputies to watch over the place. But if his concerns about the man turned out to be true—if the car that had knocked him off the road had indeed been Frank's—then there was no telling what he might find when he got there.

The short drive seemed to have done him wonders. He felt almost whole again, his brain no longer banging around inside his skull. His body still ached, but he knew he could easily push past that pain, as long as he was fully cognizant.

"What time is it?" he asked the driver.

The old guy glanced at his watch. "Closing in on 7:00 p.m."

Brody nodded. He had lost more than an hour out there and was amazed that no one had come along before the driver had to scrape him up off the side of the road.

"Thanks for this," he said quietly.

"I'm a darn fool for doing it, I'll tell you that. I still think you belong in a hospital."

Brody popped his door open. "I hate hospitals."

"I guess you do," the driver said, then tipped an imaginary hat. "You stay dry out there."

Brody nodded again and climbed out, happy to find that he was able to stand now without wobbling. He closed his door then patted the side of the truck

and watched it pull away, mentally sending up thanks for the kindness of strangers.

Pulling his collar up to help protect him from the rain, he pointed himself toward Anna's house and headed up the block.

When he got there, he knew his instincts hadn't been wrong.

There was a dead deputy on her doorstep.

Chapter Seventeen

The guy had a hole in his chest about the size of a cannonball, and his eyes were glassy and lifeless.

Brody tried for a pulse anyway.

Nothing.

He knew he should call this in, but not before checking the rest of the house. This guy needed a meat wagon, not an ambulance.

The front door was ajar. Brody reached to his waistband for his gun and discovered that he had lost it in the attack. It was probably lying in the mud somewhere along the roadside.

Glancing at the body, he noted that the deputy's gun was also gone, so he'd be doing this the hard way.

He stood very still, listening to the rain fall on the roof, trying to read the house, to get a sense of what he might be facing when he stepped inside. He inched up to the door and flattened against it, peeking in through the opening.

Nothing but darkness in there.

Except for the rain, the night was still and silent. If he had to guess, he'd say that no one was home, and the thought of this both comforted and terrified him. It meant that there weren't any bad guys inside, but it also meant that Anna, Sylvia and Adam were gone, too.

And how they may have *gotten* gone was the terrifying part.

He could only hope that they'd somehow managed to run away or were hiding in an upstairs closet again, Anna nervously clutching the gun she'd pulled out of the shoe box, ready to blow the head off anyone who opened that closet door.

Not wanting to waste any more time, Brody brought a foot back, nudged the front door open then slipped inside and flattened against the wall in the foyer.

He felt vulnerable without a weapon, but what choice did he have?

He scanned the darkness. Saw no sign of movement. He had no idea how long ago the deputy was shot, but the body had still been warm to the touch—even with the chill in the air—so he knew it couldn't have been long.

Which gave him hope.

Not much, but it was something.

The only way to do this, he thought, was one room at a time.

Pushing away from the wall, he stepped cautiously

into the living room and looked off toward the kitchen. Keeping to the shadows, he crossed through the dining room and stopped just short of the kitchen doorway.

He stood still again.

Listening.

Waiting.

He heard only the faint ticking of a clock mounted on the wall above the kitchen table. He chanced a peek inside and saw that this room was also empty, everything in place, no evidence of a disturbance.

Except for one thing:

There was a half-eaten sandwich on a plate on the table, with a glass beside it, three-quarters full of milk.

A meal interrupted, Brody thought.

Adam's meal.

Not a good sign.

Stepping past the doorway, he quickly worked his way down the hall, hugging the wall as he went. After checking the family room and the downstairs bathroom, he moved on to a windowed door that led to a patio at the side of the house.

It was dark out there, but there was enough light from a nearby street lamp that he could see the body of the second deputy lying in a pool of blood.

His stomach roiled.

This was yet another bad sign.

He had hoped the second deputy had heard the

gunshot out front and managed to spirit the Sanfords away before the bad guys could get to them.

But that had only been wishful thinking.

His guess was that the deputies had been attacked simultaneously—probably by the same two men who had been here last night—and the chances that Anna and her family had gotten away were, at best, slim.

A wave of dread rolled through Brody as he left the door, moved back down the hall and circled around to the living room again.

He'd been inside the house a total of about two minutes, yet he felt as if he'd already lost too much time.

Moving past the Christmas tree, he started up the stairway to the second floor, hoping the Sanfords were hiding up there somewhere.

Please be in that closet, he thought.

Please just be there.

But as he reached the top of the stairs, the air up here was as quiet and undisturbed as the rest of the house, and the hope died inside him.

They weren't here.

He knew this. *Sensed* it.

But he had to try anyway.

He picked up speed now, crashing through the hallway from room to room, first Anna's—where the closet was dark and empty—then Sylvia's, and Owen's, and finally Adam's room—

—none of which showed any signs of life.

He looked across at Adam's bed, at the spot where he had sat the night before, reading the boy to sleep. The thought that Adam might be in harm's way was like a kick to the gut. But it was what was on that bed—what had been left behind—that really tore Brody apart.

The toy sheriff's car.

Sitting on the pillow.

He remembered Adam standing in the hallway, the car tucked under one arm.

My daddy drives a sheriff's car, he'd told Brody. *Uncle Owen says he's one of the best deputies ever.*

At the time, Brody had assumed that Uncle Owen had been talking about Frank Matson. But he realized now, with sudden clarity, that Owen had actually been talking about *him*. Had been trying to tell a son about his father.

A father who was missing in action.

Tears stung Brody's eyes, but he fought them back. This was no time for sentimentality or recriminations. The people he loved were out there somewhere, and he had to figure out how to get them back.

Still, that sheriff's car seemed to call to him. He felt the need to touch something that Adam had touched—something that meant so much to the boy—because he was suddenly afraid he might not get the chance to hold him again.

To know him.

He wanted to push that fear off as irrational, but he knew that the men they were dealing with were not shrinking violets, and they'd do what had to be done to get their hands on the thing they sought.

He couldn't let that happen.

Wouldn't let it.

Stepping forward, he moved to the bed and reached for the car, knowing that when he found the boy, Adam would want it with him. But as he got close, he was surprised by a sudden sound:

A steady *beep, beep, beep* filled the room.

Brody froze then jerked his gaze to his jacket pocket.

Shoving a hand inside, he pulled out the modified RFID reader that Coffey had given him and discovered that he'd forgotten to turn it off. It was a small miracle that the battery hadn't gone dead.

Holding it out in front of him, he waved it over the sheriff's car and the beeping sound grew in intensity, like a Geiger counter discovering a radioactive mine.

Turning it off, he tossed it aside and grabbed hold of the toy, then he moved to Adam's bed lamp and flicked it on.

Putting the car under the light, he carefully inspected it, looking for evidence of tampering—a gap in the metal or a loose screw. It was a clever hiding place. One that no one would ever think to check.

Staring at the wheels, he noticed that they were

about the same diameter as the security tag he'd found in the garment factory. Pulling each one from its axle, he pried them open, one by one.

He found what he was looking for on his third try: another RFID button.

The button.

This one worth the kind of money that men were willing to kill for.

Dropping it into his pocket, he haphazardly replaced the wheels and returned the car to the pillow. He had to strategize now. Figure a way to let the bad guys know what he had in his possession and bargain for the Sanfords' release.

Assuming, of course, they were still alive.

Please let them be alive.

Flicking off the bed lamp, he moved toward the door, but the moment he stepped past the threshold, the cold muzzle of a gun touched his temple.

"I want you to stand very still," Frank Matson said. "Or you won't be standing at all."

Chapter Eighteen

Frank pushed him face-first against the wall and patted him down. "You just bit off a whole chunka hurt, Carpenter."

"Cut the cop routine, Frank, I'm not buying it."

"What you've bought is a nice long stay at the state penitentiary. I've got two dead deputies downstairs, and it looks to me like I just caught me a killer. Where's Anna?"

"Why don't *you* tell me?"

Frank spun him around and pushed the gun in his face. "What's that supposed to mean?"

"Don't even bother, Matson. I know you're the one."

"The one what?"

"You made a mistake not making sure I was dead. I saw your car. I saw you drive away."

Frank scowled at him. "What're you, high on something? I don't know what you're talking about."

"Go ahead. Play dumb. But if you hurt Anna or Adam, I'll kill you. Plain and simple."

Frank stared at him then lowered the gun, a puzzled look on his face. "Maybe you'd better back up a little. What are you trying to tell me?"

"I'm not an idiot. I know you're behind all this—Owen, the attacks on Anna, the break-in last night. All because you want to get your hands on Owen's little souvenir."

Frank snorted. "And here I was thinking the same thing about you."

"I know Owen didn't like you much," Brody said. "So how'd you talk him into cloning his security card? You threaten him? Tell him you'd hurt Anna and Adam? Northboard must be holding some pretty valuable property for you to be going to all this trouble."

"You got it wrong, my friend."

"Do I? Are you saying that wasn't you out on the road tonight?"

"Out on *what* road? You're not making any sense."

"Somebody ran me down out there," Brody said. "And the last thing I saw was your car."

"What car? The unmarked? The patrol unit?"

Brody nodded.

"Come on, Carpenter, you know as well as I do that those units are standard-issue. They all look the same. So whoever mowed you down was either an imposter or one of our deputies gone rogue. But it sure as heck wasn't me."

"Why should I believe you?"

Frank shook his head in disgust. "I don't think you're in the position to be deciding who you should or shouldn't believe. The way I look at it, *you're* the one who set up Owen. And *you're* the one who knows where Anna and Adam are."

"You're out of your mind," Brody said. "Owen was my best friend. And you think I'd ever hurt Anna? You think I'd do anything to put my own son in danger?"

Frank was suddenly silent. Surprised.

"So she told you, did she?"

Brody nodded again. "I don't think she meant to, but yeah. And if you're crazy enough to believe I'd ever hurt either of them…"

"This isn't an act, is it?" Frank said. "You really *are* still in love with her."

"Is that a surprise?"

"No. No, I guess it isn't." He lowered the gun now. "And if it makes you feel any better, I'm sure she feels the same. It was always you, Brody. After you left she tried to convince herself that she was in love with me—doing it for Adam's sake—but it just didn't work for any of us."

Brody studied Frank's face. Saw the sincerity there.

This was, he realized, the first time the two of them had a conversation that wasn't filled with the

heat of rivalry. One always trying to upstage the other.

Could Frank be telling the truth?

Were his hands clean in this?

Was he merely a cop, a concerned ex-husband who wanted to protect the woman he loved?

"So what now?" Brody asked, eyeing the weapon in Frank's hand. "If neither one of us is behind this, then who is? And where have they taken Anna and Adam?"

"What you said about that car on the road has me thinking. We were finally able to identify Santa Claus and his buddy. They were both registered with the department as CIs."

The sheriff's department often used confidential informants to help keep the deputies apprised of what was going on in the streets. All CIs were registered in a special database and paid through a fund set aside specifically for that purpose.

"So you weren't kidding about possible rogue deputies. Who were the CIs working for?"

"That's the problem," Frank said. "The records have been tampered with. We don't know who they were assigned to. My first instinct was that they must've been connected to *you* at one point, back when you were on the force, but I can see I was wrong. I let my own prejudice get in the way of my judgment."

"Join the club," Brody told him. It seemed they'd

both jumped to conclusions. "So we could be dealing with anyone. Anyone in the department."

Frank nodded and gestured. "Which makes calling all this in a very bad idea. Looks like we're on our own from here on—"

There was a crash down below.

The front door flying open.

Frank brought the gun up and turned, starting down the stairs, Brody right at his heels.

When they reached the bottom, to their complete surprise they found Anna stumbling to the sofa, soaked to the bone and out of breath, her eyes filled with panic and terror and tears.

"They've got Adam," she sobbed. "Oh, my sweet God, they've got Adam…"

Chapter Nineteen

Anna had never been so terrified in her life. Her chest constricted and she could barely breathe. She was wet and cold and miserable, but most of all worried. Worried that she'd never see her son and her mother again.

Brody and Frank moved to her.

"*Who* has Adam?" Frank asked. "Who took him?"

She shook her head. "I don't know, I don't know. There were two of them and they were wearing ski masks."

"Tell us exactly what happened."

Anna tried her best to tamp down her panic and catch her breath. But it wasn't working.

"I took a taxi home from Owen's place," she managed. "But when he dropped me off, I saw the deputy on the porch and the door hanging open, and before I could react, they came crashing past me, dragging Adam and Mom along with them. Then they shoved them in a car and took off."

"What did you do?" Brody asked. "Where have you been all this time?"

"I started running after them. Shouting at them to stop. Screaming for Adam. I don't know why the neighbors didn't report it. I must've looked like a crazy lady."

"Forget about the neighbors," Frank said. "They probably don't want to get involved."

"I kept running and running," Anna told them. "Even after I couldn't see the car anymore. I must've run a couple of miles. I don't know what I was thinking. I was out of my mind with panic."

Brody sat down next to her and pulled her into his arms. "Easy," he said. "Take it easy."

Anna welcomed his touch. Needed it. "They've got my son, Brody. *Our* son."

"I know," he said. "I know. We'll find him. We'll get him back."

"But how? We don't even know who they—"

The phone rang, cutting her off. The landline in the dining room. Mounted on the wall next to the kitchen doorway.

They all jerked their heads toward it, listening to its shrill ring pierce the air.

Frank started toward it, but Brody held a hand up, stopping him.

"Let Anna answer," he said. "It's gotta be them."

They all exchanged glances, and Anna knew she had no choice now but to overcome her panic and

answer the phone. Adam's and Mom's lives might depend on it.

The phone continued to ring. She got to her feet, her legs trembling as she moved, a knot of dread burning in her stomach as she crossed to the dining room.

She got close to the receiver, stared at it, still trying to stifle her terror.

Then she picked it up.

"Hello?"

The voice on the other end was mechanical. Robotlike. The caller was using some kind of device to disguise it. "That was quite a display, Ms. Sanford. You should consider running a marathon."

"Who are you? Where's my son?"

"Sitting in his grandmother's arms as we speak. Cute kid you've got there."

"If you hurt them, I swear to God—"

"That's entirely up to you, now, isn't it?"

Anna tried to calm herself. "What do you want from me?"

"Come on, now, Anna, let's not play that game anymore. You know very well what we want."

"That stupid button," she spat. "The key that'll get you into Northboard."

"We know your brother gave it to you. He tried to double-cross us, back out on the whole plan. He even threatened to go to the sheriff. But we weren't about to let that happen."

"I don't believe you. You must have forced him into it. What did you threaten him with?"

The voice was silent a moment. Then: "The same thing we're using to threaten you, my dear. Your precious little Adam. And if you don't cooperate…"

Anna's panic rose again. "Don't hurt him—*please* don't hurt him."

"Then give us the button."

"But I don't *have* it. How can I give it to you if I don't know where…"

She stopped suddenly when she realized that Brody was standing next to her now, holding up a hand.

He had a disk between his fingers.

Anna knew he'd left the other disk with his friend Coffey, so this had to be a different one.

A new one.

Was it the *real* thing? Had he somehow managed to find it?

She spoke into the phone again. "All right," she said. "No games. Tell me what you want me to do."

"It's very simple," the voice said. "First, I want you to sit there for a while and think about what's at stake. If you think you're gonna get clever and call the police, try setting us up, you'll only be signing your son's death warrant. Grandma's, too."

Anna glanced at Brody then across at Frank.

"No police," she said. "I promise."

"Good, Anna. That's what I like to hear." He

paused. "Around about midnight, I want you to get into that car of yours and start driving."

"Where am I going?"

"There's a meatpacking plant on Mercer Street, the South Side, about a forty-minute drive from your house. You park just outside the front doors at twelve forty-five sharp and bring that button. We'll take it from there." He paused again. "You understand?"

"Yes, yes—and you'll have Adam and my mother with you?"

"As long as you cooperate."

"But how do I know you're telling the truth? How do I even know they're still alive?"

"That's easy enough to remedy."

Then there was a rustling sound and Mom's quavering voice came on the line: "Anna?"

"Mom—Mom—are you okay? Is Adam all right?"

"He's fine, dear. They haven't hurt us. They just want whatever it is Owen gave you and they promised they'll let us go."

Anna started to break down. "Mom… Oh, Mom…"

"Easy, hon. We'll be okay. Don't you worry, I won't let anything happen to Adam. He's safe with me."

Anna started to say something, but the rustling sound filled her ear again and the mechanical voice came back on the line.

"Twelve forty-five, Anna. Are we clear?"

Anna couldn't speak.

"Are. We. Clear?"

"Yes," Anna sobbed. "Yes. I'll be there. I'll be alone."

Without another word spoken, the line clicked.

"WE HAVE TO CALL THIS in," Frank said, pulling his cell phone from his pocket. "We should storm that place with every available man we've got."

"No!" Anna cried. "We can't take that chance. I promised him, *no police*."

Frank ignored her and started to dial, but Brody crossed to him, grabbing his forearm.

"If you call it in, you'll tip our hand. You said yourself there may be rogue deputies involved in this thing."

"I was guessing about that. I could be wrong."

"And if you aren't?"

Frank thought about this then nodded. He pulled his arm away and dropped the phone back into his pocket. "All right, then. What's the plan?"

"I go in alone," Anna said. "Just like they told me. There's no other choice."

Brody shook his head. "That's not gonna happen."

"But you *heard* me on the phone. I promised him no police."

"I'm not a deputy anymore, remember? And Frank here's just an interested party at this point. And if

you think either of us will let you go in there without some kind of backup, you're completely out of your mind."

"But you'll be risking Adam's life!"

"Listen to me, Anna. I guarantee you these people don't have any intention of letting any of you walk away from this thing alive. Adding me and Frank to the mix may be the only way to prevent you all from being killed."

Anna was torn. She knew Brody was talking sense, that the men they were dealing with were ruthless and cruel. But if anything went wrong, she'd never forgive herself.

"You have to trust me," Brody said. "I spent a year smuggling refugees out of one of the most dangerous places in the world. In all that time, I never lost a single life. Not one. And I don't intend to now."

"But he's my son."

"*Our* son. And they'll have to shoot me dead before I'll let anything happen to him."

"I'll double down on that," Frank said. "We've both got your back."

She looked from one to the other, saw the determination in their eyes. They were both good men, and she knew she was blessed to have them on her side. Any resentment she harbored toward either had vanished in the face of this nightmare.

"All right," she said softly. "How do we do this?"

"We've got a few hours before the rendezvous,"

Brody said then turned to Frank. "Are you familiar with this meatpacking plant?"

"I've never seen it, but I do know this. One of the CIs who attacked you two used to work for a place called American Beef. What do you bet we're talking about the same place?"

Brody nodded. "I'm sure it's no coincidence."

"Problem is, if they're a working meat plant, they're probably open night and day, which could be tricky."

Brody considered this then shook his head. "If they're keeping Adam and Sylvia there, I'm guessing the plant took a break for Christmas." He looked at Anna. "You have a laptop handy?"

"Sure, why?"

"I want to look at a satellite image of this place, see what we're dealing with."

"Smart thinking," Frank said. "I can hook us into the department's sat-com line."

Anna knew that at any other time it would have killed Frank to give Brody such a compliment, but they were past the pettiness now.

Brody looked out the window. "If this rain keeps up, we may be able to use it to our advantage. They won't see us coming."

"Except we don't know how many of them there are," Frank said. "That plant could be crawling with bad guys."

"They've already lost a couple of their men, and

they don't strike me as people who like to share. I figure two or three of them at the most."

"Which puts the odds at just about even. Let's hope you're right."

"Even if I'm not," Brody told him, "we've got another big advantage."

"Which is?"

"They don't know you're part of this. And they think I'm lying in a ditch on the side of the road."

Chapter Twenty

According to its internet profile, American Beef didn't deal directly with livestock but shipped in carcasses by the truckload for processing and packaging. Then another set of trucks transported those to some of the lesser grocery store chains throughout Cedarwood, Iowa, and its neighboring counties.

The plant had recently been the subject of a federal probe, after a disgruntled worker had taken video of what were believed to be unsafe food-handling practices. The video was deemed inconclusive evidence, however, and while the probe had turned up a few minor violations, the plant had been allowed to remain open for business.

The lot it stood on was dominated by a tall water tower that overlooked a seedy, rectangular brick building about the size of a small convalescent hospital. The adjacent parking structure was empty, and the loading dock was crowded with at least a half dozen idle trucks bearing the American Beef logo.

A tall, rusty chain-link fence topped by barbed

wire surrounded the place, and Anna had no idea what to expect as she pulled her car up to the gate.

There was no guard in the booth.

No lights shining in the building.

No sign of life anywhere.

Had they lied to her? Was this some kind of cruel joke being played on her for the amusement of sociopathic minds? Would she get inside and discover that Mom and Adam weren't even in there? Had *never* been in there?

No, she thought. *They're here.*

They have to be.

If they weren't, the creeps behind Owen's murder would never get what they wanted. They'd never take possession of this thing in her pocket that was so important to them.

Before she and Brody and Frank left the house, Brody had given her the button and told them where he'd found it. She had no idea why Owen had hidden it in that sheriff's car, but he must have had his reasons. Probably figured no one would ever think to look there.

And he was right. Brody had stumbled upon it only by pure luck. A small turn of fate that had worked in their favor.

The rain hammered her windshield, the wipers pumping hard but not doing a whole lot for visibility. Anna listened to that *thump...thump...thump...*and

realized the sound was working in counterpoint to her rapidly beating heart.

She couldn't remember a time when she was so scared. Adam was her life, and if anything happened to him or Mom, if those monsters touched a hair on their heads…

She didn't want to think about that.

She couldn't allow herself to go down that cold, dark alleyway. It was too bleak down there.

Too heartbreaking.

Too…permanent.

Instead she sat there silently in the darkness, listening to the thumping wipers, the ceaseless rain, feeling the vibration of the car's idling engine as her gaze drifted to the digital clock on the dash.

It was 12:41 a.m.

Four minutes to go.

Just twelve hours ago she had been sitting in a house full of sheriff's deputies as they finished up their investigation of the break-in. The deputies had been there since very early in the morning, going over and over the chain of events, Frank and Joe Wilson making it clear to everyone that they thought Brody was behind it all.

They'd wanted to take him in for further questioning, but Brody had refused, and without any concrete evidence against him, they had finally given up and gone away. Just like that.

Anna had to admit that for just the briefest of

moments she had wondered about Brody. Frank's accusations against him had managed to work their way into her subconscious, planting the tiniest sliver of doubt in her mind.

But she dismissed that doubt the moment it surfaced.

As angry as she might have been at Brody, as hurt as she was by the things he had done to her in the past, Anna had known—and *still* knew—that the father of her child, the best friend her brother had ever had, the man she had loved since she was sixteen years old, would never betray her like that.

Brody Carpenter was not a killer.

Brody Carpenter had never cared enough about money to enable him to do the kinds of things that these men were willing to do.

His time in Darfur and Chad had more than proved that. He hadn't been there as a mercenary, as someone sent into the country to exploit and abuse for profit or political gain.

He had gone there as a savior. A protector.

And that's why he had come back to Cedarwood. That's why he had answered Owen's call without hesitation. To do what he had been trained to do, selflessly and without compromise.

Trouble. Too late for me.

Protect Anna.

He hadn't asked for forgiveness. He hadn't even

expected it from her. All he had wanted was to explain, to apologize, to try to make her understand what he had been going through all those years ago when he walked out the door.

He'd made it clear that his behavior had been inexcusable and that he was sorry for what he had done to her. And when he had come to her last night and laid her across the bed, she took him with a hunger she hadn't known she possessed.

Yet she'd been conflicted about having him in her life again. She was afraid to completely let herself go, to once again fall under that intoxicating spell of his, because she feared that once his work was done, he might not stick around.

She had carefully weighed whether to tell him about Adam and had been unable to do it. She hadn't wanted to keep him in Cedarwood that way. Hadn't wanted him to feel obligated to stick around.

Now, as she sat there watching the clock, counting off the seconds, she realized just how silly she'd been. If they all managed to get through this terrifying night in one piece, she would welcome Brody back into her life with open arms.

And she would forgive him. Just as her father would have. Just as her mother had.

Without forgiveness, there is no future.

And Anna knew, with great certainty, that was exactly what she wanted with Brody.

A future.

WHEN THE CLOCK ON THE dash ticked over to 12:43, Brody said, “Two minutes. We’d better get moving.”

He was crouched low on the seat next to Anna, looking out through the rain toward the packing plant, his jaw set, his gaze unwavering. He was in work mode, all business, and if Anna had to rely on someone to save Adam, she knew there was no one better or more determined than Brody.

Frank was in the backseat. “I’ll go in first,” he said. “I’ll take the left flank, you take the right. You ready, Anna?”

“Yes.”

“Let’s do it, then.”

Bracing herself, Anna popped open her door. Using an umbrella for protection against the rain, she climbed out of the car and walked ten steps to the packing plant’s gate.

Her legs were trembling, her nerves doing somersaults in her stomach.

There was no lock on the gate. Just a wooden handle. She grasped it and rolled it aside, leaving enough room for her car to fit through, then walked back and climbed behind the wheel.

Putting the car in gear, she followed the plan Brody and Frank had laid out for them in her living room and slowly pulled through the gate.

The moment she was past it, Frank cracked his

door open and rolled out, disappearing into the darkness.

A few seconds later, Brody leaned toward her, touching her forearm.

"Remember to play your part," he said. "You're alone, you're scared and you just want to get this thing over with."

"I won't have to do much acting."

He nodded then pulled a pistol from his waistband. "I took this from your closet. If I don't come out of this thing alive, I—"

"Don't talk like that."

"We both know it's a possibility. If anything happens to me in there, I want you to use this thing. Do whatever you have to do to get your mother and Adam out of that place."

He handed her the gun. "Keep it in your waistband, at the small of your back." He started to go, then hesitated. Turned to her. "I know I've said this before—but I love you, Anna. More than anyone should ever be allowed to love someone. And I'm sorry for all the pain I put you through."

Then he squeezed her arm, cracked open his door and slipped away, disappearing into the rain.

Chapter Twenty-One

The rain didn't let up, which was both a blessing and a curse.

Brody crouched under the water tower, his gaze on the packing plant, but getting there had taken some time and he was soaked through. Hair, shoes, pants, shirt—every part of him was dripping water, and the chill in the air wasn't helping much.

Even the gun Frank loaned him was soaked. That didn't mean it wouldn't fire, but handling it wouldn't be as easy with it wet.

The plan they'd formulated was a simple one.

Maybe too simple.

But with only satellite footage available, and no blueprints or floor plans to guide them, they'd known that their best option was a quick and dirty stealth assault:

—Make entry;

—Take out anyone who got in their way;

—Find Adam and Sylvia.

Despite their differences, Brody had always

EXCLUSIVE
15% OFF ALL
ORDERS!
SEE OVERLEAF
FOR DETAILS

thought of Frank as a man who could handle himself, and he knew that the training offered by the Cedarwood Sheriff's Department was some of the best in the country. Frank was no stranger to tactical maneuvers and was bound to be an asset here.

But if the men inside that plant were rogue deputies, as Frank suspected, then they would've gone through the very same training.

And that could be a problem.

This wasn't the first time Brody had been in a situation like this. The geography had been different, and the target had been a Janjaweed compound in the middle of nowhere, but he and another man had managed to silently put down ten guards before freeing a cell full of African farm women—the compound's personal sex slaves.

He had come very close to losing his life that night, and he knew that if he miscalculated this time, if there were more people involved in this thing than his instincts told him there were...he might not walk away.

But that didn't matter as long as Adam and Sylvia were safe.

Nothing else mattered.

He kept his gaze on the building. There were no lights inside. No signs of life whatsoever. He was directly across from the loading dock, several big rigs and small refrigerator trucks sitting silently in

the surrounding darkness. He knew they'd make good cover as he worked his way toward the building.

He had no idea what time it was, but he figured no more than two minutes had passed since he'd left Anna near the gate.

She would be driving forward now, rolling up close to the front doors and waiting for someone to make contact.

He knew she was afraid. He had seen the fear in her eyes as he told her he loved her. He didn't like leaving her out there on her own, but what choice did he have? She was a strong woman, and if things went sour for him tonight, she'd do whatever it took to get their son back.

A few hours ago he had been overjoyed to hear the news about Adam. But now that joy was tempered by worry and fear, feelings he'd have to fight off if he was going to be effective here.

Just think of it as another mission, Brody. Visualize Darfur and do what you have to do.

Shoving aside all emotion, he got to his feet, checked the building one last time for any sign of movement then darted across the lot to the first truck parked near the loading dock.

Crouching low, he slipped under the container and waited near the left rear tire, all the while keeping his gaze on the building.

Still no movement.

Now that he was closer, however, he thought he

saw light in one of the windows. A faint yellow glow that was barely visible through the falling rain.

He needed an even closer look.

Steeling himself, he got to his feet and made another quick dash, hiding behind one of the refrigerator trucks. Moving from truck to truck, he made his way to the loading-dock steps and waited there a moment, staying low behind the dock's cement ledge.

There was definitely light in that window.

After a quick scan of the area, he moved up onto the dock and stood under the overhang, thankful to be out of the rain. Flattening against the rollaway door, he moved sideways to the window, stopping just short of it.

Crouching again, he got below the windowsill and carefully peeked in.

The room inside was dark, but beyond this, through an open doorway, was a narrow corridor that led to another doorway.

This was where the light was coming from.

It was hard to tell with the constant drumming of the rain, but he thought he heard voices coming from in there.

He glanced around, looking for a way inside. There was a door to his far right of the loading dock, protected by a dead bolt. He moved to check it and wasn't surprised to find it locked.

Fortunately, he'd never had much problem with

locks. Pulling out his wallet, he removed the paper clip he kept in one of its pockets then unfolded the clip and straightened one end.

Gripping the other end between his forefinger and thumb, he inserted the length of wire into the narrow part of the keyhole, carefully lined up the tumblers then pushed it deep and worked it around inside.

It took some effort, but the lock finally gave and the dead bolt turned.

A moment later he was inside the packing plant, dripping rainwater on the scarred linoleum floor. There was a corridor ahead of him, and now that the rain was muffled by the door, he could definitely hear voices. They were indistinct from this distance, but he knew what direction they were coming from.

Pulling the gun out from under his shirt, he headed toward them.

As he reached the end of the corridor, he waited, listening for footsteps. Heard none.

Shifting to his left, he raised the gun and ducked low as he pivoted into the adjoining corridor, ready to squeeze off a shot.

The corridor was empty. There were deep shadows at the far end but no movement there.

The doorway with the light was located on the right side. He rose to his full height and moved against the wall, keeping the gun ready, working his way toward that room.

He could hear the voices clearly now but realized

that there was a tinny quality to them, as if they were coming from a speaker.

Reaching the doorway, he chanced a quick look inside and saw a break room with an old tube television set tucked into one corner, tuned to a classic movie channel.

In other words, a bust.

He was about to duck away when a whisper came out of the darkness behind him.

"Glad you could make it, scooter boy."

Brody whirled.

A man wearing a ski mask emerged from the darkness at the far end of the hall, pointing a small assault rifle at Brody. The kind the local drug dealers used. He was one of the men Brody had confronted in Anna's house—the guy he'd stopped on the stairs.

"Put the gun on the floor," the man whispered.

Brody looked at the pistol in his hand then leaned down and placed it on the linoleum.

The man stepped toward him now and Brody didn't hesitate. He plunged forward, tackling the guy, grabbing his gun arm. Wrapping both hands around the wrist, Brody squeezed hard as the man hammered at him with his free hand, trying to break him loose.

The fingers slackened and the gun clattered to the floor, and they went down hard, Brody struggling to gain control. He grabbed blindly at the man, getting hold of a handful of fleece, yanking the ski mask

off his head. As they rolled into the light from the doorway, Brody got a look at the man's face and was surprised by what he saw.

It was Joe Wilson.

Frank's partner.

Wilson scowled at him and brought a knee up into Brody's stomach, knocking the wind out of him. As Brody clutched himself and rolled away, gasping for breath, Wilson got to his feet, frantically shuffled around then disappeared from view.

When he came back into the light, he was once again carrying his assault rifle, a self-satisfied grin on his face.

He pointed the muzzle at Brody. "I guess you aren't such a hotshot after all, are you, Carpen—"

A silencer *plocked.* Three holes opened up in Wilson's chest, the impact knocking him back into the darkness, his rifle skidding across the floor.

Pulling himself upright, Brody staggered to his feet and turned to find Frank Matson, dripping wet, standing at the opposite end of the corridor.

"Just goes to show you can't trust anyone these days," Frank said.

Then he pointed his silencer at Brody.

"Including me."

Chapter Twenty-Two

It was 12:49.

Still no sign of life in the building.

Anna was parked in front of American Beef's entrance, worried that something had gone wrong, wondering why her son's kidnappers hadn't yet come outside.

Were they waiting for her to make the first move?

Should she get out of the car and see if the front doors were locked?

Five more minutes, she thought. *Five more minutes, then you go inside.*

She glanced at the pistol on the seat beside her. Scooping it up, she ejected the magazine, checked to make sure it was full of cartridges then snapped it back into place.

She didn't really know what she was doing. She had no use for guns and still wasn't quite sure she could actually pull the trigger. If it came down to the

bad guys versus her family, she'd have to find a way to get past the uncertainty, point at the target and squeeze.

12:50.

The longest minute of her life, and still nothing.

Pulling the pistol into her lap now, she closed her eyes and sent up a prayer.

Help me, Lord. Help me.

BRODY COULDN'T QUITE believe what he was seeing. "What are you doing, Frank?"

"Come on, Carpenter. You're smarter than that. I'm surprised you didn't already figure it out on your own." He smiled. "I'm afraid I lied to you earlier. I *am* the guy who mowed you down on the road, and I gotta tell you, it felt pretty good."

"You think you're actually gonna get away with this?"

Matson laughed. "It took some improvising, but it looks like I already have."

"What does that mean?"

"Turns out I was right about you all along. After I shoot you—in self-defense, of course—there's gonna be an investigation. And guess what they'll find when they open up Wilson's private email?"

"No idea," Brody said.

"Enough evidence to prove that you and he were in cahoots all along. That you colluded with Wilson's confidential informants to try and get that button

from Anna. But the button I give them will be a blank, so nobody'll be quite sure what the fuss was all about."

"You're insane. What could Northboard have that's worth all this killing?"

"My ex-brother-in-law told me there are a number of things in that building that could catch a pretty penny. But what I'm looking to grab are the plans for a brand-new weapon they're developing. I've already got buyers starting to line up. And these people have deep, deep pockets."

"Even with a key card," Brody said, "you think you can just walk in there and take whatever you want?"

"That's the beauty of having an inside man. Owen told me that every Christmas Eve, Northboard throws its office party—a big old shindig—and everyone in the building is invited. Including most of the security staff. I figure that's the perfect time to slip inside and do what needs to be done."

"You're dreaming," Brody told him.

"Maybe so," Frank said, "but a man's gotta dream. The way I see it, when this is over, I'm the hero and I get the girl. Just like last time."

Brody frowned. "Last time?"

"Who do you think set you up for the fall four years ago? Made it look like you took that bribe?"

Brody felt his chest tighten. His eyes must have shown his anger.

"That's right, Carpenter. I didn't expect you to be acquitted, but it all worked out in the end. You left town and I got Anna." He smiled. "But this time out, I won't be making the same mistakes. And I don't have to worry about you coming back."

"What about Adam?" Brody asked. "Where is he?"

"He's safe. Always has been. We never made much of a connection, but I wouldn't dream of hurting that boy. He and Sylvia were just an excuse to get you out here." He paused. "And when all is said and done, Anna's gonna be telling that boy that his daddy was one of the cruelest human beings ever to walk this good green earth. Assuming she tells him you're related at all."

Brody clinched his teeth. "You really are insane."

"What I am is in love," Frank said. "But I guess that pretty much amounts to the same thing."

He smiled again and Brody sensed that this was his cue. His gaze zeroed in on Frank's trigger finger and when he saw the flicker of movement there—

—he dove sideways.

The silencer coughed, two shots in rapid succession, both of them whizzing past Brody's head as he rolled into the darkness and scrambled to his feet.

Then a third shot came, catching him in the shoulder, and he nearly went down again, intense heat ripping through him. Pushing past the pain, he ran

toward the far end of the hallway, found another doorway there and slipped inside.

He heard Frank cursing behind him, his footsteps echoing against the corridor walls. Picking up speed, Brody crossed through what looked like a packaging room and raced past a wide conveyor belt, heading toward a lighted doorway at the far end.

When he went through that doorway, the temperature dropped about sixty degrees. He was inside a massive refrigerator, surrounded by hanging carcasses of beef.

ANNA LOOKED AT THE clock on the dash.

1:00 a.m.

She had waited a lot longer than she'd intended, nervous about making a move, but now she grabbed the pistol from her lap and shoved it into her waistband at the small of her back, just as Brody had instructed.

Snatching up her umbrella, she threw the car door open and climbed out, shielding herself from the rain.

She stared at the building's entrance, hoping that her movements might have alerted someone inside. But she saw nothing but blackness beyond the glass doors, and no one came out to greet her.

She wondered about Brody and Frank.

Had they been successful?

Was that why no one was coming outside?

If so, then why hadn't they told her? Why hadn't one of them come to get her, to assure her that the bad guys had been caught and that Adam and Mom were safe?

Anna approached the entrance, moving onto a short covered walkway. Setting her umbrella on the asphalt, she moved up to the doors and put her face against the glass, peering into the room beyond.

All she saw was a rundown lobby area, bathed in shadow and moonlight. There was a reception desk and several framed posters of assorted meats hung on the wall behind it, surrounding the American Beef logo.

She tried the door, found it unlocked.

Should she go inside?

Part of her wanted to turn and flee, but she knew she really had no choice.

If anything happens to me, Brody had said, *do whatever you have to do to get your mother and Adam out of that place.*

Mustering up her courage, Anna pulled the door open and stepped into the darkness. She was only a few feet inside when she decided to throw caution to the wind.

"Hello?" she called. "Is anyone here?"

No response.

She moved deeper into the lobby, her gaze shifting to a hallway just beyond the reception desk.

"Hello? This is Anna Sanford, is anyone around?"

And that's when she heard it: a muffled cry. Someone calling for help.

Mom?

Pulling the gun from the small of her back, Anna sucked in a breath, swept past the reception desk and headed down that hallway.

Chapter Twenty-Three

Brody's shoulder was leaking.

Thanks to the refrigerated air, the initial pain had subsided somewhat, giving way to numbness, but he knew that eventually that would wear off and the pain would return full force.

For the moment, however, he could deal with it.

The problem was the blood.

Frank's shot had gone straight through his shoulder, which was leaking profusely. He was trailing blood behind him—a trail that would be hard to miss in this lighted room. He knew he'd made a mistake coming in here.

He clamped a hand to his shoulder, trying to control the flow, but it wasn't doing him much good. Worse yet, he was starting to weaken from the loss of all that fluid.

He had no idea where Frank was at this point, and being weaponless didn't give him great comfort. He stood behind the carcass of a fairly large steer, one

of at least a hundred that hung from meat hooks in this massive room.

He kept his gaze on the doorway, knowing that sooner or later, Frank would walk through it.

It didn't take long for his prediction to come true.

Frank was carrying Wilson's assault rifle now, keeping it tucked close to his body.

"I know you're in here, Carpenter. You're leaking oil like a rusty old Buick." His gaze went to the floor, scanning it for signs of blood. "We both know how this is gonna end, so you might as well come out and get it over with."

Brody didn't move.

"I can't wait to see the look on Anna's face when she realizes you betrayed her again." He laughed. "And the sex. Can't wait for that, either. Comfort sex is the best, isn't it? Especially when you've got a woman like Anna in your bed."

Brody knew that Frank was trying get a reaction out of him. Keeping his hand clamped on his shoulder, he stepped backward, crossing to the protection of another carcass. He glanced at the floor and didn't see blood this time.

"Woman really knows how to please a man, wouldn't you say? We had us a whole lot of fun after you ran away, and she took me places I've never been before."

He was working his way toward Brody, following

that trail of blood. Brody stepped sideways now, moving on to yet another carcass.

"There's no question she'll be devastated after tonight," Frank said. "But I'm at my best when a woman is vulnerable. And don't you worry. I'll make her forget about you this time."

ANNA FLEW DOWN THE hallway.

"Mom?" she shouted. "Is that you?"

She heard the muffled cries again and turned a corner, spotting a closed door at the end of another short hallway. The sounds came from behind it.

She rushed to the door, tried the knob, found it locked. Pounded her fists on the wood.

"Mom? Are you in there? Is Adam with you?"

More muffled cries. She couldn't make them out, but she recognized her mother's voice.

Stepping back, she brought a foot up high and kicked at the door, right near the knob. It buckled but didn't crack.

She tried again, and then again, and the wood finally began to splinter. After she gave it three more solid kicks, the door finally broke loose and swung open.

Mom and Adam were bound and gagged, tied to a chair. Both of them were wearing blindfolds.

Anna rushed to them, ripping at the bonds, pulling away the blindfolds, and when she had them free,

she grabbed Adam and hugged him with everything she had.

"Oh my God, baby, are you all right?"

Adam was crying now. She could tell that he was terrified. But he nodded in answer to her question. "I'm okay, Mommy."

She turned to her mother. "What about you?"

"I'm a little shook up," Sylvia said. "But I'm fine. Is Brody with you?"

Anna nodded. "Frank, too. They're somewhere inside. But I need to get you two out of here. Get you to my car."

Sylvia returned the nod and they headed out the door.

MATSON HAD FINALLY stopped talking. Probably figured he'd get the job done easier if he wasn't constantly telegraphing his position.

The good news: Brody was still alive.

The bad news: he was losing energy fast, and he had no idea where in this sea of beef Frank might be.

He found out soon enough.

Deciding it was time to move again, he circled backward and crossed toward another slab of beef. But the moment he reached it, it suddenly exploded, a hail of bullets shredding it to pieces.

Narrowly missing being hit, Brody dove to safety, scrambling to a corner of the room. He crouched

there, renewing his grip on his shoulder, his strength draining with every breath he took.

As he looked at the floor again, he realized he'd left another trail of blood. And just beyond the row of carcasses in front of him, was Frank—

—headed in his direction.

ANNA WAS HUSTLING MOM and Adam into the front seat when she heard the gunshots.

She jerked her head toward the building.

Brody and Frank. One of them was in trouble. Maybe both.

"Lock yourself in," she said to Sylvia. "And if I'm not back here in five minutes, get Adam out of here and call the sheriff."

Sylvia looked stricken. "What are you going to do?"

Anna pulled the pistol from her waistband again. "Whatever I have to."

"I'VE GOTTA ADMIT I'M a little disappointed, Carpenter." Frank was moving toward Brody, the assault rifle aimed at his chest. "I was expecting a little more fight out of you."

Brody was trapped in the corner. Every syllable he uttered was an effort for him. "She'll never…believe you, Frank."

"Oh, she'll believe me. I'm pretty convincing when I'm motivated."

"The only thing motivating you…is money."

"What—you don't think I'm capable of loving someone?"

"You're a sociopath," Brody said, feeling his adrenaline rise. "You don't even know what love is. Owen used to be your brother-in-law. He meant everything to the woman you claim to care about, but did you feel anything when you shot him?"

Matson shrugged. "I was a little annoyed he wouldn't tell me what I wanted to know."

"That just proves my point. You're incapable of emotion. And I'm betting that's why Anna divorced you. She could see right through the facade. Imagine what'll happen when she takes a deeper look and sees your black heart."

Matson frowned at him now. "You got a lot to say for a dead man." His eyes narrowed. "I think it's time we got this over with. Your buddy Owen is waiting for you in the after—"

"Frank?"

Matson flinched and took a step backward. Anna stood at the far end of the row of carcasses, staring at Frank in disbelief.

Frank did his best to cover, gesturing to Brody. "It's him, babe. He's the one who set this all up. He tried to jump me in the hallway."

Anna wasn't buying it. It was obvious by her expression that she'd heard more than enough to know

that he was lying. She brought the pistol up and pointed it at him.

"I can't believe you killed Owen." She shoved her free hand into her pocket, pulled out the security tag Brody had given her. She held it up. "And for this? This is worth that much to you?"

"I did it for us, babe. You and me. Owen could've had part of it, too, but he got stupid."

"So you shot him."

"We're gonna be rich, Anna. Don't you get that? You won't have to slog in that shop every day, trying to get ahead. We can do whatever we want. Go wherever we want to."

Anna's face hardened. "I wouldn't cross the street with you," she told him then dropped the RFID tag to the floor and raised her foot over it. "And you can kiss that money goodbye."

As she brought the foot down, Frank's face filled with panic.

"No!" he shouted and swung the assault rifle toward her, fingering the trigger.

In the split second before Frank fired, Brody used every last ounce of strength he had and sprang from the corner, grabbing Frank's legs.

They went down hard and the assault rifle chattered wildly, sending bullets into the air. Then Brody was on top of him, pummeling Frank's face, his chest, hammering him over and over again, channeling his rage into the effort, until Frank was out cold.

Then Brody staggered to his feet, and Anna rushed to him, pulling him into her arms, hugging him, kissing him, murmuring in his ear.

"I love you, Brody. I'll always love you. And I forgive you for everything. Everything."

Pain shot through Brody's shoulder, and he knew he was leaking blood all over her. But he didn't care.

He was back in the arms of the woman he loved.

And that was all that mattered.

Chapter Twenty-Four

Frank Matson refused to confess to his crimes, but it didn't make a difference. It turned out that Joe Wilson had survived the gunshots in the hallway and was all too happy to cooperate in exchange for a chance at parole.

Frank, however, would never get that chance. The D.A. was predicting multiple life sentences, and nobody involved in the case wanted to take odds against her.

On Christmas Eve, Anna found herself caught in the whirlwind of the investigation, answering questions, looking at photographs. She'd been asked to identify the two men in the van—all part of the evidence against Frank—and she'd had no trouble picking them out of a photo array.

Brody spent Christmas Eve, and several days after, in the hospital, getting his wounds stitched up and telling his version of events.

A lot of the sheriff's office brass came to see him,

and one of them even mentioned the possibility of Brody going back to his old job.

"You got a lousy deal, Carpenter. Maybe we can make up for that. Put you where you belong—on the homicide squad."

Brody didn't make any commitments. He told Anna that he wasn't sure he wanted to go back to the department, and she didn't really blame him.

Too much history there. For both of them.

She didn't care what he did with his life, as long as he stayed with her here in Cedarwood and got to know his son.

Adam had come through this trauma like a champ. He hadn't even complained when Anna told him they were going to delay Christmas a bit, waiting for Brody to get out of the hospital. She hadn't told him that Brody was his father, yet. Figured that was too much, too soon.

But the time would come, and she knew that Adam would be thrilled by the news.

THEY CELEBRATED Christmas on New Year's Day.

This seemed appropriate to Anna. The beginning of a new year and a new life. They all still had an empty spot in their hearts for Owen, but they knew he was with them in spirit and always would be.

As they sat by the tree, exchanging gifts—Mom, Adam, Brody and Anna—Brody, still wearing a

sling, handed a box to Adam, the wrapping paper covered with multicolored dinosaurs.

"Is this mine?" Adam asked.

"Sure is," Brody said then tousled his son's head. "A little something to make up for breaking the wheels on your sheriff's car."

Adam grinned, unceremoniously ripping the wrapping paper free. When he got the box open, he paused and sucked in a breath, his eyes going wide with surprise and excitement.

Then he dove in, pulling out a toy motorcycle.

A black Harley-Davidson.

Anna's heart filled with joy as she watched him pull the motorcycle to his chest then jump into Brody's arms, giving him a thankful hug.

She knew that everything would be all right from here on out. That the fantasy she'd had so many years ago was finally coming true.

* * * * *

THE LAWMAN'S NANNY OP

BY

CARLA CASSIDY

First published in Great Britain 2011
by Mills & Boon, an imprint of Harlequin (UK) Limited,
Eton House, 18-24 Paradise Road, Richmond, Surrey TW9 1SR

ISBN: 978 0 263 88561 3

46-1111

Harlequin (UK) policy is to use papers that are natural, renewable and recyclable products and made from wood grown in sustainable forests. The logging and manufacturing processes conform to the legal environmental regulations of the country of origin.

Printed and bound in Spain
by Blackprint CPI, Barcelona

Carla Cassidy is an award-winning author who has written over fifty books. Carla believes the only thing better than curling up with a good book to read is sitting down at the computer with a good story to write. She's looking forward to writing many more books and bringing hours of pleasure to readers.

To Ann and Bruno,
for finding love again after all these years.

Chapter 1

Four cartons of crayons, a ream of construction paper, ten glue sticks and a dozen boxes of tissues. Portia Perez smiled to herself as she pulled up in front of the discount store.

Her best friend Layla West would think it was pathetic that Portia's shopping list didn't include a pair of three-inch red heels and something skimpy and sparkly, but Layla had never spent eight hours a day entertaining twelve little kids.

As the owner and operator of Portia's Playpen, a day-care facility, Portia would much rather have enough crayons and glue sticks than shiny high heels any day.

As she got out of her car, the hot, early-morning

August air felt like a slap in her face. There were times she didn't think the sun shone any brighter in any other town on earth than it did in August in Black Rock, Kansas.

The concrete pavement beneath her sandals already radiated with heat and she reminded herself to add a couple of tubes of sunscreen to her shopping list.

She was almost to the store when she saw the first flyer. It hung on a light pole and as she glanced at it she froze. Her own face stared back at her.

"What the heck?" She moved closer to read it and as she did her heart banged hard in her chest and all her breath whooshed out of her body. *Portia Perez—Baby Beater and Child Abuser. If You Love Your Kids, Don't Use Her Day Care.* The words swam before her eyes, for a moment making her nauseated.

She yanked it from the pole and then looked down Main Street, stunned to see more flyers on other poles. Shopping forgotten, she hurried down the street, taking down the flyers as she fought against the angry tears that threatened to erupt.

Who would do this to her? Who would be so cruel? This wasn't just cruel; it was criminal. Somebody was trying to destroy her business, her very livelihood.

It took her fifteen minutes to take down all the flyers she saw in the immediate area. She held them

in a trembling hand and stared across the street at the sheriff's office.

She needed to report this. It was slander at its worst. Surely Sheriff Tom Grayson would do something, find the person responsible.

Who could be behind this? Her head whirled as she marched across the street and into the sheriff's office. The minute she opened the door and stepped inside the tension that already coiled tightly in her stomach increased as she saw who sat behind one of the desks.

Deputy Caleb Grayson.

For almost ten years of her life Portia had gone out of her way to avoid any real interaction with the man. In a town the size of Black Rock they'd had occasions to run into each other, but any conversation had been polite and impersonal.

It amazed her that after all these years just the sight of him created a faint twinge in her heart. But she couldn't think about that now. She had more important things on her mind than an old heartbreak.

"Portia," he said in obvious surprise and stood from the desk.

"Is Tom in?" she asked.

"No, it's his day off. What's up?" He stepped closer to her, close enough that she could smell the scent of his cologne, a familiar scent that would

always remind her of high school prom and things she'd never wanted to think about again.

"This is what's up…up all over town." She handed him one of the flyers.

He frowned as he read it aloud. "Portia Perez neglects and abuses your children that you put in her care. Portia's Playpen is a place of pain for little ones without a voice. Don't let this woman watch your kids." He whistled low beneath his breath and looked at her once again. "You've apparently made somebody very mad."

"You have to do something," she exclaimed. "They're everywhere, each one more slanderous than the next."

"Did you see who posted them?" he asked.

"No, but it's…it's all lies." Once again she felt the pressure of tears welling up, but the last person in the world she would cry in front of was Caleb Grayson. "I want whoever did this arrested."

"Unfortunately this is more of a civil matter than a criminal one," he replied. "I'll ask around, see if anyone saw somebody putting them up, but there's really nothing more I can do."

It wasn't what she wanted to hear. In fact his apparent lackadaisical attitude about the whole thing irritated her. She wanted him outraged on her behalf. She wanted him out beating the streets to find the guilty and she wanted that person lynched at high noon in the hot sun.

More than anything she wished Caleb wasn't so darned handsome. She wished that his shirt didn't stretch so neatly over his broad shoulders, that his slacks didn't hug the length of his long legs and that that lock of his dark brown hair on his forehead didn't look as if it were begging for female fingers to gently push it back into place.

"You'll call me if you find out who did this?" she asked curtly.

"Yeah, but I wouldn't wait by the phone if I were you. These were probably put up sometime in the middle of the night and I doubt that anyone saw who hung them."

"So that's it?" she asked, not attempting to mask her anger.

Caleb shrugged. "Sorry, there's not much else I can give you."

Portia whirled around on her heel and left the office without another word. Still stunned by the flyers, irritated that she had to have any dealings with Caleb Grayson, she stalked across the street and down the block to Black Rock Realty.

Even though it was early, Layla would be in and Portia needed to talk to somebody who would be properly outraged and lend support. Her best friend since childhood would do just that.

As she entered the office Layla looked up from her desk with a smile. "Hey, girl, what are you doing

in town so early? Most Saturdays you aren't even dressed until noon."

"I came to pick up some supplies. Take a look at these." Portia threw the flyers on the desk then flopped down in the chair facing her friend.

Layla scanned a flyer then looked up at Portia, her green eyes wide. "Where did you get these?"

"They were taped to light poles around the discount store."

Layla looked back at the piece of paper in her hand. "But who would do something like this? Have you had a fight with any of the kids' parents?"

"No, nothing like that. I can't think of anyone who would have a reason to put them up."

"What are you going to do about it?"

"I already did it. I marched myself into the sheriff's office."

"What did Tom say?" Layla twisted a strand of her long blond hair between two fingers.

Portia frowned. "Tom wasn't in. I had to talk to Caleb."

Layla raised a perfectly formed blond eyebrow. "And how did that go?"

"He told me it was a civil matter, not a criminal one. I think he just didn't want to be bothered with the whole thing. He probably couldn't work my crime into his busy schedule."

Layla smiled at her knowingly. "Now that wouldn't

be a little ancient history aggression coming into play, would it?"

"Don't be ridiculous, I don't harbor any ill will toward Caleb. What happened between us happened a long time ago. I've certainly moved on since then."

"Yeah, right, and I'm going to be six feet tall when I wake up in the morning," Layla replied dryly. "Admit it, you've carried a torch for Caleb Grayson ever since high school."

"That's the most outrageous thing you've ever said," Portia exclaimed.

"Really?" Layla dropped the strand of hair she'd been twisting. "You think it was more outrageous than that time I told you I had sex with Ralph Davidson in the front of his pickup and my hip bumped the shift knob so we ended up in his pond?"

Portia laughed, which she knew had been Layla's intention all along. "You're crazy," she said.

"And that's why you love me." Layla leaned forward and covered one of Portia's hands with hers. "Don't worry about the flyer nonsense. Everyone in town knows those kids at your day care are your life and you'd never do anything bad to any of them."

"I hope you're right," Portia said.

Layla grinned. "Of course I'm right. I'm always right. Now get out of here. Go buy your supplies. I have a client due to arrive any minute and I'm hoping to schmooze him into buying the old Miller property."

"That old dump?" Portia said as she stood.

Layla grinned. "By the time I finish with my sales pitch my client will think it's Buckingham Palace."

Portia was still smiling as she left the realty. Layla was always good for cheering her up no matter what the circumstances.

Of course, that whole thing about Caleb and a torch was utterly ridiculous. If she had a torch and Caleb came too close to her, he'd definitely get burned. She'd given him not one, but two chances years ago, and he'd blown them both.

"Fool me once, shame on you. Fool me twice, shame on me," she muttered as she headed to the store to pick up her supplies.

Caleb Grayson was as much a part of her past as teenage blemishes and pep rallies. She'd outgrown all of them, most of all the very hot, handsome Deputy Caleb Grayson.

He dreamed about her Sunday night. A wild, hot dream that combined part past and part fantasy and woke him with a yearning he hadn't felt in years.

Caleb Grayson pulled himself out of bed Monday morning, irritated that Portia Perez had invaded his sleep in any way, shape or form. Minutes later, as he stepped into his shower, he tried to shove thoughts of her out of his head, but they kept coming.

She'd been his first love and he'd never loved like that again. A year ago he'd thought he'd finally found

love with Laura Kincaid, but that had ended so badly he still felt a burn of anger when he thought of her. A swell of grief threatened to sweep over him, but he consciously shoved it away and instead focused back on Portia and her current problem.

The flyers had been a nasty piece of business, but he'd spent most of the morning on Saturday asking around to see if anyone had seen who'd posted them and as he'd suspected, nobody had a clue who might be responsible. There wasn't much else he could do about the situation.

Stop thinking about her, he commanded himself as he got dressed in his khaki uniform. Besides, all the Grayson men had more important things on their minds than ugly flyers hung around town.

Their sister, Brittany, had been missing for almost five weeks. Caleb strapped on his gun and grabbed his keys from the kitchen table and tried to still the thundering in his chest that began whenever he thought of his younger sister.

She'd disappeared the week of the sixth anniversary of their parents' death and for the first two weeks or so Caleb and his brothers Tom, Benjamin and Jacob had just assumed she'd gone off alone to get through the difficult anniversary. But too much time had gone by without any of them hearing from her.

His brother Tom, the sheriff of Black Rock, had been doing what he could to find some answers. He'd issued a BOLO alert on her vehicle and was

monitoring her bank account and credit cards. There had been no sign of her car anywhere but what was more troubling was that her accounts hadn't been touched since the day of her disappearance.

This wasn't the first time Brittany had disappeared, but before it had always been only for a few days, a week at the most, then she'd turn up with explanations and apologies.

Caleb knew all his brothers felt the same as he did, that they didn't care about apologies or explanations; they just wanted to know that she was okay.

He got into his car and headed for the office. Caleb lived in a small rental house in the heart of the small town of Black Rock. He'd moved there seven years ago from the family ranch when he'd gotten the job as deputy when he turned twenty-one.

Law enforcement in Black Rock was definitely a family affair. Tom was the sheriff, and Caleb, his brother Benjamin and his sister, Brittany, were deputies. His brother Jacob had been an FBI agent, but had returned home almost two months ago and shut himself up in a small cottage on the ranch property.

He refused to talk about what had brought him home and didn't want anyone except family to know he was there. It was bad enough when Caleb just had Jacob to worry about, but now he had Brittany, as well.

No wonder he couldn't get Portia out of his head.

She was the least of his worries. Despite the fact that they shared the same town, he rarely saw her.

Still, there had been a moment yesterday when she'd first stepped into the office when his heart had done a little dance in his chest.

"Indigestion," he muttered as he pulled up in front of the two-story brick building that was his home away from home. Surely that was all that he'd felt when he'd seen Portia.

It was only a few minutes before seven in the morning but already the sun was warm on his shoulders as he got out of the car.

"Good morning, Sam," he said as he entered the office.

Deputy Sam McCain gave him a sleepy smile and raised his coffee cup in greeting. "Coffee's fresh and I brought in some homemade cinnamon rolls that Loretta baked this morning."

"You're a lucky man, Sam," Caleb said. "Not only is your wife gorgeous, but she cooks, as well."

Sam's teeth flashed white against his cocoa-colored face as he grinned. "You stay away from my Loretta. You with your legendary charm might turn her head."

Caleb laughed. "You know I save my charm for the single women in town. Besides, for reasons I can't understand, Loretta seems to be madly, crazy in love with you."

Sam chuckled. "Yeah, I can't explain it, either."

At that moment the phone rang and Sam answered. Instantly his broad forehead creased in a frown. "Okay, all right. We'll get somebody right over there."

He hung up the phone and looked at Caleb. "That was Portia Perez. Somebody broke into her day-care center last night."

"I'll go," Caleb said. "First those flyers and now this. I wonder what's going on?"

Minutes later he was in his car and headed to Portia's place. She lived on the north edge of town, not far from the house where she had spent her childhood.

Caleb had spent many nights of his high school years visiting Portia and her mother. In fact, he and Portia had been inseparable all through high school.

On warm summer nights he'd sat on the porch swing with Portia and they'd talked about their future together, made plans for a lifetime of happiness. They'd been best friends, and on the night of their senior prom they had become lovers.

He thought of the dream of her he'd had the night before. It had been hot and wild and when he'd finally awakened he had imagined he could smell the scent of her still lingering in the sheets, on his skin.

Crazy, he thought. Crazy that after all these years she should invade his dreams. And just as crazy

that the thought of her could still bring the taste of bitterness to the back of his throat.

Her house was a small ranch, painted the color of cinnamon and with gingerbread trim in beige that gave it a fairy-tale look. Colorful flowers lined the sidewalk leading up to the front door and baskets hanging from the porch ceiling spilled blossoms of red and purple.

He turned in to her driveway and followed it to the detached garage where he knew her day-care facility was housed.

As he pulled up he noticed several things. Melody Markfield, Portia's assistant, was in a fenced play area next to the building with several toddlers, and Portia stood at the front door, her face unusually pale in the early-morning sunshine.

He parked the car and as he opened his door to get out, she approached him. He couldn't help but notice the way the sun sparked on her copper-colored hair and that her legs beneath her denim shorts were just as shapely as they'd been when she'd been a cheerleader in high school.

"What's going on?" he asked.

"Somebody broke in." Her voice trembled slightly and her hazel eyes appeared larger than usual. Her chin tilted upward. "And if you tell me this is a civil matter I might just punch you in the stomach."

"Let's take a look inside," Caleb said. As he walked toward the door of the building he was conscious of her

just behind him. The floral scent of her perfume eddied in the air and reminded him of his dream of her.

But all thoughts of dreams fled from his head the moment he stepped into the day care. Destruction and vandalism were everywhere.

The mattresses on two of the cribs had been slashed and the stuffing pulled out. Books had been thrown from shelves and toys had been smashed and littered the floor in colorful plastic shards.

"Not civil, definitely criminal," Caleb murmured as he walked around the room and tried to take it all in.

He checked all the windows looking for a point of entry and finally found it in the small bathroom. The window had been broken inward and pieces of glass glittered on the floor in the sunlight.

He left the bathroom and returned to the main room. A laptop computer sat on the adult-size desk in the corner, along with a stereo system, letting him know that robbery hadn't been the intent.

It was a malicious crime scene. Whoever had broken in had been hell-bent on causing damage and nothing else. Who would have done this and why?

He turned to look at Portia, who leaned against one wall with her arms wrapped around her waist. Her eyes held the hollow look of someone who had taken a hard hit to the head and wasn't quite sure where she was or how she had gotten there.

"When was the last time you were out here?" he asked.

She raised a hand to her temple, as if she had a headache. “Last night. I came in around six to make sure everything was ready for this morning and then I went back into the house.” Her voice still held a faint tremor.

“And you didn’t hear anything out here?”

She shook her head. “Nothing.”

“Do you have any idea who might be responsible for this? Have you had a fight with somebody? Maybe one of the parents of one of the kids?”

She shook her head again, this time more forcefully. “No, nothing like that. Layla asked me the same thing Saturday morning when I found those flyers, but I can’t imagine who might do something like this.”

Caleb pulled his cell phone from his pocket. “I’ll get some of the boys over here to fingerprint the area around the broken window in the bathroom. Maybe they can lift some prints that will let us know who’s responsible.”

“I hope so,” she said. He turned his back to make the call and then when he had finished turned back around to face her. She looked small, and tears brimmed in her eyes.

He wanted to reach out to her, to take her in his arms and soothe the tears away, but he knew better. He knew he was the last man she’d want to hold her for any reason.

She wrapped her arms around her middle once

again, as if trying to warm an insidious chill. "I know it sounds crazy, but I have this awful feeling that this is just the beginning."

"The beginning of what?" he asked.

"Something terrible," she replied, her voice a mere whisper.

Chapter 2

It was just after nine when the deputies Caleb had called in finished up what little they had been able to do. There had been no fingerprints around the window, although they'd found a black thread stuck on one of the shards of glass, a thread they assumed was from whatever the intruder had been wearing when he'd broken in.

Portia knew there was no way they'd be able to figure out who had smashed the window and crawled inside by a single thread of cotton.

As Caleb walked with the other men out of the day care, she looked around the room and wanted to weep. She'd worked so hard to make this a place of

fun and love for the little ones who were in her care, and now it was all nothing but a big mess.

Melody had all the kids outside in the play area, but she needed to get them inside before the sun grew too hot and at the moment this was no place to bring children.

Caleb came back inside. "You have a broom?" he asked.

She looked at him in surprise. "Cleaning up a crime scene isn't your job."

He shrugged. "You've got a yard full of kids out there who are going to need to get inside pretty soon. Two sets of hands will make the cleanup go more quickly."

"They aren't coming back in here," Portia exclaimed. "I'll make arrangements for Melody to have them at her house until we figure out what's going on."

"You still need this mess cleaned up, now where's the broom?"

As he began to sweep the floor Portia went outside to speak to Melody. All the children had arrived for the day and she gave Melody the keys to the minibus they used for field trips to transport the children to Melody's house.

Melody assured her the children would be fine at her place for however long it was necessary and Portia knew she could trust her assistant with all the details.

By the time she returned to the garage, Caleb had finished sweeping up the floor. "You sure you can't think of anyone who's mad at you?" Caleb asked as he stopped pushing the broom and leaned on the handle.

She frowned and bent down to pick up the picture books that had been thrown off the toddler-size bookshelf. "I spent all day yesterday trying to figure out who might have hung those flyers, who might have such a big problem with me that they'd want to hurt me like that."

She straightened and looked at Caleb. She'd spent most of her time since high school trying not to look at him, trying not to think about him, and most of the time she'd succeeded.

She'd finished college with a degree in early childhood development and had devoted herself to her business, but that didn't mean she hadn't had time to date.

"Joe Castle," she said.

Caleb frowned. "What about him?"

"He's the only one I can think of who might have an issue with me."

"Why? What did you do to him?"

Portia felt the heat of a blush filling her cheeks. "It's not what I did to him, it's what I didn't do with him." She broke eye contact with Caleb to place the books on the shelf. "Joe and I have been seeing each other for the last month. You know, dinners out or

an occasional movie, nothing serious. Last week at the end of one of our dates he tried to take things to the next level, but I told him I wasn't interested. I told him I thought it best if we didn't see each other anymore."

"How did he take it?"

She met his gaze once again. "He was irritated, told me if I didn't intend to get in a serious relationship then I shouldn't have wasted his time."

Caleb frowned, his expression inscrutable. "I've known Joe for a long time. I know he's got a hot temper, but this definitely doesn't feel like something he'd do."

"I know, that's why I hadn't mentioned him until now, but he's the only person I can think of who I've had any kind of issue with."

"I'll have a talk with him, see if he knows anything about this." Caleb swept the last of the plastic trash into a pile and then grabbed the dustpan.

They worked for another few minutes, putting some of the things back where they belonged and not speaking. Tension gripped her and she told herself it was because of Caleb, because this was the first time in years that they'd spent any time together.

The old saying was that you never forgot your first love and Portia knew it was true. She'd never completely been able to distance herself from the love they'd shared in high school.

Despite the fact that he'd broken her heart years

ago, she still remembered how it had felt to be held in his arms, how his mouth had plied hers with a heat she'd never known before or since.

"That's good," she finally said. "I'll call a carpenter and see about getting the bathroom window replaced and things will almost be back to normal."

"Except that you're afraid." Caleb stepped closer to her, so close she could see the golden flecks in his dark brown eyes, so close she could smell the dizzying, familiar scent of him.

His words gave the tense feeling inside her a name. Fear. She'd thought it was because she was close to Caleb, but since the moment she'd walked in here and seen the senseless destruction she'd been gripped by a simmering fear.

"This feels like such hatred," she said. "It's creepy to think that somebody could possess this much hatred directed toward me."

He reached out and touched her chin, a familiar gesture that might have ushered in a million memories if she allowed it. "Maybe you're taking this all too personally," he said softly.

A disbelieving laugh escaped her. "It's hard not to take this personally."

He dropped his hand back to his side. "It could be kids, some teenagers with too much time on their hands looking for a little excitement. If that's the case somebody will talk to somebody else and eventually I'll hear about it."

"I hope you're right," she said and for just a moment she wished he'd pull her into his arms and hold her, take away the chill that refused to go away.

And for just a minute she thought she saw in his eyes the desire to take her into his arms. It was there only a moment, a soft yearning that quickly disappeared and made her wonder if she'd only imagined it.

"I'll have a talk with Joe and see where he was last night and if he had anything to do with this," Caleb said, all business as he started to back toward the door. "And if you think of somebody else who might want to cause you trouble, call me."

"I will, and thank you for all your help in cleaning up," she said.

He nodded once and then walked out. As she watched him go she felt a small stab in her heart, a faint echo of the way she'd felt years ago when she'd watched him walk away that final time.

Crazy.

They'd had their chance at making it work and he'd blown it. He'd obviously moved on. She knew he'd been engaged a year ago to Laura Kincaid, a statuesque blonde who was two years younger than Portia and Caleb. The engagement had fallen apart and Portia had just assumed it had been Caleb who had called it off, who had probably cheated on her. After all, that was what he'd done to Portia—cheated on her and broken her heart and there was nothing

to indicate to her that over the years he'd changed his ways.

Laura had left town soon after the broken engagement and Portia had heard through the grapevine that Caleb was once again playing the field.

Portia wasn't sure now if her rapid heartbeat was because she was still just a little bit afraid or if it was because Caleb Grayson still had the capacity to touch her in a way no other man ever had.

The rest of the day passed in a haze. For the first time in years the day care was silent on a weekday. No childish laughter, no sloppy kisses, just a silence that pressed in on her as she finished trying to clear up the last of the mess. The carpenter arrived late in the afternoon to put in a new window.

Maybe it would be best to keep the kids at Melody's for the next couple of days until they could figure out who was behind all this. She could take the time and give the walls a new coat of paint, she thought as she closed and locked the door.

She'd been wanting to put a fresh coat of paint on the walls for a while now, but had never found the time. There was no way she could have the children come back until she was certain there was no danger to them.

She hoped Caleb solved this issue quickly so she could get the day care back up and running, but in

the meantime she'd use the time with the children absent to do some grunt work.

It was just after five when she went inside her house. She would sleep with one eye and her bedroom window open tonight to make sure she'd hear anyone who tried to break into the garage again. On second thought, she'd keep her windows closed and locked. Anything that was destroyed in the day care could be replaced, but she couldn't be.

The kitchen smelled faintly of fresh oranges and the chicken salad she'd made early that morning for the children's lunch. She tossed her keys on the table and then walked from the kitchen through the living room and into her bedroom.

What she wanted more than anything was a quick shower, her favorite robe and maybe a quart of chocolate ice cream for dinner. She positively didn't want to think about break-ins or vicious flyers—or Caleb Grayson.

Minutes later as she stood beneath the warm spray of water she found thoughts of Caleb creeping into her mind. She wondered who he was dating at the moment.

He'd promised to love her forever, had promised she was the only one he wanted in his life, and then she'd gone out of town for her grandfather's funeral and the rumors had begun, rumors of his betrayal.

She frowned and shut off the faucets, then reached for the fluffy towel that awaited her. Ancient pain,

she thought. She wasn't that naive young woman anymore, and she'd learned her lesson well where Caleb was concerned.

Once she was dry she pulled on her short, green silk nightgown and a matching robe. It was not quite seven when she settled on the sofa in front of the television with a tray holding a plate of chicken salad and a tall glass of iced tea.

She'd just finished eating and carried the tray back into the kitchen when the doorbell rang. She went to the front door and peered out, surprised to see Caleb standing on the porch.

Maybe he had news, she thought as she cracked open the door. "Caleb," she said in greeting.

"Hi, Portia. Mind if I come in?"

She unfastened the chain and opened the door to allow him entry. As he walked into her living room, he looked around with interest.

She followed his gaze, wondering what he thought of her bright color scheme, the oversize throw pillows on the gleaming wooden floors and the bookshelf jammed full of books, knickknacks and pictures of kids who had passed through her care.

"Nice," he said as his gaze went first around the room, then slid down the length of her body, making her unsure what exactly he thought was nice. He sank down in the overstuffed chair next to the sofa.

Self-consciously she belted her robe more tightly around her waist and sat on the edge of the sofa.

"What's up? Please tell me you've solved the crime and the vandal is behind bars."

"Not even close," he replied with obvious reluctance. "I just wanted to let you know that I talked to Joe this afternoon. He insists he had nothing to do with the flyers or what happened here last night. I also talked to several high school kids to see if they knew anything about it, but nobody seemed to have any information."

"You didn't have to make a trip here for that. You could have called me," she replied. She wasn't at all sure she liked him being here in her personal space. She didn't want to smell his cologne when he was gone, didn't want a mental picture of him sprawled in her chair as if he belonged here.

"You were upset when I left here earlier. I wanted to stop by to make sure you were okay." His gaze was too warm as it lingered on her, on her throat, on her lips.

"You know me, Caleb, I always bounce back from things."

One of his dark eyebrows lifted slightly. "That's just the thing, Portia, I don't know you. We've been sharing this small town for a long time and we never talk."

She shrugged. "We say hello, we talk about the weather. There's never been a reason for us to have a real conversation before now."

"We definitely need to have more than a passing

conversation now. Joe told me that you were dating Eric Willowby before you dated him."

"Eric and I dated for a little while," she agreed. "But that was months ago. Surely you can't imagine that he'd have anything to do with this." She rose from the sofa, unwilling to share anything else personal with him. "I appreciate you coming by to check on me, but as you can see, I'm fine." She looked at the door, giving him the nonverbal message that she was finished with the conversation.

Caleb rose slowly from the chair, as if reluctant to leave. She walked with him to the front door and he turned back to face her.

"Are you sure you're okay? You still look upset," he said.

She was upset, but it had less to do with the break-in and more about how his presence affected her. "I'm fine," she replied, surprised to hear a slight tremor in her voice.

He reached up and touched a strand of her hair. "You are so beautiful," he murmured.

For a moment they simply looked at each other and Portia felt the past rising up between them. A mix of emotions cascaded through her. A snapping electricity combined with a heady rush of desire and mingled with a bittersweet pain.

His eyes darkened and softened and as he stepped closer to her she knew with a woman's instinct that he intended to kiss her.

Her brain told her to step back, to stop it from happening, but her feet remained frozen in place and as he leaned down to taste her lips, she raised her head to receive the kiss.

Hot and half-wild, that's how she remembered his kisses, and this one was no different. His lips were soft and yet commanding, but as he raised his arms to embrace her, she broke the kiss and took a step back from him, angry that he would try to kiss her, even angrier that she'd let him.

"That was stupid," she exclaimed.

He grinned, the boyish smile she'd once loved to see. "Maybe," he agreed. "But sometimes stupid tastes good. Good night, Portia."

As he stepped out on the porch she slammed her door and locked it behind him, angry that he could still make her want him after all these years.

She was right. It had been stupid to kiss her, but she'd looked so damned kissable in that sexy green robe that allowed the tops of her creamy breasts to peek out and displayed her gorgeous legs.

He got into his car and gripped the steering wheel with both hands to allow the wave of desire that gripped him to slowly ebb away.

When he felt more in control, he started his car and pulled out of her driveway. He'd spent much of his day not only trying to find out who had broken into

her day care, but also asking questions about Portia, trying to get a feel for the woman she'd become.

Loving. Generous and *kind:* those were words that had been used again and again to describe her. So why hadn't she married and started a family of her own?

Yes, it had been foolish to kiss her, but he'd wanted to taste her mouth, see if she still had the capacity to stir him. The answer was a definitive yes.

But years ago he hadn't been enough for her. She hadn't trusted him, hadn't trusted in his love, and there was nothing to indicate that another round with Portia would have different results.

He wouldn't put his heart on the line with her again, but he definitely wouldn't mind laying her down in a bed of fresh, scented sheets and making love to her until they were both gasping and sated.

She'd allowed him the kiss, but he had a feeling there was no way she'd be agreeable to a night of wild, mindless sex.

She'd thought he'd cheated on her when she'd been out of town and then again when she'd left for college. She'd allowed rumors and innuendoes to crack them apart. It hadn't mattered that he'd proclaimed his innocence loud and long; ultimately she hadn't believed him.

He'd never quite been able to forgive her for that, and that betrayal from her, coupled with the killer

blow that Laura had delivered to him, made him wary of attempting any serious relationship ever again.

As he entered his small house, the first thing he thought about was how gray and dismal his surroundings appeared compared to the rich, bold colors of Portia's living room.

Her living room had been filled with life, as if a burst of laughter was ready to resound within the walls. He threw his keys on the coffee table and sank down on the gray sofa.

Gray. That was how he'd felt lately, as if he were just going through the motions of life without any real emotion or joy.

Over the last month he'd watched his oldest brother Tom find love with a beautiful woman and her infant daughter, and Caleb had been surprised by the yearning his brother's happiness had pulled forth in him.

With a grunt of dissatisfaction, he pulled himself off the sofa and went into the kitchen to grab a beer from the fridge.

He popped the tab and took a long swallow as he eased down into a chair at the kitchen table. As always when he had a quiet moment to himself, thoughts of his sister jumped into his mind.

"Brittany, where are you?" he muttered aloud.

He knew with gut instinct that she was in trouble, although he refused to believe she might be dead. A missing persons report had gone out to all the

news outlets in a four-state area and the brothers had checked her house for any signs of foul play, but there had been none. They had conducted search parties for days that had yielded nothing. The worst part was not knowing what happened and not knowing where to begin to look for her.

With a sigh he took another sip of his beer. His cell phone rang and caller ID let him know it was his brother Benjamin. "Hey, bro, what's up?"

"Tom wants us to meet him at the Miller place as soon as possible," Benjamin said.

"The Miller place?" Caleb said in surprise. "Why?"

The Miller place was an abandoned farmhouse on the north edge of town. It had been a foreclosure that had been for sale for a couple of years.

"He said Layla was showing the place to some out-of-towner and called him a few minutes ago to tell him there's a vehicle parked in the old barn. That's all I know, but Tom wants us there."

"Be there in ten," Caleb said and clicked off.

Caleb set the beer on the table, grabbed his car keys and headed out. It wasn't unusual for the Grayson men to act as backup for each other when something came up that didn't sound right.

Tom was a cautious man, which was one of his strengths as sheriff. Caleb, on the other hand, had a tendency to be impatient. He knew it was a fault of

his, one that he'd have to work on to become the kind of deputy he wanted to be.

Even though it was almost eight in the evening when he pulled down the dirt lane that led to the Miller place, the sun was still warm and bright, although lowering in the western sky.

Tom's car was already parked in front of the house, along with a car he recognized as belonging to Layla West, Black Rock's most aggressive real-estate agent and Portia's best friend since high school.

"What's going on?" Caleb asked as he approached where the two of them stood in the front yard.

"Layla was just about to tell me," Tom said.

"I had an out-of-town client, and I brought him here on Saturday to look at the house. Today he wanted to come back and check out all the outbuildings." Layla pointed to the barn in the distance. "We went into the barn and in the back of it, underneath some blankets, is a car."

"What kind of a car?" Caleb asked.

"I'm not sure. It freaked me out and I got my client out of the barn and called Tom." She looked at Caleb's brother. "Nobody should be parked in there, Tom. This property belongs to the bank and it definitely wasn't there when I showed this place a couple of months ago."

At that moment Benjamin pulled up and Tom quickly filled him in on what had occurred. "You

go on home, Layla," he said. "We'll let you know what's going on when we know something."

It was obvious she would have preferred to linger and find out the scoop. "Come on, Layla, I'll walk you to your car," Caleb said. Tom shot him a grateful smile.

"Portia told me about the break-in," she said as they walked across the tall grass. "Are you going to find out who did it?"

"I'm doing my best," Caleb replied.

"You need to do better than your best," Layla said with a touch of censure.

Caleb opened the driver's side door of her car. "We'll figure out who's bothering Portia, but in the meantime we need to figure out what's going on here."

"Be sure and let me know," she said as she slid into the driver's seat. "And be nice to Portia," she added as she started the engine with a roar.

Caleb didn't wait to watch her drive away, but rather turned and hurried back to Tom and Benjamin. "Shall we check it out?"

Tom nodded and the three brothers walked side by side to the barn. "I haven't received any reports of stolen vehicles," Tom said as he pulled open the doors.

"Maybe somebody just didn't want to pay to have it hauled away," Benjamin said.

"Or it's being hidden from creditors," Caleb added. "Nobody likes the repo man."

They found the car in the very back of the barn, and just as Layla had said, it was covered with old blankets. Only the grill was showing and the sight of it sent a chill through Caleb.

As Tom and Benjamin yanked the blankets off, the chill deepened. Brittany's car. For a moment none of them said a word.

It was Benjamin who broke the silence. "I'll go get some gloves," he said and hurried out of the barn.

Caleb peered into the driver's window, careful not to touch the side of the car. "Her keys are in the ignition, but I don't see her purse anywhere."

Caleb felt sick and one look at Tom let him know his brother felt the same way. Tom's face was pale and his jaw clenched tightly.

There was no way to believe there wasn't foul play involved. Brittany wouldn't hide her car and just walk off with somebody.

Caleb's gaze lingered on the closed trunk and a rising fear thickened in the back of his throat. As Benjamin came back into the barn, half out of breath from running, he handed each of them a pair of latex gloves.

Caleb pulled his on and opened the driver's side door. Carefully he leaned in and pulled the keys from the ignition.

His feet felt as if they weighed a thousand pounds

apiece as he walked to the back of the car. Benjamin and Tom joined him there as he carefully put the key into the trunk lock.

For a moment it was as if the entire universe held its breath. He could smell the fear in the air. Caleb twisted the key and the trunk lid popped open.

He nearly fell to his knees in relief.

It was empty.

"I'll call the men," Tom said, his voice deeper than usual. "We need to process this car and see if we can find anything that will let us know what's happened to Brittany."

None of them spoke of the fact that it might be too late, that if the car had been hidden here right after Brittany disappeared, then it had been five weeks since anyone had seen their sister alive.

Chapter 3

At ten the next morning Portia was back in town to buy paint. She hadn't slept well. Every creak and groan of the house had put her on edge, but thankfully the night had passed without further incident.

It was Ed Chany in the hardware store that told her about Brittany's car being found at the Miller place. Her heart ached for what all the Graysons must be going through.

Portia knew what it was like to have somebody disappear from your life, to wonder where they had gone and if they were still alive. Her father had walked out on Portia and her mother when she'd been twelve and for years she'd wondered where he'd gone, what he was doing and if he were still alive.

She'd never tried to find him, had believed that if he had wanted a relationship with her, he would have contacted her.

She hoped there was a logical explanation for Brittany's disappearance, but the fact that they'd found her car hidden in a barn at the Miller place certainly didn't promise a happy ending.

She'd just loaded the cans of paint into the trunk of her car when she heard Caleb call her name. As he hurried toward her she couldn't help but notice the shine of the sun in his rich, dark brown hair, how he walked with a confident stride that was instantly appealing.

"Caleb, I heard about Brittany's car. I'm so sorry," she said when he stood just in front of her.

His eyes darkened and he nodded. "Thanks. We're doing what we can to find her, but so far all the leads go nowhere."

Portia fought the impulse to reach out and take his hand, to offer comfort to the man she'd once loved with all her heart and soul. "Hopefully she'll turn up safe and sound," she replied.

"We can only hope. Tom is still out at the Miller place conducting a search but he sent me back here to hold down the fort with Sam." An edge of frustration tinged his voice and she knew he'd rather be out actively involved in the search than on duty in town. "And speaking of Sam," he continued, "he thought

he saw somebody this morning who might be behind the trouble you're having," he said.

"Who?" she asked curiously.

"Dale Stemple."

The name blew a cold wind through her. "Oh, my God, I hadn't even thought about him." She frowned. "But isn't he in prison?"

"After Sam told me he thought he'd seen him drive by I did some checking. He was released from prison two weeks ago."

"What about Rita? Where is she?" The sun overhead seemed less bright, less warming as Portia thought of the couple she'd turned in to Child Protective Services two years before.

"Who knows? The minute Dale was arrested she left the area. I imagine Rita has probably remarried. She didn't seem like the kind of woman who would be okay on her own."

Portia nodded and had a hard time summoning up a vision of Rita Stemple in her mind. The woman had been thin and mousy and had rarely been seen in town.

"I just wanted to give you a heads-up that he'd been released and might have come back into town to give you some grief. I'm going to try to find out where he is, but you need to keep an eye out, too."

"Thanks, Caleb. I can't believe he didn't even cross my mind. I guess because I just assumed he was still in jail. You'll let me know what you find out?"

"Of course."

"And I hope Tom and the others find out something about Brittany."

His eyes darkened with pain and his shoulders slumped forward. "Thanks. Me, too." He straightened and drew a deep breath and then glanced into her trunk. "Planning a little work, I see."

"I decided with the children at Melody's for the time being, it was a good time for me to do a little redecorating in the day care."

"So you'll be home all day?" he asked.

"Off and on. I'm planning on stopping by Melody's on my way home to see the kids, then I'll be home until this evening. Tuesdays I always have dinner with my mother. But, if you find out something and need to get hold of me, let me give you my cell phone number."

He wrote the number on a small notepad and then shut her trunk for her. "There's no reason to believe that you're in any imminent danger," he said. "No threats have been made on you and it's possible it wasn't Dale that Sam saw. Sam said he just got a quick glance at the driver. I just wanted you to know that I'm on top of it and you need to be aware."

"Thank you, Caleb. I appreciate it, especially with you having Brittany's disappearance on your plate."

He smiled, although the gesture didn't reach the brown depths of his eyes. "At the moment Tom is

working Brittany's disappearance and I'm doing everything possible to fix your world. Besides, I'm afraid if I don't you'll sic Layla on me."

She laughed, and it felt good. "Layla is a good friend."

"She's like an attack pit bull when it comes to you," he replied. He jammed his hands into his pockets. "Anyway, I just wanted to let you know about Dale. I'll be in touch if I find out anything else."

"Thanks, Caleb."

She watched him walk back toward the sheriff's office and couldn't help but notice that he looked as good going as he had coming.

As she got into her car she told herself that the tingly feeling she got whenever he was near was nothing more than an old memory playing itself out in her mind.

Did anyone ever really forget their first real love? Their first sexual awakening? Did the memory of that person always evoke the kind of yearning, the kind of electric sizzle that Caleb still managed to pull from her?

They'd both moved on. She knew he dated often and so did she, although no man had ever been as important to her as Caleb had once been.

She dismissed thoughts of him as she pulled away from the curb and headed home. Instead her head filled with thoughts of the Stemples. Dale and Rita had had two children, a three-year-old little boy

named Danny and a four-year-old little girl named Diane.

The two children had only been in Portia's care for two days when she saw the signs of abuse. There had been bruises on Diane's forearm in the distinctive pattern of fingers and when Danny had called for her help in the bathroom on the second day, Portia had seen that his bottom was not only marked with lines from a belt, but also scabbed over in several places.

She'd immediately called Child Protective Services and a woman had shown up at the day care and had taken the children into custody. Portia had never seen Dale or Rita again.

She'd heard through the grapevine that Dale had been arrested for threatening a social worker and for keeping illegal guns in his house. Rita had left town and Portia had put the whole incident out of her mind except for occasionally wondering what had happened to Danny and Diane.

There had been some speculation that Dale's parents might step in and request custody, but at the time Dale's mother had been battling cancer and so the children had disappeared into the foster care system.

After a visit to Melody's where she got enough hugs and kisses to last for the day, she drove home. She unloaded the paint into the day care and then went into the house for lunch. Her plan was to spend

the afternoon moving everything into the center of the room to prepare for painting the next day.

She supposed she was probably overreacting to the break-in by moving the children to Melody's, but she'd rather err on the side of caution where their safety was concerned.

Besides, she'd been wanting to repaint the interior of the day care for months and this seemed like a perfect opportunity to get it done.

When she left her house to return to the day-care facility, she carried with her a knife from the kitchen drawer and her cell phone. She felt slightly foolish with the knife in her hand and wasn't even sure she could use it on anyone, even to protect herself. But she was reluctant to be there with no weapon at all while she worked.

At five o'clock she knocked off working and went inside to shower and change for dinner with her mother.

As usual, a faint edge of dread coursed through her as she thought of spending time with her mother.

Doris Perez was a bitter woman who had never gotten over her husband walking out on her and with each year that had passed, her bitterness had grown.

It was duty that drove Portia to the weekly dinners. Her mother had no friends, her health was failing and Portia was an only child. She loved her mother, but there were times she didn't like her very much.

At six she got into the car to head to her childhood home eight miles away. As she drove she thought of the brief kiss she'd shared with Caleb. It had stunned her to realize that after all these years there was still magic in his kiss. His lips had held an intoxicating warmth, a faint edge of hunger that had excited her.

Although she'd halted it before it had gotten too deep, too breathtaking, there had been a part of her that had wanted to pull him back into her house, take him to her bed and make love with him. But the rational part of her knew that would be inviting heartache back into her life.

As she turned down the tree-lined, narrow country road that would eventually lead to her mother's farmhouse, she couldn't help but admire the play of the evening sunshine through the trees.

It wouldn't be long and the leaves would begin to turn red and gold and fall to the ground. Portia loved autumn, but it was always in that time of the year when she thought of the babies she wanted—not babies who belonged to somebody else that she watched during the day, but rather babies that were from her heart, a twenty-four-hour part of her life. The fall always reminded her that another year was about to pass and she still wasn't pregnant.

"You have to find a husband before you can have babies," she said aloud. Although she knew some women chose to be single moms, that wasn't a choice she wanted to make.

As the daughter of divorced parents and as someone who hadn't had a relationship with her father since he'd walked out on them, she wanted her children to have something different, something more.

Her mother sat in a rocking chair on the front porch. The swing where Caleb and Portia had spent so many nights of their high school years had been taken down years ago.

As Portia pulled up in front of the house and parked, her mother stood. Doris Perez would be an attractive woman if bitterness hadn't etched frown lines into her face.

"Hi, Mom," Portia said as she got out of the car.

"About time you got here. I imagine the salad is soggy by now."

"I'm sure it will be fine. I told you I'd get here around six-thirty." Portia joined her mother on the porch and gave her a quick hug.

"Come on in and let's eat," Doris said. "When your father was here we always ate at five o'clock sharp. I'm not used to eating this late."

It was the same litany every time Portia had dinner with her mother. She swallowed a sigh as she followed Doris into the cheerless kitchen, where the table was already set.

As Portia slid into the chair where she'd sat every night for meals while growing up, Doris opened

the oven door and took out a homemade chicken potpie.

"How's work?" Portia asked once they were both seated at the table and eating.

Doris scowled. "I never thought I'd have to work. If your father hadn't left I would be spending my days having lunch with friends and puttering around the house instead of selling cosmetics to snotty teenagers at the local five-and-dime."

"You only work four days a week. That still leaves you three days to putter around and have lunch with friends," Portia countered.

Doris didn't reply, but Portia knew the truth: her mother had chased off all her friends long ago with her negativity.

"Did you hear about them finding Brittany Grayson's car in the Miller barn?" Portia asked.

"I heard." Doris shook her head. "Terrible thing. You know that poor girl is probably dead."

Portia's heart constricted as she thought of Caleb grieving for his sister. "I hope not."

"Have you heard any more on the break-in at your place?"

"I spoke to Caleb this morning about it. He mentioned that Dale Stemple just got out of prison. Remember him? I turned him and his wife in for child abuse."

Doris nodded. "A nasty piece of work, that man was. I always thought he probably beat up on Rita,

too. She acted like she was half-scared to move or talk whenever I saw her."

"Of course we have no idea if Dale is even back in town or not," Portia replied.

"I'm sure Caleb has other things on his mind with his sister's car being found," Doris replied with a knowing gaze. "But the way I remember it you were always on a back burner when it came to Caleb Grayson. He's just like your daddy. Loves the women."

"Mom, please, that was all a long time ago. Why don't we talk about something a little more pleasant?" Portia exclaimed. The last thing she wanted to do was rehash Caleb's betrayal of so long ago.

For the rest of the meal they talked about the kids in Portia's day care, local gossip and the winter months that weren't so very far away.

After eating, Portia helped her mother clear and wash the dishes. "You aren't leaving right away, are you?" Doris asked when the dishes were finished. "I thought I'd fix some coffee and you could maybe help me on my newest puzzle."

Although the last thing Portia wanted to do was spend another hour or so working on a jigsaw puzzle with her mother, she agreed. In truth, Portia felt sorry for her mother, who spent her evenings working puzzles and hating the man who had left her so long ago.

There had been no secrets in the Perez family. Doris had shared with her daughter at a very early

age that her father, Pete, had not been faithful. There was a part of Portia that resented that her mother had made her party to adult issues when she should have been a carefree, happy child.

She remembered her father as a big, affable man with a booming laugh and big, strong arms. When she'd been young she hadn't understood why when he'd left her mother, he'd also left her. As an adult she suspected that her father had been unable to sustain a relationship with Portia because that would have meant he'd have had to deal with his ex-wife.

He'd paid child support every month until Portia turned eighteen, and to this day Portia wondered if she would ever see him again.

It was almost ten and dark outside when her mother walked her out on the porch to tell her goodbye. Portia hugged her mother and wished things could have been different for her, wished that Doris had found some sort of happiness in her life, but she'd clung to her bitterness like it was a warm familiar lover and had refused to let it go.

"I'll call you tomorrow night," Portia said as she headed to her car.

It was a beautiful night. The temperature had dropped to a pleasant level and as Portia started her car she rolled down the windows for the drive home.

The road she travelled between her mother's house and her own was a narrow two-lane stretch of

highway that was rarely used and lined with thick-trunked old trees.

The night air drifted through the window and caressed her face. She turned the radio on and tuned it to her favorite oldies station.

Portia hadn't gone far when she noticed the headlights of another vehicle approaching quickly behind her. Irritation surged up inside her as the truck drew close and its brights shimmered in her rearview mirror.

"Jerk," she muttered and flipped the mirror up to diminish the blinding glare. "Dim your lights."

Before she had her hand firmly back on the steering wheel she felt a jarring bang. "Hey!" she cried as she realized she'd been hit from behind.

She started to brake, assuming that it had been an accident, but before she could she was hit again, this time with enough force to wrest the steering wheel out of her hands.

A single moment of panic soared through her as she realized her car was out of control and one of those beautiful, big oak trees was directly in front of her.

She heard the impact just before her head snapped forward and made contact with the steering wheel and darkness sprang up to grab her.

Caleb had just shucked his jeans to go to bed when his cell phone rang. It was the deputy on duty, Sam McCain. "What's up, Sam?" Caleb asked.

"I just got a call from Gus Swanson. He and his wife were driving down Old Pike Highway and found Portia Perez's car wrecked and her unconscious. They're near Doris's place and I've called for an ambulance, but thought you might want to know."

Sam had barely gotten the words out of his mouth before Caleb hung up. He grabbed his jeans and pulled them back on, his heart thundering with urgency.

He snatched his car keys and was on the road within seconds. *Unconscious:* that didn't sound good. What had happened? He knew that stretch of highway was narrow, but Portia had driven it enough times to know it like the back of her hand.

So, what had happened? How had she wrecked? And how badly was she hurt? He squeezed the steering wheel tightly and stepped on the gas, unable to get to the scene fast enough.

No matter what their past, Portia had never moved far out of his heart. Even the love he'd thought he'd had for Laura hadn't rivaled what he'd once felt for Portia.

As always, thoughts of Laura created a hot ball of anger in his chest. What she'd done to him was unforgivable and even though it had been a little over a year ago, the rage he felt toward her hadn't diminished.

But he couldn't think about that now. He had to get to Portia.

His heart nearly stopped as he rounded a curve and came upon the scene. The front end of Portia's red car was smashed against a tree trunk.

Gus Swanson and his wife, Martha, stood next to the car and Portia was prone on the ground next to them. A sigh of relief escaped Caleb as he saw Portia raise a hand to her head. At least she was conscious now.

He jumped out of his car and approached at the same time he heard the sound of a siren in the distance. Good, the ambulance would be here within moments.

The air bag had deployed and as Caleb assessed the damage to the front of her car he knew her seat belt and the air bag had probably saved her life.

"Caleb." Gus greeted him with obvious relief. "She's conscious now but she was unconscious when we found her. We didn't want to move her but were afraid to leave her in the car with all the hissing and smoke."

"Did you see what happened?" Caleb asked.

"No, it must have happened just before we got here," Gus replied.

As the sound of the ambulance siren grew louder, Caleb hurried toward the car. Martha nodded to him as he approached Portia.

Her forehead was red and sporting a big lump, her face was as pale as the moonlight overhead and her eyes were big and vaguely unfocused.

A band squeezed his chest as she once again reached a hand up and rubbed her forehead. "I'm fine," she said before he could say a word. "I just want to go home."

"You're going straight to the hospital," he replied, worried when she once again closed her eyes. "Portia, can you tell me what happened?"

Her eyes fluttered open once again and in the bright silver moonlight he saw the fear that darkened the hazel depths. "Somebody hit me from behind and I spun out of control."

At that moment two paramedics moved in to get her on a stretcher. Caleb stepped back to allow them to do their job.

When she was loaded up Caleb walked at her side to the open door of the ambulance. "I'll meet you at the hospital," he told her as they were about to load her into the vehicle.

"Caleb, someone hit me on purpose. It was a pickup truck and it rammed me not once, but twice. Definitely on purpose." With that, she was loaded in and Caleb watched the ambulance pull away.

Her words rang inside his head like a deafening bell. *On purpose.* Was it possible she was confused about what had happened?

He thanked Gus and Martha for their help and then grabbed a flashlight from the back of his car. He approached Portia's wrecked car once again and shone the light on the back bumper.

There was no question that it had been hit from behind. The back bumper was smashed in as well as a portion of the trunk. He leaned closer and noticed flecks of black paint on the bumper.

When he straightened, a chill waltzed up his spine. If what Portia had told him was true, and the physical evidence certainly supported her story, then he wasn't investigating a hit-and-run accident, he was investigating a case of attempted murder.

Chapter 4

Portia just wanted to go home. She'd been X-rayed and examined by the doctor and now sat alone on the examining room table waiting the doctor's return with the results.

Her head ached. Heck, her entire body felt as if it had been beaten by a gang of thugs with bats and she just wanted the comfort of her own bed.

The room was cool, Portia being clad only in the open-backed gown. But she didn't know if her chill was from the room temperature and her attire or thoughts of what had happened out on the road.

She heard footsteps approaching and breathed a sigh of relief. Good, maybe she was finally going to be released. The curtain swung open and Caleb came in.

"I thought you were the doctor here to release me," she said.

"He's looking at your X-rays now. You feel up to answering a few questions?" He stepped closer to her and his eyes radiated with a sympathy that made her suddenly feel like crying.

"Okay," she replied and wrapped her arms around her middle, seeking some warmth. Her chill intensified as she prepared herself to answer his questions.

"How are you feeling?"

"On a scale of one to ten, with ten being the worst I've ever felt in my life, I'm about a twelve," she replied. "I'm sore in places I didn't know I had muscles." *And scared,* she mentally added. As she thought of those moments on the dark, narrow highway when the truck had hit her, fear overwhelmed any soreness in her body.

"Before they loaded you in the ambulance, you said whoever hit you did it on purpose." His gaze was intense as it lingered on her.

"He did." The chill intensified. "It was a truck. I'm pretty sure it was a pickup. It tapped me in the rear end the first time but I managed to maintain control, then it hit me again harder and the wheel spun out of my hands." A sob crept up the back of her throat, but she swallowed hard against it.

She was surprised to realize that what she wanted more than anything at the moment was Caleb's strong,

warm arms around her. But she had to remind herself that it had been years since she'd found comfort in his arms.

"Could you see the driver?"

"No, it was too dark and whoever it was had the brights on. There was a terrible glare. But it was definitely a dark-colored truck."

"Black," he replied. "There were black paint chips on your bumper."

"Gee, that should narrow things down," she said wryly. Half the men in Black Rock drove black pickup trucks. "Joe drives one," she said suddenly.

"I'll check it out. Whoever hit you will have damage on their vehicle. We'll alert all the body shops in the area and check every truck that fits the description."

At that moment Dr. Debar walked in. "Caleb," he said with a nod. "If you could excuse us, I need to talk to my patient."

"It's okay. I don't mind if he stays," Portia replied. She doubted that the doctor had any information about her condition that she'd hate for Caleb to hear.

"You've suffered a mild concussion. I'd like to keep you overnight for observation," Dr. Debar said.

"No, I don't want to stay. You said it was a mild concussion. I just want to go home," she replied.

"You shouldn't be alone," Dr. Debar said.

"I'll be fine," she said more firmly. "Please, I really just want to go home."

"You want me to call your mother?" Caleb asked.

"Are you offering to make things worse?" she retorted. He knew that her relationship with her mother was trying at best. The last person she wanted to deal with at the moment was her mother. "Really, I'm all right. I just want to go home and go to bed."

Dr. Debar shrugged and looked at Caleb. "I can't force her to stay." He looked back at Portia. "While you get dressed I'll get your release papers signed, but if you have any dizziness or nausea you need to come right back."

Portia nodded wearily and breathed a sigh of relief as they left her alone to get dressed. What was happening to her life? She could have died if she hadn't had her seat belt on, if the air bag hadn't deployed.

Had the Swansons saved her life by being there? Had the driver of the truck had intentions of stopping to see if she'd died in the crash? And when the driver had found her still alive, would he have ensured her death somehow?

This was a nightmare with a very real, but shadowy, boogeyman she couldn't imagine the identity of. All she knew was that for the first time in her entire life she was truly afraid.

A glance at the clock let her know it was almost

one. If it wasn't so late she would call Layla and invite her to stay with her, but she hated to bother her friend at this time of night.

Surely she'd be safe in her own house until morning. She had good locks and strong windows. Still, the idea of being alone for the rest of the night scared her more than she wanted to admit.

"Are you decent?" Caleb's voice called from behind the curtain.

"As decent as I get," she replied.

He swept the curtain aside. "You're all set to go. Dr. Debar said to contact him tomorrow if you feel like you need some pain meds and he'll call in a prescription."

"I don't need pain meds, I just need you to find out who's doing this to me," she exclaimed.

"I've already got Benjamin checking the system for anyone who has a black pickup registered in their name in the area." He took her by the arm. "In the meantime, I'll take you home."

"What happened to my car?" she asked as he led her down the hallway to the exit.

"I had it towed to Wally's. He'll keep it in the garage until we get samples of the paint chips off the bumper and it can be fixed." He tightened his fingers around her elbow. "You could have been killed."

"That thought has crossed my mind more than once in the last half hour," she said. Although she'd never really quite forgiven Caleb for breaking her

heart years ago, she was grateful for the warmth of his hand on her, the nearness of his body as they stepped out of the building.

She was beyond exhausted and had yet to really process what had happened. The idea that somebody had intentionally tried to kill her was as alien as the spaceships old Walt Tolliver, the town kook, insisted landed in Black Rock on a regular basis.

Who could want to hurt her like that? What had she done to make somebody so angry with her? Question after question tumbled in her aching brain.

Caleb led her to the passenger's side of his patrol car and opened the door for her to ease inside. The minute he closed the door she was enveloped by the familiar scent of him, a scent that instantly reminded her of carnation corsages and hot kisses and a night of making love that she'd thought was the beginning of her future.

She leaned her head back and closed her eyes, weary beyond words as a headache banged in the center of her forehead.

"You okay?" he asked as he got in and started the engine.

She looked at him beneath half-closed eyelids. "Of course I'm not okay," she snapped irritably. "My head aches, my body hurts and somebody tried to kill me."

Everything felt wildly out of control and she didn't know how to cope, what to do to make herself regain some modicum of control.

He pulled away from the curb and was silent. "Sorry, I didn't mean to snap at you," she said apologetically.

He cast her one of his charming half smiles. "If anyone has a right to snap right now, I'd say it was you. You've had a rough night."

"It's not just tonight. It's a combination of the flyers and the break-in and now this. I just don't understand what's happening to my life right now."

"We're going to figure it out," he replied.

She leaned her head back and once again closed her eyes, comforted by the ringing confidence in his voice. Despite any personal reservations she might have about him, she knew he was a good lawman. All the Graysons were good at what they did.

Within minutes they were at her house and she breathed a sigh of relief.

"Thanks, Caleb, for everything," she said as she opened the door and got out of the car. "You'll stay in touch with me as far as how the investigation is going?"

"Absolutely," he agreed as he got out of the car. He hurried around to her side and grabbed her elbow to escort her to the front door.

With each moment that passed, the aches in her body grew more pronounced and she felt as if her feet each weighed a hundred pounds.

"How's your head?" he asked as they reached the front door and she dug into her purse for her key. She

was grateful that he'd thought to grab her purse from the car before it had been towed away by Wally.

"I have a headache, but I'm not feeling dizzy or nauseated or anything like that." She pushed the door open and turned back to him. "I'll be fine now," she said.

"I know you'll be fine. Because I have no intention of leaving you alone for the rest of the night." He moved past her and into the house. "Come on, Portia, let me help you to bed."

Caleb saw the faint glint of fire that lit her eyes at his words and realized at that moment there was still something between them, something hot and crazy that the years hadn't managed to douse.

"That's not necessary," she protested, but it was a weak protest.

"You heard the doctor. You aren't supposed to be alone now. You don't want to call your mother and I'm here, so that's that."

She closed the door and locked it. "I have to admit, I was kind of dreading being alone tonight." She walked over to the sofa and sank down on the cushions. "I'm not quite ready to go to bed yet. My head is still spinning with everything that's happened."

She looked small and vulnerable and a surge of anger filled Caleb as he thought of the person responsible. He walked over and sat next to her,

fighting the impulse to pull her into his arms and promise to spend the rest of his life keeping her safe.

"I contacted Dale Stemple's parents yesterday to see if they'd seen or heard from Dale since his release from prison. They insisted they haven't had any contact with their son since he went to prison. I asked around town and nobody else has seen him. It's possible Sam was mistaken."

"Which puts us back to square one—who can hate me enough to try to kill me?" She rubbed the center of her forehead and released a sigh that pierced through to his heart. "Maybe Sam wasn't mistaken and Dale is here in town but just hiding really well."

"Maybe, but, Portia, we aren't going to solve anything tonight. You've been through a pretty major trauma. What you need right now is rest."

She nodded and winced. "You're right. I'm going to bed. The guest room is made up and you can help yourself to whatever." She stood and sighed once again. "Hopefully this headache will be gone in the morning."

He stood, as well, wishing he had some words of comfort to offer her, some assurance that no more danger would come to her. But he refused to offer her false promises. "You can get into bed all right on your own?"

She offered him a faint smile. "I've been doing

it on my own for a long time," she replied and then headed down the hallway.

It was ridiculous how her words hinting that she'd always slept alone filled him with an unexpected pleasure. He knew she dated a lot, but apparently those dates hadn't led to any real intimacy.

Since Laura, Caleb had dated, as well, but he'd also avoided any intimacy with the women he casually dated. He didn't want to get close, knew that lovemaking could evolve into heart involvement and he simply didn't intend to ever go there again with any woman.

At the moment his lack of a personal relationship in his life was the last thing on his mind. He needed to find out who was after Portia and why. And the disappearance of Brittany continued to haunt his mind.

Knowing that nothing could be accomplished until morning, he checked the locks on the doors and windows, then headed down the hallway to the guest bedroom.

The room was as inviting as her living room with a bright red spread across the bed and throw pillows in yellow and sky-blue.

He grabbed a pillow from the bed, checked the hall closet and found a sheet and then went back into the living room. He'd bunk on the sofa and sleep with one eye open.

Even though he didn't really anticipate any more

trouble for the rest of the night, he'd err on the side of caution.

It took him only minutes to make up the sofa, then take off his jeans and T-shirt and slide in beneath the sheet.

It was late and he was tired, but sleep refused to come as his head filled with thoughts of the woman in the next room. Were there secrets in her life she hadn't told him about, secrets that might hold a clue to what was happening to her now?

Black Rock was like any small town; the gossips loved to talk and everyone listened. He'd always assumed there were few secrets in Black Rock, but the truth was that nobody knew what went on behind closed doors or in somebody's mind.

He then realized that he'd always thought of Portia as his. She'd been his first love, his first lover and even though they'd only had a single night, prom night, together, it had indelibly written her name on his heart.

Even though it had been years since they'd been a couple, even though he had no hope that they would ever be a couple again, he wouldn't rest until the person who was tormenting her was behind bars.

He must have fallen asleep for he awoke with a start and immediately checked his watch. Just after six. Despite the shortness of his sleep, he felt rested and ready to face a new day.

He pulled on his jeans and then crept down the

hallway to Portia's bedroom. Her door was open and he peeked inside. She slept on her side facing him, her features soft and relaxed in slumber. Her hair was a spill of brown and copper against the pillow and the sheet had slipped down to expose the skimpy top of her emerald-green nightgown.

She looked beautiful and there was nothing he wanted to do more than crawl in next to her and kiss her awake. He'd love to stroke her silky skin until she was gasping with pleasure, but that would be the biggest mistake he could make. Instead he turned and headed back to the bathroom where he washed up and then went into the kitchen to make some coffee.

When the coffee had brewed he poured himself a cup and then stood at the window and frowned. The house backed up to a wooded area and there were trees on either side of the house, as well.

It had been easy for somebody to break into the day care without being seen. Her neighbors were far enough away that nobody would have heard the noise. It would be relatively easy for somebody to break into the house without being seen or heard, as well.

He needed to figure out what in the hell was going on, he thought as he sipped the coffee and watched the sun begin to peek over the horizon.

He was on his third cup of coffee and had made several phone calls when he heard the sound of water running and realized Portia was awake and taking a shower.

She was probably going to be sore, he thought as he checked the refrigerator and pulled out everything he needed to rustle up some bacon, eggs and toast.

Although he was eager to get out and start checking trucks and asking questions, his first order of business was to make sure she was okay.

The bacon had just finished frying when she made an appearance. "Over easy or broken yolks?" he asked. He tried not to notice how the lime-green T-shirt she wore clung to her breasts and transformed her hazel eyes to the color of lush grass. White shorts hugged her shapely behind and displayed her gorgeous long legs.

"Caleb, what are you doing?" she asked from the doorway.

"I'm making you breakfast. How are you feeling?"

She left the doorway and walked over to the cabinet to get herself a coffee cup. "Actually, better than I thought I would. My body is a little sore but at least my headache is gone. And over easy would be terrific."

"Sit," he commanded and pointed to the table. "This will be ready in just a few minutes."

She sat at the table. "I didn't know you could cook."

He crooked an eyebrow upward. "There's probably a lot of things about me you don't know. Just like

there are probably a lot of things about you that I don't know."

She wrapped her slender fingers around her cup and looked at him. "Why do I get the feeling you're not just making small talk?"

He broke the eggs into the skillet and pressed the bread down into the toaster. "What are your plans for the day?" he asked, intentionally changing the subject. He'd just needed to remind himself that they had no real connection, that they'd been two different people when they'd been young and crazy in love.

"I'm thinking of doing something completely shallow and out of character and calling Layla to see if she wants to go shopping and have lunch."

"I think that sounds like just what the doctor ordered," he said, glad that she didn't intend to stay here all day alone.

The toast popped up and he flipped the eggs onto the awaiting plates, then he set the plates on the table and joined her there.

"What are your plans for the day?" she asked.

"This morning I'm going to coordinate with Benjamin and we're going to check out the black pickups in the area and look for front-end damage. This afternoon I plan on stopping in at Harley's Bar to see if Harley has seen or heard from Dale. If I remember right, the two men were friends before Dale went to prison."

"Maybe Harley is behind this," she said.

Caleb thought of Harley Danvers, the owner of a raucous bar on the edge of town. The big bald man was mostly muscles and tattoos and wore his badass attitude on his broad, ex-boxer features.

"I don't know," he finally replied. "Everyone knows that beneath Harley's gruff exterior is a big heart. I can't imagine him risking everything he's built here in town to do something like this for a friend, but I'll check it all out."

For a few moments they ate in silence. Caleb tried not to notice the play of the sun in her hair and the floral scent that emanated from her. He tried not to remember that single night of passion they'd shared so long ago.

He needed to solve this thing and fast. The more time he spent with Portia the more she stirred something inside him that was definitely unwelcome.

"After you eat I want you to make a list for me of anyone you've dated, anyone you've flirted with in the last year. I want to know anyone who was rude to you, anyone who made you feel uncomfortable even for a second."

"So you don't think it's Dale Stemple come back to get revenge on me?" she asked.

"I think the worst thing we can do is have tunnel vision and just assume it's Dale to the exclusion of anyone else." He ate the last bit of his toast and then got up and carried his plate to the sink.

"I don't see why we need to go back a whole year. Surely whoever is angry with me, if it isn't Dale Stemple, is mad about something that's happened recently," she replied.

"Not necessarily." He leaned with his back against the cabinet and gazed at her thoughtfully. "Emotions aren't always that clean and clear. Sometimes things simmer just beneath the surface for months, for years, and then they explode."

She held his gaze for a long moment and he realized he didn't know if he was talking about whoever was after Portia or his own unresolved feelings where she was concerned.

He shook his head as if to dispel such thoughts. "And another thing, I think it would be best if you stayed away from the day-care kids." Her eyes widened at his words. "Let's face it, Portia. I don't want any of the kids to become collateral damage and at the moment, it looks like somebody has targeted you."

Chapter 5

"He was surprised when I wrote down all the names of the men I'd dated in the last year," Portia said as she stabbed her fork into a piece of celery in her salad.

"We all know you're nothing but the town slut," Layla said with a teasing grin. "Besides, isn't that the pot calling the kettle black? Caleb hasn't exactly been a recluse. He dates a lot, too. He was even engaged for a while, although he managed to screw that up."

Portia looked around the café for the tenth time since they'd come in for lunch, wondering if one of the men at the counter, if somebody at one of the tables, had been the person who had run her off the road the night before.

She'd been targeted, that's what Caleb had said. But why? And by whom?

She returned her attention back to Layla and released a sigh. "It would be nice if all the dating I've done would have led to a Mr. Right, but I'm beginning to think there is no Mr. Right for me in this town."

"Tell me about it," Layla said dryly. "The only difference between you and me is that I *am* the town slut and I still can't find my Mr. Right."

Portia laughed and shook her head, as always half appalled and half delighted by Layla's outrageous sense of humor. Layla wasn't exactly promiscuous, but she'd definitely had more sexual experiences than Portia.

"I thought maybe after lunch we'd check out that new dress shop that opened down by the hardware store. I've been meaning to go in for the last week but haven't done it," Layla said.

"Surely you need to get back to work," Portia protested. "I don't want to take up your entire day."

"Seriously, do you realize how bad the real-estate market is here in Black Rock? I'm just lucky that I had a good inheritance from my parents, otherwise I'd be starving."

"Or buying fewer clothes," Portia said teasingly.

"Trust me, I'd rather stop eating than stop shopping," Layla replied with a grin.

An hour later the two were in Bernie's Boutique.

Bernice Clinton, aka Bernie, was a plump housewife who had decided to open the store in an effort to bring better fashion to the small town. She had an eye for what was hot and trendy and her store carried not just clothing but also shoes and handbags.

Layla was in heaven, sorting through the racks with a discerning eye and pulling out a half-dozen things to try on. Portia had no need for new clothes and was more than aware of the fact that until the children returned to the day care, her life would feel incomplete and no amount of shoes or purses could make it right.

When Layla disappeared into the changing room Portia sat on a tufted bench and visited with Bernie, but her mind was on Caleb.

Sometimes things simmer just beneath the surface for months, for years. His words played and replayed in her head. Had he been talking about the person who was after her or had he been talking about the two of them?

What could have possibly simmered in him about her through the years? He'd promised to love her forever, yet when she'd gone out of town he'd cheated on her.

Several of her friends hadn't been able to wait to tell her that he'd spent the evening at the café with Jayme Cordell, a lovely blonde who'd been two years younger than Portia and Caleb. Those same friends

had told her that at the end of the evening the two had left together.

He'd proclaimed his innocence strongly and Portia had forgiven him. They'd resumed their relationship, but it had never been the same. She refused to make love with him again and he seemed okay with that, seemed to understand that she wanted to take things slowly.

She'd left for college and had only been gone a week when rumors began to circulate again about Caleb and Jayme and she didn't give him another chance.

Once a cheater, always a cheater, her mother would say. But her mother thought all men were cheaters and just needed the right opportunity to prove their vile natures.

Now, after all these years, Portia found herself wondering what had really happened between Caleb and Jayme. With the benefit of age and maturity, she recognized how twisted things could get when delivered from gossipers.

She also could admit that at eighteen years old her mother had been an enormous influence in her life and the memory of her cheating father had certainly played a role in her decision to kick Caleb to the curb.

She frowned. Why was she thinking about all this now? She couldn't go back and change the past and

Caleb was only in her life now as the deputy trying to solve a crime.

It was just after four when Layla dropped her off at her place. "You sure you're going to be okay here alone?" she asked, concern evident in her voice.

"I'll be fine," Portia replied. "Caleb said he'd check in with me later and besides, I'm not going to be chased out of my own home by some boogeyman," she added with a touch of false bravado.

"You go, girl!" Layla exclaimed. "You know, I could get you a gun if you think you need one. One of my old beaus has a revolver."

"No, thanks," Portia instantly exclaimed. "It would be just my luck that I'd shoot myself in the foot or somehow an intruder would get it away from me and use it on me. I'll be fine."

"Call me later," Layla said as Portia got out of the car.

Portia waved as Layla pulled out of the driveway. The two women had been best friends since fifth grade, their friendship challenged by their differences and nurtured by their sameness.

There had been no father in Portia's life and Layla's father had been a cold, critical man who had punched holes in Layla's soul with harsh words, a backhand and a lack of love. They were holes Layla tried to fill by jumping into bed and into relationships with men too quickly.

Portia started to head to her front door but paused

when a familiar car pulled in to her driveway. She smiled at the pretty blonde who got out.

"Hey, Peyton," she said to the woman who was dating Caleb's brother, Tom, and whose little girl was in Portia's day care.

"Hi, Portia. I heard about all the trouble you've been having and thought I'd stop by to see if there's anything I can do to help."

"Not that I can think of," Portia replied. "You want to come in?"

"No, thanks. I was just on my way to Melody's to pick up Lilly and thought I'd stop here for just a minute. I know Caleb is worried sick about all this. So is Tom."

"I feel a little guilty taking Caleb away from his search for Brittany," Portia said.

Peyton frowned. "Unfortunately there isn't much they can do about it right now. Tom told me that so far they haven't found anything in the car, no fingerprints, nothing that would tell them what might have happened. It's been terrible."

"Caleb didn't mention that to me."

"Caleb is the type who keeps things bottled up inside. I checked with Tom a little while ago and the search of the Miller property didn't turn up anything. Anyway, that's neither here nor there, I just wanted to check in on you." Peyton reached out and touched Portia's forearm. "I've been where you're at, Portia.

I know all about fear. If you ever need to talk, just give me a call."

It was no wonder that Tom Grayson had fallen in love with Peyton. She was not only beautiful, but she was warm and caring, as well.

"Thanks, Peyton, I appreciate it." The two women said their goodbyes and then Peyton got back in her car and Portia went into the house.

Peyton was right. She knew all about fear. It hadn't been so very long ago that her baby had been kidnapped and her life threatened by an unknown assailant. Tom had investigated the case and had not only managed to get baby Lilly safely back into Peyton's arms, but had also fallen in love with them both. The man behind the crimes had been Peyton's ex-boyfriend, who was also Lilly's father.

There had been rumors that a wedding was imminent between Black Rock's sheriff and the beautiful Peyton and everyone in town was happy that Tom had found the woman to complete his life.

The house was too silent and Portia found herself wandering from room to room, checking the locks on the windows, fighting the jangling nerves that threatened to take hold of her.

She'd told Layla the truth, that she refused to be chased away from her home. But, she had to consider that the person who had run her off the road probably also knew where she lived. She told herself she was safe behind locked doors and windows, with the

promise of a patrol car in the area, but still she felt on edge, with a touch of fear simmering inside her.

It was just after six when Caleb called to check in. "How are you feeling?" he asked.

"Fine, tired," she replied, surprised by how the sound of his deep voice chased away a little bit of her fear. "Busy day?"

"Busy but unproductive," he replied, his frustration evident in his voice. "So far we haven't been able to locate the truck involved in the accident last night. I'm heading to Harley's Bar now to see if I can catch up with him. Are you okay there? I think maybe I should come by there when I'm finished at Harley's. I don't like the idea of you there by yourself."

Yes, a little voice screamed in the back of her head. *Yes, please come and stay with me.* But she refused to allow the words to leave her lips.

"No, that's not necessary. I'm fine. The doors and windows are locked, I'll sleep with my cell phone right next to the bed and there's no reason to believe anyone would try to break in here."

She couldn't let her fear rule her life, couldn't allow it to make decisions for her that she might later regret. She couldn't very well have Caleb move in with her for protection, nor did she want to.

His hesitation let her know he wasn't happy about her being alone. "I'll make sure a patrol car drives by periodically through the night," he finally said.

"That's fine. I'm sure I'll be okay," she replied.

It was long after they'd hung up, after she'd eaten dinner and gotten ready for bed, that she started to regret the fact that she'd told him she was fine.

She wasn't fine. The house that had always felt so warm and inviting now seemed alien. Each floor creak sent a wave of alarm through her. The sound of the air conditioner whooshing on nearly shot her up out of her chair.

At nine o'clock she finally decided to go to bed. She'd read until she got sleepy. She was in the middle of a good book and hopefully it would keep her mind off her fear and off Caleb.

She read until eleven, then, realizing sleep was the furthest thing from her mind, she decided to get up and fix herself a cup of hot tea.

As she went by the front door she peeked outside, and was surprised to see a car parked by the curb in front of her house.

Caleb.

What was he doing out there so late? The answer came with a swell of her heart. He was watching her house. He was protecting her.

Who was the man Caleb Grayson had become in the years since those high school days when she'd been so in love with him? And why, for the first time since those long, lost days, did more than a little bit of interest fill her?

What did he intend to do, park in front of her house for the entire night to ensure her safety? A

warmth coupled with a sweet peace filled her. How easy it would be now to go back to bed and sleep, knowing Caleb was on duty.

And yet she knew it wasn't his duty to sit all night on front of her house. How on earth would he function tomorrow after spending the night in the cramped confines of his car?

You could make it easier on him, a little voice whispered. She hesitated only a moment and then unlocked the front door and stepped out on the porch.

In the shine from the nearby streetlight she saw his face and knew that he saw her. She raised a hand and motioned him toward the house, unsure if she was welcoming in her protector or the only man on the face of the earth who had the power to hurt her again.

He'd had a bad day. Caleb felt as if he'd been spinning his wheels all day long with no forward movement on Portia's case.

His talk with Harley at the bar had yielded no answers as to Dale Stemple's whereabouts. With no indication that the man was even in the small town, Caleb had once again focused on all the men who had been in Portia's life over the last year.

If that wasn't enough, thoughts of his sister had filled him with despair. When they'd found the car Caleb had hoped it would yield some clue as to her

whereabouts, but that hadn't happened. He knew that there were missing persons cases that never got solved, but he didn't want his sister to be one of those statistics. Still, until something broke in the case, there wasn't much more they all could do.

He'd finally gone home, but had only been there a few minutes when he'd been filled with a nagging concern for Portia. He hadn't been able to quell the feeling of imminent danger.

He'd finally given up trying and had driven to her house with the intention of spending the night in his car. The minute her front door had opened he'd tensed, wondering if something was wrong.

She'd stepped out on her front porch in that sexy, little green nightgown and had stared at his car for a long moment. When she'd finally raised a hand to motion him to the house, it hadn't been alarm that had shot through him, but rather a stir of something very different.

He now got out of his car and headed toward where she stood on the porch, his heart thudding a rhythm that had nothing to do with duty or protection.

God, she looked hot with her thick hair tousled and the green gown barely skimming the middle of her thighs and exposing the swell of her breasts.

"Evening, Portia," he said as he reached where she stood.

"It's not evening, it's the middle of the night,"

she replied. "Did you plan on staying out there until morning?"

"That was the plan," he replied. He tried not to allow his gaze to slide down the length of her.

"Wouldn't you be more comfortable in my guest room or on my sofa?"

I'd be more comfortable in your bed. The thought jumped unbidden into his brain. "Definitely," he agreed.

"Are you expecting trouble?" Her hazel eyes appeared more green than brown as she gazed at him somberly.

"Not really." There was no way he could explain to her that faint thrum of anxiety about her safety that had been with him all evening. He had no facts, nothing concrete to go on except the gut instinct that rarely led him wrong. If the person who had hit her car had murder on his mind, then he hadn't been successful and Caleb didn't know if he might try again. "I just decided safe was better than sorry."

"I like the way you think," she said dryly and opened the door to allow him inside. She relocked the door behind him and motioned him to the kitchen. "I was just about to make myself a cup of hot tea before trying to go to sleep. You want something?"

"No, but I'll sit with you while you drink yours." He sat at the table and watched as she filled the teakettle and placed it on a stove burner to heat. It

surprised him just a little that she didn't seem self-conscious about her night attire.

Once the kettle was on she joined him at the table. "Nothing new?"

He frowned, irritated that he couldn't tell her the case was solved and she had nothing more to fear. "Nothing. I talked to Harley and asked around town about Dale Stemple, but nobody has seen or heard from him. I also spoke to Joe Castle who says last week he lent his truck to his son, who lives in Oklahoma City."

She narrowed her eyes. "Sounds a bit suspicious, doesn't it?"

"I thought so. I have the authorities there checking it out. I should hear something by tomorrow. Walt Tolliver also owns a black pickup and I went to his place to check on it, but it was undamaged."

She smiled. "Walt is too busy seeing aliens to worry about trying to kill me. Besides, he and I have never exchanged a cross word."

He shrugged. "He's a bit out of it most of the time. I thought maybe he'd hit your car accidentally while prowling for his aliens, but it wasn't him. Oh, and I had a talk with Eric Willowby. You know he's still in love with you." He watched her expression closely, but at that moment the teakettle whistled and she jumped up from the table.

"Eric is a nice man," she said as she poured the hot water over the tea bag in her cup. After a moment

she pulled her tea bag and added a dollop of milk and then returned to the table. "He'll make somebody a terrific husband."

"Then why didn't you keep dating him?" he asked.

She took a sip of her tea and eyed him over the rim of the cup. She released a small sigh as she lowered the cup back to the table. "Because he wasn't the one."

"The one?"

A whisper of impatience flashed in her eyes. "You know, the one I want to go to bed with each night. The one I want to wake up to each morning. He wasn't the one I wanted to tell my hopes and dreams to." She shrugged. "As nice as he is, as well as he treated me, he just wasn't the one."

"Maybe you're looking for somebody who doesn't exist."

"Then I'll just stay single because I don't intend to settle," she exclaimed. "Besides, why are you asking me these questions? You certainly aren't an example of marital bliss."

"At least I got closer than you have been," he replied and felt the burn of anger that thoughts of Laura always evoked.

"I didn't know we were in a contest." She took another sip of her tea.

"We're not," he replied easily. "I was just curious, that's all."

"What happened with you and Laura? I heard through the grapevine that the two of you had set a date for a wedding and the next thing I heard was that she'd left town."

He hadn't told anyone about what had transpired between him and Laura and he sure didn't intend to tell Portia now. "It just didn't work out." He forced a smile to his lips. "She just wasn't the one."

Portia stared down into her cup and then looked back at him. "Like I wasn't the one?"

He sat back in his chair, surprised that she'd bring up their past and equally surprised by the faint surge of resentment that filled him at her words.

Her cheeks flushed with color and she averted her gaze from his. "Sorry, I shouldn't have said that," she said. "The last thing I want to do is rehash the past. I have enough to worry about with the here and now."

"I agree, although there is a little bit of our past I wouldn't mind rehashing." His gaze slid down the length of her and he knew there would be no question in her mind about what he meant.

Why not let her know he still desired her? They weren't kids anymore, but rather two consenting adults who didn't need promises of forever to indulge in a little shared passion.

He leaned forward and breathed in her scent, that delicious burst of sweet floral and clean soap. "I think about prom night sometimes," he admitted.

Her eyes shimmered with an emotion he couldn't begin to identify. "Sometimes I think about it, too. But we were nothing but kids, Caleb, and what we shared that night was magical because it was our first time." She finished her tea and got up from the table and carried her cup to the sink. "There's no way to recapture that magic, Caleb," she said as she turned to face him.

He got up from the table, as well, and for a moment he forgot why he was here in her house in the middle of the night. He forgot that he'd come here to protect her from some unknown assailant.

All he could think about was how shiny her hair was in the artificial light overhead and how no other woman's kisses had ever stirred him the way hers had done. His head filled with the memories of the slide of his hands across her breasts, the throaty moans that had issued from her as she'd helped him with a condom on that night so long ago.

He'd had an older friend rent the motel room for them and for that single night it hadn't been a seedy, rented room, but rather a love nest for the two of them to explore the desire that raged out of control between them.

"Maybe we don't need the magic. I mean we aren't kids anymore," he said as he stepped closer to her. "Aren't you curious, Portia?" He took another step toward her, close enough now to see the flecks of gold in her eyes, feel her quickened breath on his face.

He reached out and swept a strand of her silky hair away from her face, then ran his index finger across her lower lip. Fire leaped into her eyes and emboldened him and he didn't give himself a chance to change his mind, didn't give her a chance to protest, but rather took her mouth with his in a searing kiss of hunger.

She stiffened against him, but didn't step back, didn't withdraw. As his tongue touched her upper lip and then slid into her mouth, the tenseness left her body and she seemed to melt against him.

He wrapped his arms around her, his heart crashing wildly in his chest as she entwined her arms around his neck. The kiss grew wilder, hotter, as it continued and she pressed her body against his.

Kissing her was the same…and yet different than it had been years ago. She felt sweetly familiar in his arms and yet it wasn't a boy's desire that swelled up inside him, but rather that of a man.

His hand slid up her back, reveling in the feel of the cool silk and the radiating heat of her body beneath. His mouth left hers and slid down the length of her neck as he remembered the sensitive spot just behind her ears.

Her breath caught as he kissed her there and then continued down the length of her throat. She tossed her head back in a familiar gesture from so long ago, and in that moment Caleb knew he'd been mistaken when

he'd told himself he'd rarely thought about her over the years, that he'd stopped wanting her long ago.

She'd never moved completely out of his blood, out of his heart, and at the moment the resentment he'd felt toward her seemed distant and impossible to summon.

It wasn't until his hand slid around to cup her breast that she released a small gasp and jumped back from him. Her breasts rose and fell with rapid breaths and her eyes were dark and turbulent.

"Is this why you came here tonight? You've gone through all the other women in town and have now decided to start all over again?"

Any desire that Caleb felt was doused by the surge of old resentment that sprang alive inside him. He stepped back from her and shoved his hands in his pockets. "You never did understand the kind of man I was…I am."

"I'm sorry, Caleb. That was uncalled for," she said, obviously contrite. "I'm tired and it's late. Maybe it would be best if we just called it a night."

"You go to bed. I'll just bunk on the sofa for the rest of the night," he said.

She nodded and without another word she left the kitchen. Caleb watched her go, his emotions a curious battle between anger and want.

Had he come here tonight following a need to protect her, or a need for something else altogether? Curiosity, that's all it had been, he told himself as he

left the kitchen. He'd just wondered if that crazy, hot magic they'd once shared would be there again with her.

And it had…for just a moment as he'd held her in his arms, tasted the sweet fire in her kiss, he'd felt that same yearning to be her everything, to be the one.

Her words to him had been an unwelcome dose of reality and reminded him that what they'd once shared had been broken ultimately by her inability to trust him, her inability to believe in him.

Apparently nothing had changed and he'd be a fool to attempt any kind of a relationship with her. He'd keep her safe. He'd do his duty as the deputy assigned to her case, but there was no way in hell he intended to let Portia or any other woman into his heart.

Chapter 6

Despite the lateness of the night before, Portia awoke at dawn with the taste of regret lingering in her mouth. Shame washed over her as she thought about what she'd said to Caleb.

Her words had been hateful and had nothing to do with the truth. Caleb wasn't a womanizer. Sure, he dated a lot, but why wouldn't he? He was handsome and single and, besides, he probably didn't date any more than she did.

She'd been wrong to say what she had, but she'd been desperate to create a chasm between them, had needed a defense against the incredible want that had built up inside her with his touch.

As he'd kissed her, as he'd held her so tight against

the lean heat of his body, all she'd wanted to do was take him into her bedroom and make love. The desire had been so intense it had frightened her and she'd had to do something to douse the fire.

She sighed and rolled over on her side to look out the window where the light of morning was just beginning to creep across the sky.

It was too early to get out of bed and so she remained beneath the fresh-scented sheet with only her thoughts as company. Maybe Caleb was right, maybe she'd never really understood what kind of man he was—what kind of man he'd become.

What if he'd always been telling the truth? What if he hadn't cheated on her with Jayme Cordell? She couldn't even remember now who had told her about Caleb's betrayal. She sighed once again. What difference did it all make now?

It had been ten years ago. There was no going back in time to change things. She'd once believed that Caleb was the one, but now she sensed a simmering anger in him that occasionally flashed in his eyes, that hardened the line of his jaw.

Maybe it was because his sister was missing, or perhaps it was some damage that Laura had left behind when she'd moved from town. Surely he couldn't have any residual resentment toward Portia for something that had happened years ago when they had both been kids.

Portia only knew that as much as she wanted Caleb

and he might want her, she didn't believe he was the one, didn't believe he wanted to be the one.

She frowned irritably. What was she thinking? She didn't want another chance with Caleb. She just wanted him to find out who was after her and to get her life back to normal.

She needed her kids back in the day care. She missed their happy faces, their smacking kisses and their hugs. They had been the most important people in her life and without them there was a huge hole in her heart.

She desperately wanted a child of her own, but for now she had to be content with her children on loan, and at the moment she didn't even have them. Caleb had been right, until they knew exactly what was happening it was best that she stay away from the children she loved.

Sick of her own thoughts, she got out of bed and headed for the adjoining bathroom, hoping a hot shower would banish all thoughts of Caleb and how close she'd come to making love to him the night before.

But as she stood beneath the hot spray of water all she could think about was how Caleb's kisses had thrilled her, how his touch had torched through her with a desire she hadn't felt for any other man.

She certainly hadn't remained celibate during the last ten years. There had been two men she'd dated with whom she'd been intimate, one who had

eventually moved out of town for his business, the other eventually moving on with her blessing.

But neither of those men had affected her like Caleb did. He made her feel as if her skin was on fire and he was the only one who could put the flames out. She had to admit to herself that there was something strong between them, at least on a physical level.

By the time she was out of the shower and dressed she smelled the scent of coffee and knew Caleb was also up and about.

She owed him an apology and it was on the tip of her tongue as she found him in the kitchen standing before her window with a cup of coffee in hand.

He turned as he heard her, his expression guarded and distant. "Good morning."

"Good morning," she replied. "Caleb, I'm sorry about what I said last night, about you starting all over with the women in town."

A smile curved his lips but didn't reach the darkness of his eyes. "Don't worry about it. I've already forgotten it."

"It wasn't a nice thing to say and in any case that's not what I believe about you."

He shrugged. "It doesn't matter." He took a sip of his coffee. "Have you talked to Wally about your car?"

"Yesterday. He told me he hopes to have it back to me by the first of next week." She walked over to

the coffeemaker and poured herself a cup of the fresh brew and then turned to face Caleb once again.

The deep frown that cut across his forehead did nothing to alleviate his attractiveness. His hair was mussed, that charming, errant lock falling down precariously close to his left eyebrow. She fought the desire to step forward and push it back into place.

"I don't like the idea of you being here all alone without a car. Maybe it would be best if I stay here on your sofa at night until we figure out what's going on," he said.

The idea of having him here with her at night both exhilarated and terrified her. There was no question that there was still an overwhelming passion between them and she feared allowing that passion to boil over. And she knew instinctively that if he stayed here at night, eventually it would explode.

"Actually, I was going to invite Layla to spend a couple of days here with me," she replied, although it hadn't been a thought in her head until that moment. "I'm hoping to get in a little girl time with her and convince her that it would be good for her soul to help me paint the interior of the day care."

"Why don't you go to her place and spend a couple of days there," he suggested.

"Can't. Mr. Whiskers and I don't get along."

Caleb raised a dark brow wryly. "I hope that's a cat and not the newest man in Layla's life."

She smiled. "A big, long-haired cat who for some

ungodly reason loves me. Unfortunately it only takes about ten minutes in her house for me to suffer a major allergy attack."

His features gave away nothing of his thoughts. "Whatever, I just don't feel right with you being here alone until we figure things out. Call and let me know if Layla can't come over."

"I will," she said. "You want breakfast?"

"No, I need to get out of here and head back to my place to shower and change for work." He drained his coffee cup and carried it to the sink.

It was early enough that he could have stayed for breakfast and still had plenty of time to go back to his place and get ready for the day. It was obvious he was eager to leave and she wondered if he hadn't really accepted her apology. Or maybe he was regretting his own lapse in judgment in the heated embrace and kisses they'd shared the night before.

He didn't say another word as she walked with him to the front door. When they reached the door he turned to face her. "I'm not going to lie to you, Portia. I want you." His eyes smoked with a hint of a flame. "Since the moment you came into the sheriff's office about those flyers, I've been thinking about making love to you again, dreaming about it when I go to sleep." He shoved his hands into his pockets, as if afraid of what they might do if not contained. "But make no mistakes, I'm not in the market for a meaningful relationship or any kind of relationship

at all. Still, if you're interested in indulging in a little strictly physical pleasure, keep me in mind."

With that he turned and walked out of her house. She watched him go, her mouth slightly agape in shock at his words and the realization that beneath the shock was a renewed burn of want for him.

Caleb was in a foul mood and didn't know if it was because he couldn't figure out who had it in for Portia or because she'd gotten to him the night before, her sexy curves melting against him and her mouth hot and sweet beneath his.

And then there had been her cutting comment that she'd apologized for, but was an indication that she still had trust issues where men were concerned.

Portia called just after ten to let him know that Layla had agreed to stay with her for the next couple of days. His irritation rose higher as he realized he was slightly disappointed that her friend had stepped in to help.

Despite everything there was a part of him that wanted to be her hero, a part that wanted to guard her through the long, dark nights.

At noon he left the office and walked down to the café to grab lunch. The officials in Oklahoma City had called that morning to let him know that Joe Castle's black truck had no damage on it. Everywhere he turned was a dead end.

He and his brothers Tom and Benjamin felt the

same way about Brittany. No clues, no direction to look, and with each passing day a sinking feeling that they'd never know what happened to their sister.

At noon most of the tables and booths in the café were filled with people. Caleb took a stool at the counter and forced a smile as Linda Wyatt, one of the waitresses, came over to take his order.

"Tough day?" Linda asked.

"Does it show?"

She smiled. "You look tired, Caleb." She pulled her order form from her apron pocket. "Working too hard?"

"Maybe thinking too much," he replied. "Just give me a burger with extra pickles, fries and a glass of iced tea."

"No news on your sister?" she asked and then blew upward to move a wisp of gray hair that clung to her forehead.

He shook his head. "Nothing."

She gave him a look of sympathy and then left to place his order. A wave of depression swept over him. His sister was missing and things didn't look good. He couldn't even figure out who had nearly killed Portia in a car accident.

"Hey, Caleb." The deep voice pulled him from his thoughts as he nodded to Larry Norwood. Larry and his family had moved to Black Rock two months before and he was quickly gaining a good reputation as the town's vet.

"Larry. How's it going?"

Larry sat on the stool next to Caleb and offered him a friendly smile. "Good. Every day that passes, Black Rock feels more and more like home."

"It's a good place to live with good people," Caleb replied, a sense of pride for his hometown filling his chest.

As the two men ate their lunches they talked about the town, their work and the relentless heat that was forecast for the next several days.

It was a respite for Caleb to talk about ordinary, mundane things for a while, with the conflicted emotions that filled him when he thought about Portia and the fear that thoughts of Brittany always brought shoved to the back of his mind.

When he left the café, instead of heading back to the office he got into his car and pointed the nose toward the Grayson homestead on the edge of town.

It had been a couple of days since he'd checked in with his brother Jacob and he decided to take a few minutes and stop by the cabin where Jacob was staying.

Benjamin lived in the large house where they'd grown up and he made sure their brother had the supplies he needed. As Caleb drove through the entrance onto the Grayson property, signs of a working ranch were everywhere. Cattle roamed

the pasture on the left and on the right a field of cornstalks waved in the hot breeze.

Benjamin enjoyed being a deputy, but his heart was in ranching. Caleb wouldn't be surprised if eventually his brother quit his law enforcement work to become a full-time rancher.

He drove by the house and onto a gravel road that led to a wooded area some distance away. As he entered the woods the cabin came into view when he was almost on top of it. He parked and got out, wondering for the hundredth time what had happened to Jacob that had him hiding out in a cabin cut off from the rest of the world.

He knocked twice and heard Jacob's deep voice tell him to come in. Jacob sat in a chair with a lamp on the end table turned on. Sunshine couldn't pierce through the thick canopy of trees that sheltered the cabin.

"Little brother," Jacob said and smiled, although the gesture didn't reach the darkness of his eyes. "What's going on?"

"Not much. I'm feeling frustrated and decided to take a few minutes and come out here to see you. How are you doing?" Caleb sat in the chair across from his brother. He knew better than to ask what was going on in Jacob's world, in his head, because he'd already asked a million times and Jacob refused to share anything with anyone.

Jacob raked a hand across his whiskered jaw and

leaned back in the chair. "I'm fine. Tom stopped by last night and told me there's nothing new on Brittany's disappearance."

"I'm trying to stay optimistic, but it's getting harder and harder with each day that passes," Caleb replied.

"So, tell me what else is going on in town."

For the next few minutes Caleb told his brother about the mayor's plans for a fall festival, Walt Tolliver's latest supposed encounter with aliens and Portia's problems.

"You two had quite a thing when you were younger," Jacob said. "I remember Mom and Dad worrying that the two of you would run off and get married before either of you had a chance to experience life."

Caleb emitted a dry laugh. "They worried for nothing."

"Portia hasn't married, has she?"

"No, she's still single."

Jacob gazed at Caleb with a directness Calcb had found daunting since he had been a small child. Jacob was the older brother who had always been able to get Caleb to confess to whatever mischief he'd made. One look from Jacob's dark gray eyes and Caleb had always crumbled like a cookie.

"So are there any sparks between the two of you?" he asked.

Caleb felt the scowl creep over his features. "Of

course not," he exclaimed. One of Jacob's dark brows rose and he smiled. "Okay, maybe a few," Caleb added. "But it's just a physical thing. Nothing is going to come of it. We got it wrong before and there's no reason to think that we'd get it right this time."

"You were nothing but a couple of kids before. Both of you have some years of experience and wisdom under your belts now." Jacob reached over and picked up the bottle of beer that had been sitting on the table next to him. "Want a beer?"

"No, thanks. I'm still on duty. In fact, I need to get out of here." Caleb stood.

"Let me know how those sparks work out," Jacob said with a wry grin.

Caleb walked to the door and then turned to face his brother. "Trust me, they won't work out. I'm a man meant to live alone."

A burst of laughter left Jacob, the sound rusty as if from lack of use. Caleb hadn't heard his brother laugh since he'd returned to Black Rock and for a moment he savored the sound. Then he straightened his shoulders and glared at his brother. "What's so damned funny?"

"The idea of you being alone the rest of your life. I've never known any man less inclined to choosing to be alone than you." Jacob's eyes darkened. "And trust me, I know all about being alone." Jacob raised the bottle of beer toward his lips. "Go on, get out of here. I'll talk to you later."

As Caleb opened the door Jacob took a deep drink of the beer and raised a hand in goodbye. Caleb frowned as he got back into his car.

Jacob had become another concern on his radar. He was drinking too much, spending far too much time alone, and it was rare that Caleb saw glimpses of the man he had been before whatever events had brought him back home.

Tom and Benjamin had jokingly mentioned that they needed to have an intervention for Jacob, force him out of the cabin and back into the world with love and concern. But Caleb knew that wasn't going to happen. All of them respected Jacob's need at the moment to stay reclusive. It was obvious he was working something out in his mind. Hopefully, eventually he'd rejoin the world or at least tell them what had happened to him.

As he headed back to town his thoughts skittered over the members of his family. Fear gripped his throat as he thought about Brittany and concern filled him when he considered Jacob. At least Tom had found love with Peyton, and Benjamin was just a laid-back, happy soul whose goal in life was to see everyone else just as happy.

The afternoon passed with more of the same, chasing down false leads and fighting against a frustration that threatened to be all consuming.

He left the office at dusk but before heading home he swung by Portia's place. He wanted to make sure

that Layla was really there and that Portia wasn't all alone.

With each day that passed and in which nothing more happened, he wondered if maybe there was no further danger for Portia. Perhaps the crash on the road had truly been some sort of accident and the person responsible had simply been too scared to stop.

Whoever had a beef with Portia, maybe their anger had been vented with the posting of the flyers and the vandalism in the day care. Maybe he was looking for trouble where there was none.

Maybe he was inventing trouble in order to have a purpose in her life. The thought hit him square in the stomach and nearly stole his breath away.

Immediately he shoved it away. That was not what he was doing. There had been three incidents of violence directed at Portia. He'd be a fool and completely irresponsible not to expect a fourth.

He breathed a sigh of relief as he pulled up to the curb in front of her house and saw Layla's sports car in the driveway.

Good, at least Portia wouldn't be alone.

An old rush of feelings swept through him, a bittersweet pang of loss, of broken dreams and unrealized hopes. The familiar bitterness crawled up the back of his throat and he swallowed hard against it.

As the emotions swelled inside him, he knew his brother was wrong about him. No matter how many

sparks there were between him and Portia, no matter how lonely he found his life, he was never going to give his heart to another woman.

Jacob was wrong. He was meant to be alone.

Chapter 7

"It's going to look awesome," Portia said as she stepped back from the bright yellow wall that they'd finished painting over the last couple of hours.

"To heck with the walls, what I want to know is what are you going to feed me for dinner? I'm starving," Layla exclaimed as she laid down her paint roller. "You've practically worked me to death this afternoon."

Portia laughed. "And just think, we get to do it all again tomorrow. We still have three walls left to paint." She threw an arm around Layla's shoulder. "And dinner is going to be pizza delivery. I'm too tired to cook."

Together the two women cleaned up their brushes

and rollers and left the garage and headed for the house. Once inside, Layla plopped onto the sofa while Portia grabbed the phone to order the pizza. When the pizza order had been placed Portia joined her friend on the sofa.

"I can't tell you how much I appreciate you taking some time off and hanging out here with me," Portia said.

Layla smiled and shoved a strand of her long blond hair behind one of her ears. "Work has been slow and I had vacation time coming, and I can't think of anyone I'd rather spend it with than you." She wrinkled her nose and frowned. "And I think it sucks, that I don't have some Prince Charming begging me to spend a couple of days with him."

"This town is definitely short of Prince Charmings," Portia agreed and her head immediately filled with a vision of Caleb.

He might have been her Prince Charming years ago but she'd believed his crown had tarnished and there was no way to get the shine back. All day long she'd wondered if she'd been wrong about him back then. Had it been her heart that had tarnished and not his princely crown?

She jumped up from the sofa. "Come on, let's go into the kitchen and get some sodas and get ready for our pizza." She didn't want to think about Caleb anymore. She didn't want to think about how much

she'd wanted him the night before, how much that want still sizzled inside her.

Once they were in the kitchen Layla sat at the table and Portia pulled out plates and got their drinks. They talked about their work in the day care the next day, Layla's lack of real-estate sales and the fact that she might have to consider a new career path because of the current economic times.

"What would you like to do if you don't work in real estate?" Portia asked.

Layla paused a long moment. "I know it sounds totally out of character for me, but what I'd really like is to be somebody's wife, somebody's mother. I'd like a couple of years of being a stay-at-home wife and mother and building a home and then when the kids went to school I'd decide what I wanted to do with the rest of my life." She flashed Portia a grin. "Lame, huh?"

"Not lame at all," Portia replied with a new burst of warmth for her friend, "although maybe a little politically unpopular nowadays."

"I've never been one for following the politically correct path," Layla replied. "You know I had a giant crush on Jacob Grayson when I was young."

"Really?" Portia replied in surprise. "He was definitely nice looking but he always seemed kind of scary to me."

Layla grinned. "Your scary, my sexy."

"That should be the pizza," Portia said when the

doorbell rang. She hurried to the door and threw it open and gasped as she saw the tall blond man standing on her porch. "Joe!" she said in surprise as a tiny edge of fear sprang to life. "What are you doing here?"

Joe Castle was a handsome man with piercing blue eyes, blond hair and a tanned, weathered face. At the moment his eyes were cold and hard and his mouth was a thin slash of displeasure as he glared at her. "Do you have a problem with me?" he asked.

Portia held tight to the edge of the door, unsure what Joe might be capable of. "Of course not," she replied.

"Then why do I have Caleb Grayson on my ass?"

Portia breathed a small sigh of relief as Layla stepped up next to her. "Hi, Joe," Layla said. "What's going on?"

"I just want Portia to know that I had nothing to do with what's happening to her. I'd never hurt a woman and I'm definitely not into vandalism."

"Joe, I'm sorry if all this has made you uncomfortable, but Caleb has to investigate and the first thing he asked me was who had been in my life lately. I had to tell him we'd dated and unfortunately that put you on his potential-suspect list," Portia said. "I never even considered it might be you," she added. It was a fib, but one that instantly dispelled some of the tension in Joe.

"I'm glad to hear that," he replied gruffly. "We dated long enough that you should know what kind of man I am, and I'm not a woman abuser."

At that moment the pizza-delivery car pulled up to the curb and a young boy got out carrying a carton. "Looks like you're getting ready to eat. I just wanted to tell you to your face that I had nothing to do with all this." Joe didn't wait for a response but instead turned on his boot heels and strode back to his car.

Portia paid for the pizza and the two women returned to the kitchen. "You think he really came here to apologize?" Layla asked as she grabbed a slice of the gooey pizza and put it on her plate.

"Why else would he have come?" Portia asked.

Layla shrugged her slender shoulders. "Maybe for attack number four?"

"That's ridiculous. Surely he saw your car in the driveway and knew I wasn't here all alone."

"Maybe he thought the car in your driveway was a rental since yours is in the shop," Layla countered.

Portia took a bite of her pizza and frowned. Surely Joe didn't feel that kind of rage against her just because she'd decided they weren't right for each other.

The news is filled with stories of women being murdered because of unrequited love, a little voice whispered inside her head. "I just can't believe this is all happening," she finally said. "I keep thinking this is a nightmare and eventually I'm going to wake up."

"If it is a nightmare I don't appreciate you involving me in your bad dreams," Layla said, making Portia grin.

For the remainder of the meal the two indulged in a little gossip. They placed bets on when Tom Grayson and Peyton would get married, how long it might be before Walt Tolliver needed to be committed and Layla's penchant for bad boys.

"I think Benjamin Grayson is pretty hot," she said, "but he's just too nice for me."

Portia thought about Caleb's brother. Like all of the Grayson men, Benjamin was definitely a hunk but he was also the most easygoing and good-natured of all the brothers. Layla was right, she was far too tempestuous for a man like Benjamin. She'd eat him up and spit him out.

"Benjamin doesn't date much. If fact, I can't think of anyone he's dated," Portia said thoughtfully.

Layla tore a piece of crust in half and popped it into her mouth and chewed thoughtfully. "I can't think of anyone he's dated, either," she finally added. "I wonder what happened to Jacob? I haven't heard anything about him in years."

"Who knows? Maybe we are both meant to be old maids with lots of cats and only memories of our old boyfriends to keep us warm," Portia said.

"Mr. Whiskers is my baby, but he's no substitute for a man. Besides, I don't know about me, but I

definitely know you're meant to get married and have a dozen babies. That's all you've ever wanted."

A faint depression settled over Portia's shoulders. Yes, that's exactly what she'd always wanted—and that's what Caleb had once promised her, love and family.

"Sometimes I wonder how different my life would have been if I hadn't broken up with Caleb when I was in college," she said.

Layla reached for another piece of pizza. "Maybe not so different, except that you'd be watching your own kids along with everyone else's."

"I sometimes wonder if I was wrong to listen to gossip instead of listening to Caleb."

"Possibly," Layla replied easily. "There were a lot of girls who were jealous of you in high school. Caleb was one of the hottest guys in the school and you had him wrapped around your little finger from your sophomore year on. Lots of girls would have loved to see the two of you break up so they could have a chance with him. But it's all water under the bridge now, right?"

"Right." Portia frowned thoughtfully. "But I have to confess that I have just a little bit of regret inside me."

"Regret is kind of a wasted emotion unless it brings some sort of lesson with it," Layla replied. "Of course it would be nice if we could go back and fix all the things we regret."

Portia thought of the hardness she'd seen in Caleb's eyes that morning. Was she partially responsible for that faint edge of anger she occasionally saw in the depths of his eyes?

She didn't know, but what she suspected was there was no way to fix what had gone wrong between them, no way to reclaim the magic that they had had before. Besides, he'd made it clear that he was only interested in having sex with her again, not in having a real, meaningful relationship.

They finished eating and moved into the living room for more girl talk. The phone rang at eight-thirty. It was Caleb checking in to make sure they were okay.

The sound of his deep voice caused a whisper of a shiver inside her, a shiver of the sweet desire she'd felt for him the night before. She assured him they were fine, that Layla was staying with her for the rest of the week and the call ended.

"I know I have a reputation as a party girl, but all that painting and moving furniture wore me slick," Layla said as she stifled a yawn with the back of her hand.

"I'm pooped, too," Portia admitted, although she thought her exhaustion came more from too many thoughts about Caleb than from the physical work she'd accomplished that day.

"You aren't going to get me up at the crack of dawn, are you?" Layla asked as the two headed down

the hallway to the bedrooms. "You know how much I need my beauty sleep."

"I promise I won't wake you too early," Portia replied as she turned on the light in the guest bedroom. She gave Layla a grateful hug. "Thanks."

"For what?" Layla asked.

"For being here. For being my friend."

Layla grinned. "I have to be your friend, you know all my secrets."

Portia laughed and released her. "You know where everything is, but if you need something you can't find just let me know."

"I'll be fine," Layla assured her. The two said good night and Portia headed for her bedroom at the end of the hallway.

Like Layla, she was exhausted. Her arm muscles and back ached from the strain of wielding a paint roller, and a hot shower sounded like heaven at the moment.

Minutes later as she stood beneath the spray of hot water, she thought of the work they'd accomplished that day. The yellow paint had easily covered the drab beige that had been on the walls and when finished would give the area a cheerful atmosphere that the children would enjoy.

She'd called Melody that morning to check on how the children were doing at her house. Melody assured her everything was fine but the kids missed Ms. Portia.

While she couldn't put her life on hold forever, she explained to Melody that she just didn't want to take a chance being around the kids until this matter was resolved. She would die if one of the children got hurt or worse because some nut was after her.

When would she know if it was safe to have the children back where they belonged? When would she be safe to resume her normal day-to-day activities?

Maybe she and Caleb had overreacted to everything that had happened. Sure, it was obvious that somebody was mad at her, somebody didn't like her, but maybe that bump on her car had been the last gasp of somebody's ire.

Finished with her shower, she pulled on her nightgown and got into bed with only the lamp on her nightstand aglow. There was no other sound in the house so she knew Layla was also in bed.

Warmth filled her heart as she thought of her friend. When she'd called Layla and asked her to stay with her for a couple of days, Layla hadn't hesitated. Within an hour she'd arrived with a suitcase and a smile, ready to support Portia in whatever she needed.

Portia wished Layla would find a man who would love her to distraction, a man who could manage her volatile nature, who would see beyond her flaws and find the gold inside.

With a deep sigh Portia reached out and turned off her lamp. The room was plunged into darkness with

just the faint cast of the moon spilling in through the window.

She thought that it would take her forever to fall asleep, but almost immediately she not only slept, but dreamed. And in her dream it was prom night and she was in the motel room with Caleb.

Her stomach was knotted with a delicious tension as she saw the rose petals on the bed, saw the desire that flamed hot and wild in Caleb's eyes. This was it—in the next few minutes she would give her virginity to the man she loved.

Although she was nervous, she wasn't afraid. She knew Caleb would be gentle, that he would take good care of the gift she was about to give to him. She knew this was the right thing to do, what she wanted to do more than anything else.

As he gathered her into his arms, her heart tap-danced a quick rhythm of desire. And when his mouth claimed hers, hot and greedy, she returned the kiss with fervor.

The kiss chased away any lingering doubt that might have entered her mind. He had her heart and now it was finally time to give him the whole of her body.

They fell to the bed where the scent of roses filled her head and his mouth found the spot behind her ear that always made her gasp with pleasure.

"I love you, Portia. I'll always love you," he whispered into her ear.

His words made her heart sing. "I love you, too. Forever and always," she replied.

"I promise you that there will never be another girl for me. I'll love you until the day I die." His voice trembled with emotion.

His arms wrapped around her and his fingers found the top of the zipper that ran down the length of the back of the royal-blue prom dress. The sound of the zipper hissing downward shot shivers of anticipation down her spine. However, as the sound continued on…and on…a niggle of anxiety weighed in her chest.

It shouldn't be taking so long to unzip the dress and yet that faint hissing sound continued. When it finally stopped she snapped awake and her heart thundered in her chest in a fight-or-flight response she didn't understand.

She lay for a long moment, eyes closed and every muscle in her body inexplicably tensed. What about the dream had created such an intense sense of unease? A sense of danger?

She cracked open her eyes and in an instant her mind took in two things. The first was the screen at the window that had been cut and hung askew. That was the sound she'd heard. The second thing she saw was the dark shadow that rushed at her.

Before she had a chance to scream the figure was on top of her with strong hands wrapped around her throat. Portia could tell that the hands were covered

by latex gloves, the cool plastic chilling her to the bone.

She struggled, but found herself trapped by the sheet covering her. Frantic, she tried to escape the cotton cocoon but couldn't get loose.

The hands around Portia's neck squeezed tighter and fingers tore into her skin as panic screamed inside her. She thrashed her arms and legs in an effort to get free, to be able to fight back.

She couldn't tell anything about her attacker other than the fact that the face was covered with a ski mask and there was almost inhuman strength in the hands at her throat. She saw the glitter of eyes, but couldn't discern the color in the darkness of the room.

The attacker didn't say a word but emitted raspy, rapid breathing as those hands continued to strangle Portia. She wished for a voice, something she could hear that would identify the person.

Tears blinded her as she realized if she didn't do something she was going to die right here in her bedroom with Layla only a room and a scream away.

She couldn't breathe and a new darkness was closing in all around her as the fingers pressed tighter and tighter into her throat. Tiny stars exploded in her head as her brain begged for oxygen.

Finally she managed to get an arm free from the sheet and she swung it hard at the side of the head of

the attacker. The hands around Portia's throat slipped slightly and she drew in a deep breath as she struck once again with her fist.

She tried to summon a scream, but nothing came out. Again and again she slammed her fist against the attacker's face and shoulders and then she managed to get a leg out from beneath the sheet and began to kick, as well.

The intruder drove a fist into Portia's jaw, snapping her head back against the pillow and finally, a scream ripped from her throat.

"Portia!" Layla's voice sounded from the distance. "Portia, are you all right? I'm coming in there and I've got my gun."

In the flash of an eyeblink the attacker was up and off the bed and back through the torn window screen to the outside.

Portia gulped in deep breaths of air and sat up at the same time her bedroom door flew open and the overhead light went on.

If she hadn't been so terrified, she might have laughed at the sight of Layla in a hot-pink camisole and matching bikini bottoms and wielding not a gun, but a hair flatiron in her hands.

She was crouched as if ready to spring and looked like a high-fashion ninja warrior. But instead of laughing, Portia grabbed her burning throat and hoarsely cried out to her friend.

Layla threw down the hair iron and ran to the

window and closed and locked it, then rushed to Portia's side. "Are you okay? Oh, God, Portia. Who was here? Did you get a look at who it was?"

Portia shook her head as she rubbed her aching neck and then moved her hand to touch her jaw. Cold. She was so cold.

It had only been a couple of hours ago that she'd wondered if she and Caleb had been overreacting to the events of the last couple of days.

Caleb.

She had to call him. She needed to tell him what had happened. A sob wrenched up her aching throat as Layla helped her out of the bed, but she swallowed it as she desperately tried to stay in control.

She needed to get out of this room, away from the window. She was afraid the person might come back to finish the job, afraid that this nightmare would never be over.

Layla seemed to sense her need and led her to the bedroom door. She didn't say anything but held tight as if aware of how close she'd come to losing her friend.

If Portia hadn't managed to release that scream, there was no doubt in her mind that Layla would have found her dead in her bed in the morning. She leaned weakly against Layla, her body trembling violently as she played and replayed the last few minutes in her mind.

Those hands had been so strong and so intent on

squeezing the life from her and they'd come so close to success.

When they were in the living room Portia grabbed the phone and quickly dialed Caleb's cell phone number. Layla sat next to her on the sofa, her face pale with shock and worry.

Portia held it together until she heard the sound of his deep, sleepy voice.

"Caleb," she said. "I need you." The control she'd tried so hard to maintain snapped and she began to weep.

Chapter 8

Caleb had never driven so fast down the streets of Black Rock. Thankfully at two-thirty in the morning there were no other cars on the road to get in his way.

The phone call from Portia had scared the hell out of him. All he'd managed to get out of her was that she needed him before Layla had gotten on the phone and told him somebody had come through the bedroom window and had tried to strangle Portia.

He gripped the steering wheel tightly as he made a right turn down the street that would take him to Portia's place.

Dammit, whoever had broken in her house had balls of steel. They had to have seen Layla's car in

the driveway and that still hadn't deterred them from trying to get to Portia.

He'd called Tom and Benjamin and asked them to meet him at Portia's. It was a crime scene and he couldn't take care of the situation on his own.

When he pulled up to Portia's every light in the house shone and he jumped out of his car and hurried to the door. "Portia, it's me," he said as he banged on the door. Layla let him inside and he strode into the living room. Portia was up and off the sofa and into his arms in an instant.

She trembled violently and cried into the front of his shirt. He tightened his embrace and looked at Layla, who sat on the sofa. She wore a short pink robe and a look of horror. Portia wore her robe, too, the silk material cool against him.

"He came in through the bedroom window," Layla said. "He cut the screen and got the window open and came inside and he tried to strangle her." Layla's voice rose an octave. "He tried to kill her, Caleb. If I hadn't been here I don't know what would have happened."

"You're sure it was a man?" he asked as Portia's sobs began to subside.

She finally moved from his embrace and looked up at him, her eyes filled with turbulent emotions. He saw the redness of her jaw and throat and wanted to hit somebody, wanted to smash the perpetrator in the face.

"I don't know. All I can tell you is that whoever it was, was strong." She raised a hand and touched her neck. "He wore a ski mask and it was so dark I couldn't tell anything about him." She moved to sit on the sofa and at that moment Tom and Benjamin arrived.

For the next hour the men processed the window and the bedroom, questioned Portia and Layla over and over again and tried to find something that might lead them to the identity of the intruder.

An ambulance arrived and the paramedics checked out Portia, looking at her throat and jaw and making the assessment that she didn't need emergency care, and at Portia's insistence had finally left.

Unfortunately, everything had happened so fast, she hadn't gotten a really good impression of the person who'd attacked her. She wasn't sure about height or weight and couldn't tell them hair or eye color.

Throughout this time all Caleb could think about was how close she'd come to being killed. His heart beat an unnatural rhythm throughout the questioning, a combination of fear for her and suppressed rage.

If he looked at her red jaw and bruised throat for too long he feared losing himself in that rage. He knew if that happened he wouldn't be able to do his job properly.

It was after four when Tom and Benjamin were finished. They'd collected her bedding to be checked

for any trace evidence. The window had yielded no fingerprints, but they hadn't expected to find any since Portia was certain the person had worn gloves.

"You're coming home with me," he said to Portia as Tom and Benjamin went out the front door.

She hesitated and it was Layla who took her by the hands. "Go, Portia. Go home with Caleb and let him keep you safe for the rest of the night. I love you dearly, but I can't keep you safe like he will."

"I'll just get some things together." She got off the sofa but hesitated.

"I'll go with you," Caleb said, easily guessing that she didn't want to go into the bedroom alone. She gave him a grateful smile. "Layla, just hang tight and we'll follow you home," he said as he headed down the hallway with Portia.

He stood in the doorway as she pulled a small suitcase from her closet and began to gather some clothes. They didn't speak. He had a feeling that at least for the moment she was all talked out.

Again a wealth of anger filled him as he glanced at the window and the bare mattress. "When I find him, I'll kill him." The words fell from his mouth before he realized he was speaking out loud.

"No, you won't," she replied. "You'll arrest him and do it the right way because that's the kind of honorable man you are." She went into the adjoining

bathroom and he stared after her, surprised and touched by her assessment of him.

She returned a moment later carrying a makeup bag, hairbrush and a bottle of shampoo. She added those to her clothes and then shut the suitcase. "I'm ready. Let's get out of here."

When they returned to the living room Layla had changed into street clothes, had her bags ready to go, and they all left the house. As Caleb and Portia got into his car and Layla got into hers, Caleb looked around the neighborhood, hoping that nobody was watching them, yet wishing he'd see the perp hiding in the shadows so he could chase him down and smash his face in as payback for the bruised jaw and neck on Portia.

"I underestimated the person who is after you," he said once they were on the road behind Layla's car. "I assumed having somebody with you, anybody with you, would keep you safe." He slammed a hand against the dashboard. "Dammit, I can't believe he tried to get to you with Layla in the next room."

"If I hadn't awakened when I did, he would have succeeded. He would have been on top of me and strangled me to death before I could make a sound." She wrapped her arms around her middle, as if possessed by a deep chill. "Thank God I managed to scream. And when Layla yelled that she was coming, that she had a gun, that sent him back out the window."

They pulled up in front of Layla's house and she got out of her car and walked back to passenger side of his vehicle. Portia lowered her window.

"I would have flat-ironed his ass," Layla said and Caleb was grateful for the sharp burst of laughter that left Portia's lips. It lasted only a second, but it let him know she was going to be all right. He admired the strength she possessed in not falling into hysterics about what she'd endured.

"Thanks, Layla," she said. "I can't tell you how much I appreciate you. You saved my life tonight."

Layla flashed Portia a bright smile. "When this is all over buy me lunch and we'll call it even."

"Done," Portia replied.

Caleb remained in the driveway until Layla was safely inside her house and then he pulled out and headed toward his place.

The drive to his house was silent. Portia leaned her head back and closed her eyes and Caleb tried desperately not to look at the marks around her throat.

She was wrong about one thing. If he'd been in that bedroom when the person had been throttling her, Caleb would have killed him. There would have been no arrest, no judge and jury, just justice done with a vengeance.

The attacker had been stupid to try to get to her tonight when she hadn't been alone. Maybe he'd thought he was big enough, strong enough to take

them both out. Whatever the case, it spoke of a hatred so intense the potential killer was willing to take big chances.

As he pulled into his driveway and turned off the engine, Portia opened her eyes and sat up. "What happens now?" she asked, her voice holding a weariness he'd never heard before.

"Right now we get some sleep and then we figure things out in the morning," he said. He got out of the car and she did, as well, her gaze furtive as she looked around the immediate area.

Caleb grabbed her suitcase from the backseat and then took her by the elbow and led her to the front door. "You'll be safe here, Portia," he said, not a hint of doubt in his voice. There was no way in hell he'd allow anyone to get to her while she was under his roof.

She raised a hand to her throat and nodded as he unlocked the door and ushered her into the living room. "Do you need some ice to put on that?" he asked as he dropped her bag to the floor.

"No, it will be okay," she replied and lowered her hand to her side.

"What about your jaw? It looks like it's going to bruise, too."

"It's all right. I just need to get some sleep. I'm sure things will look brighter in the morning." She tried to smile but tears filled her eyes. "Won't they look brighter in the morning, Caleb?"

Although he absolutely refused to fall in love with her again, there was no way he could see the need, the fear in her and not respond.

He pulled her toward him and she burrowed into him, pressing her trembling body tight against his. He knew the emotion that drove her into his arms was nothing more than fear and the residual horror of what she'd just been through, but that didn't stop him from responding to her nearness.

As he stroked his hand down her back in an effort to soothe her, his head filled with the dizzying scent of her hair, and the warmth of her sweet curves lit a tiny fire in the pit of his stomach.

He held her for only a moment, then stepped back, afraid she might feel his arousal. "Let's get you settled in," he said. He picked up her suitcase from the floor and carried it down the hallway to the guest room.

"It's not much," he said as he set the suitcase on the bed. He followed her gaze as it tracked around the room. There wasn't much to see. A single-size bed was against one wall covered in a drab, brown bedspread. A dresser stood against another wall, the top holding only a small vase with plastic yellow daisies.

"It's fine," she said.

"The bathroom is right across the hall," he said.

"I'll be right back." She left the room and went into the bathroom. While she was gone Caleb pulled

off the bedspread and turned down the sheet. What he wanted to do was lay her down and make love to her until that fear in her eyes was replaced with passion. But he knew that wasn't what she needed. By the time he finished with the bed she came back into the room.

"Thank you, Caleb, for bringing me here. There was no way I could go back to sleep in my room, in my house." She wrapped her arms around her waist and looked at him with those beautiful hazel eyes. "Would you mind sitting in here for just a little while, maybe until I go to sleep?"

He hated the fear that darkened her eyes, the slight tremble of her lower lip. Those lips were made for laughing, for kissing, not for trembling with fear.

"I'll stay here as long as you want me to," he replied.

She took off her robe and laid it on the end of the bed, then slid in beneath the sheet. Caleb turned off the light and then sat on the edge of the bed.

The light from the hallway allowed him to see her face and even though she closed her eyes he saw the tension that rode her features and knew sleep wouldn't come easy for her. "Want to talk about it?" he asked softly.

She opened her eyes and looked at him. "I just wish somebody could tell me why this is happening, what I've done to deserve this."

"You don't deserve this, no matter what you might have done," he replied.

"Maybe this is the end of it," she said as her eyelids drooped with sleepiness. "Maybe after tonight whoever it is will give up and go away."

"Maybe," he agreed, although he was certain that wasn't the case.

He couldn't forget that the person who wanted to harm Portia had taken a chance tonight by attempting to get to her with somebody else in the house. That move smelled of desperation and mindless rage.

Caleb's stomach twisted into a cold, hard knot. As much as he'd like to assure her that he saw a swift and just ending to all this, he didn't. What he did see was darkness and danger and a cunning assailant with murder on the mind.

As Portia drifted off to sleep, fear twisted in Caleb's heart.

Portia awoke with a gasp, for a moment disoriented as she took in her surroundings. Then the events of the night before came crashing back into her mind. The intruder, the hands around her throat, the fight for her life—the horrible visions flashed like a horror movie and all she wanted to do was leave the theater.

You're safe, a voice whispered in the back of her head. She sat up and drew a deep steadying breath.

Her last memory before sleep had overtaken her was of Caleb's presence next to her on the bed.

Hopefully nobody saw him take her out of her house the night before. Hopefully nobody knew she was here. Surely she'd be safe now.

Although there was no clock in the room she could tell by the cast of the sun streaming through the window that it was late. The house was silent and she assumed that Caleb had probably left to go to work.

As she got out of bed her jaw ached and her throat hurt, but it was a manageable pain. She grabbed her robe and pulled it on, then left the bedroom with coffee on her mind.

She'd scarcely looked at her surroundings the night before and so as she entered the living room she gazed around with interest. There wasn't much to see.

In between a nondescript beige chair and matching sofa was a wooden table with a beige lamp. An entertainment center held a television and stereo system and on one shelf was the only thing that indicated who lived here. That shelf contained photos of the Grayson family.

She stepped closer, her heart constricting as she gazed at a picture of Caleb and Brittany. She couldn't imagine the pain the Grayson men were all going through as they wondered what had happened to their sister.

"Good morning."

She jumped as Caleb appeared in the kitchen doorway. "I didn't know you were here," she exclaimed. He motioned her into the kitchen and to a chair at the table. She glanced at the clock on the stove and saw that it was just after ten. "Shouldn't you be at work?"

"You are my work for now," he replied as he poured her a cup of coffee and set it in front of her. "In fact, you're going to be my work until we figure this all out."

She looked at him in dismay. "Oh, Caleb, I don't want to take you away from everything else you should be doing."

His eyes were almost black. "I don't want you alone now, Portia. I want you here with me until we figure out what's going on. Nobody but Layla knows you're here and that's the way I want to keep it."

"But that's crazy," she protested. "You need to be working on finding your sister. You can't just drop everything because of me."

"I can't do anything right now to help Brittany. We've reached a dead end at the moment." His voice rang with a hint of his agony. "Until that changes I can try to keep you safe from harm."

Portia wrapped her fingers around her coffee mug and gazed at him intently. "And you would go to all this trouble for anyone in town?"

"You're not anyone," he said. "You're somebody I

once loved, somebody I still care about although not in the same way I once did. Now what do you want for breakfast?"

"Nothing, I'm really not hungry," she replied. She wasn't sure why his words hurt her just a little bit. After all, she felt the same way about him. He was somebody she still cared about but not in the romantic, loving way she'd once felt.

She couldn't deny that there was a strong physical attraction to him, but that had nothing to do with love. The idea of being cooped up here with him for the next few days filled her with a sense of peace and a simmering sense of anticipation.

She had no doubt that Caleb would keep her safe from whoever wanted to do her harm, but she wasn't sure who would keep her safe from Caleb. And did she really want to be kept safe from him?

"I forgot to tell you, Joe Castle stopped by my house last night," she said in an attempt to banish thoughts of Caleb and sex from her mind.

His eyes narrowed and he sat in the chair next to hers. She caught his scent, a pleasant fragrance of minty soap and his familiar cologne. A flicker of desire lit in the pit of her stomach.

What was wrong with her? Her life had fallen apart, somebody wanted her dead and all she could think about was making love to Caleb. Maybe she was in some sort of shock, she thought.

"What did he want?" Caleb asked.

She took a sip of her coffee, hoping the warm liquid would banish her crazy thoughts. "He wanted to assure me that he had nothing to do with anything that's been happening to me. He was upset that I would even think him capable of doing anything to hurt me."

Caleb frowned. "Maybe I need to have another talk with him, find out where he was at two this morning."

She wanted to protest, to assure him that Joe couldn't have been the person who had crawled through her window, the person who had wrapped his hands around her throat and tried to squeeze the life from her. But she didn't. Other than Caleb and his brothers and Layla, she didn't know whom to trust in the town of Black Rock.

Portia finished her coffee and got up from the table. "I need to take a shower and get dressed for the day. What are the plans?"

"I'm going to get Benjamin to come over and sit for a while and I'm going to head over to Joe's and have a chat with him, then when I get back we'll go out and get some lunch."

"Surely I'll be okay here alone for a little while," she said halfheartedly. She hated taking another deputy away from his duties.

"You might be willing to gamble with your safety but I'm not," he said firmly. "Besides, it's our job to keep the people of Black Rock safe and Benjamin

won't mind hanging out here with you. Now go shower, and I'm going to give Benjamin a call."

Even though she hated that she was being a burden on anyone, she was also relieved that Caleb wouldn't be leaving her all alone. Although she'd tried not to think about what had happened the night before, the truth was that the taste of terror still lingered in her mouth, still chilled her to her bones.

She didn't want to be alone for any length of time. She wanted small talk and somebody else's presence to keep away the fear that threatened to overwhelm her.

She felt better after a long, hot shower and dressed in a pair of white shorts and a bright yellow blouse. When she returned to the kitchen she was surprised to find Caleb already gone and Benjamin pouring himself a cup of coffee.

"Portia, you look surprisingly good for what you went through last night," he said in greeting.

She smiled and shook her head as he offered to pour her a cup of coffee. "No thanks, I'm jittery enough without too much caffeine."

There was definitely something reassuring about a man in a khaki uniform with a gun strapped to his hip. Portia had always liked Benjamin, who was soft-spoken and always pleasant.

"I appreciate you being here, Benjamin. But I hate that I'm taking you away from your job," she said as she sat at the table.

He smiled and sat in the chair opposite her. "This is my job," he replied, "although Caleb has taken this on like a personal crusade. I pity the perp if Caleb gets to him before any of the rest of us. Have you been able to think of anything else that you didn't tell us last night?"

She frowned and shook her head. "It all happened so fast and the room was so dark. I wish I would have thought to try to get that ski mask off."

"You were too busy trying to stay alive," he replied. "Sooner or later whoever it is will make a mistake and we'll get him."

"I hope it's sooner rather than later. I want my life back." And she wasn't at all sure she liked the idea of spending her days and nights here in Caleb's house, where his scent permeated everything and his presence reminded her of a passion she'd only experienced with him.

Benjamin leaned back in his chair and took a sip of his coffee, his warm brown eyes gazing at her over the rim of the cup. "You doing okay?"

She nodded. "I guess as well as can be expected. I'm just frustrated because I have no idea who's behind these attacks. Maybe it's one of those aliens Walt Tolliver is always talking about."

Benjamin laughed and then frowned thoughtfully. "Walt's always been an odd duck, but lately he seems to be more obsessed about an alien invasion than usual. I'm worried about him."

"I know his wife died three or four years ago. Does he have other family?" she asked.

"A granddaughter. Her name is Edie Burnett and she lives in Topeka. I called her yesterday and got her voice mail and left her a message to get back to me, but so far I haven't heard from her."

"It's still early. I'm sure you'll hear from her before the day is over."

"I hope so. I just want some family member to check in with him and make sure he's doing okay."

"You're a nice man, Benjamin. How come you aren't married?" she asked.

He wrapped his large hands around the coffee mug and smiled ruefully. "I'm a one-woman man and I guess I just haven't found my one woman yet. And I could ask you the same question. Why aren't you married with a bunch of your own kids running around?"

"Because I think loving Caleb ruined me for ever loving another man." She stared at him, appalled that she'd actually spoken those words aloud.

"Don't worry, I won't tell him what you said," he assured her with a soft smile. "And for what it's worth, I think maybe it's the same way for him."

"That's not true," she scoffed. "He apparently loved Laura Kincaid. They were engaged to be married."

Benjamin leaned back in his chair and once again frowned thoughtfully. "Whatever he had with Laura,

I don't think it was real love. He didn't have that sparkle in his eyes, that spring to his step that he always had when he was around you. When she left town he wasn't heartbroken. He was just angry. I think Caleb has been angry since the time you two broke up."

She leaned back in her chair and released a deep sigh. "Oh, Benjamin, Caleb's and my past is like a big white elephant in the room. We've never really talked about what happened and why. There's never been any real sense of closure between the two of us."

He smiled at her. "Then maybe it's time to get out the great big hunting gun and shoot down that elephant. Maybe what you two need is a second chance."

A whisper of warmth swept through her, the warmth of possibility. Could she and Caleb somehow move away from their past and find each other again? Was it possible they could have a second chance?

Almost immediately the warmth that had tried to take hold of her was overwhelmed by the chill of her reality as she remembered that somebody didn't want her to have a second chance. Somebody simply wanted her dead.

Chapter 9

It was just after one when Caleb pulled back in to his driveway. He parked the car but instead of getting out he leaned his head forward and released a weary sigh.

He was exhausted. Sleep had been nearly impossible after Portia had fallen asleep the night before. He'd sat on the edge of the bed and watched her as she'd slept and he'd admitted to himself the truth, that he did still care about her deeply.

He would have married Laura and he would have done his best to ensure that they had a happy life together, but his feelings for the pretty blonde had never been the same as what he'd felt for Portia.

He tried to tell himself that his intense attraction

to Portia was based on nothing more than memories of what had been, but he knew that wasn't completely true. In the last couple of days he'd come to admire her inner strength, had been reminded again and again by the people he'd interviewed of what a warm and loving woman she was, how much so many of the other people in town liked her. She was a good woman who deserved a good man, but he refused to consider that he might be that man.

He raised his head and got out of the car, the August sun scorching on his back. The idea of being cooped up with Portia in the house for the next couple of days made him feel just a little bit crazy.

How long could he smell her scent, see that occasional flicker of flame in her eyes, and not explode? How long could he see those lips of hers and not want to take them again in a kiss that left them both gasping and wanting?

More than anything he wanted to make love to her again and almost more than anything else in the world the very idea scared him. Although he was determined to keep her from walking into his heart, he was terrified that somehow she'd manage to slide in beneath his defenses.

He found her and his brother in the kitchen and seated at the table playing cards. "Thank God, you're back," Benjamin exclaimed as he scooted his chair back from the table. "She's a regular cardsharp. She's beat me nine games out of ten."

"Poker?" Caleb asked.

Portia grinned. "Go Fish."

Benjamin threw his cards on the table and stood. "What did you find out about Joe?"

"He left Portia's last night and hooked up with Ann Tyler. They had a few drinks at Harley's and then she went back to his place with him. I confirmed the story with Ann, who said Joe didn't leave his bed all night."

"So you're back to square one," Benjamin said.

"Unfortunately yes," Caleb agreed and fought to keep the frustration out of his voice.

"I'm heading back to the office. Is there anything else you need me to do?" Benjamin asked.

"It's too early for anything to have come in from the bedding we took last night." Caleb shook his head. "No, I guess there's nothing."

"Then I'll see you both later."

As Benjamin left, Caleb turned to Portia. "How about we head to the café for some lunch?"

"Should I be seen out in public?" she asked, a touch of fear darkening her beautiful eyes.

Caleb had been considering their next course of action since the moment he'd left the house earlier. He leaned with his hip against the counter and gazed at her intently. "Initially my first thought was to hide you here, to make sure that nobody knew you were here in an effort to keep you safe."

"And now?"

"And now I'm wondering if it's a better idea to let everyone in town know that you're staying here." He saw her eyes narrow and then widen in sudden comprehension.

"Use me as bait," she said. She reached up and tucked a strand of her hair behind one ear, and he noticed that her slender hand trembled slightly.

"It's your call, Portia. If I didn't think I could keep you safe, then I'd never suggest it in the first place," he said.

She frowned thoughtfully, her gaze never leaving his. "I trust you," she finally said. "Besides, it might be the only way to pull the person out of the shadows. I want this done and over and if this is the way to accomplish it, then I'm in."

"Then let's head to the café," he said. Two minutes in his kitchen with her alone and he was already eager to escape the small confines.

Minutes later they were in his car. "He presumably hung the flyers at night and slammed into your car on a dark, isolated road. Last night he hoped to find you asleep and vulnerable. I'm guessing that as long as you're out in the daylight and surrounded by other people you'll be safe," he said as he backed out of the driveway. "It's obvious he's not crazy enough to make an attack where somebody might be able to identify him."

"What makes you think he'll come after me at your house? I mean, it's one thing for him to think

he could get to me with just Layla standing in the way, but it's another for him to think he can get past an armed deputy to get to me."

"We'll figure it out," he replied. "All I want to focus on now is a big juicy hamburger with extra pickles."

She smiled at him. "Remember that night you and I sat at your mother's kitchen table and you ate a whole jar of sweet pickles and she got so mad because she was going to use them to make potato salad?"

The memory pulled a burst of laughter to his lips. "She was so mad, she said I'd ruined the meal she was going to take the next day to poor Mrs. Whittaker, who was recovering from back surgery."

"You got a bellyache and poor Mrs. Whittaker got macaroni and cheese instead of your mom's signature potato salad." Her eyes sparkled in a way he hadn't seen for what seemed like a hundred years and that sparkle lit a flame of want deep inside him.

He focused on finding a parking place in front of the café. "Things seemed so easy then," he said as he pulled the car to a halt and cut the engine.

"We thought we had the world by the tail," she replied. "We were so young and so ridiculously arrogant."

"Yeah, we were." He opened the car door. "Let's go eat."

He didn't want to share memories with her. He didn't want to think about that time when he'd had

her in his arms, in his heart, and it had felt right. He'd thought he'd known exactly what his future would be with her.

They entered the café and he spied an empty booth toward the back. He led her there and he took the side facing the door. If trouble walked into the café he wanted to see it instantly.

Immediately Linda the waitress arrived at their table with water glasses and menus. "I don't need one of those," Caleb said as Linda started to hand him one of the menus.

Linda smiled. "Let me guess, a big burger with no onions and extra pickles, curly fries and a soda."

"You've got it," he replied.

"And what about you, Portia? You good without a menu, too?" Linda asked.

"I'll have the same thing he's having and just put my pickles on his burger," she said.

"Got it," Linda said and left the booth.

Almost immediately an awkward silence descended between them. Caleb focused his attention around the café, trying to notice if anyone was paying them unusual attention. But he felt Portia's gaze lingering on him and finally returned his focus to her.

"Last night right before the person broke in through my window I was dreaming about prom night," she said.

Shock stuttered through him. Of all the things he'd

expected her to want to talk about, that night wasn't even on the list. "Oh, yeah?" he replied carefully.

She held his gaze with an intensity that stirred more than a little nervous tension inside him. "I was dreaming that we were on the bed in the motel room and you were unzipping my dress."

His throat went dry as he remembered the silk of her bare skin, the way her heart had beat a rapid tattoo against his own. "Why are you telling me this?" he asked, his voice holding a slightly rough edge even to his own ears.

"Because I think we need to talk about it, about us and what happened years ago," she replied. "I don't want it to be taboo between us anymore."

"There's nothing to talk about," he exclaimed. "We dated, we broke up, end of story. Most high school romances don't last. We weren't that different than a million other couples at that age."

"But I have things I want to talk about," she replied.

He glanced around the busy café and then looked back at her. "This isn't the time or the place for any kind of personal conversation. Let's just eat and then if you still want to we can talk about it later."

He hoped that she'd just forget whatever it was she thought she had to say. He didn't want to revisit any of it. There was no fixing it. What was done was done and he didn't even want to think about it, let alone talk about it.

Their lunch was delivered and the awkward silence that had appeared earlier returned between them. Caleb tried to keep his focus on the other people in the café rather than on the woman across from him.

Larry Norwood, the town vet, sat at the counter chatting with Margie Meadows, a tough-talking widow who worked at the convenience store at the edge of town. At a nearby table a bunch of high school–aged girls giggled and shot longing gazes to a handsome young man who sat alone at the counter.

He wanted to tell the young man to run hard and fast from teenage heartbreak, but knew that it was possible that teenage angst was a part of the painful rite of passage into adulthood.

They were nearly finished eating when Tom walked in. He spied Caleb and Portia and approached their booth. "Portia," he said in greeting. "How are you doing today?"

"Better than I was doing last night when you saw me," she replied.

"My little brother taking care of you okay?"

"Maybe too well. I feel more than a little guilty taking him away from other work."

Tom smiled, but the gesture didn't quite reach the darkness of his eyes. "Keeping you safe is his job."

"That's what I keep telling her," Caleb said.

"How're Peyton and Lilly doing?" Portia asked.

"They're great." Joy sparked in Tom's eyes and

despite Caleb's desire to remain alone, he felt a small touch of envy strike him.

"When are you going to make an honest woman out of Peyton?" Portia asked.

The light in Tom's eyes dimmed. "When Brittany is home and can attend the wedding," he replied.

"I pray that happens," she replied.

He nodded and focused back on Caleb. "You'll keep me posted on what's going on?"

"You know it," Caleb replied easily.

With a murmured goodbye Tom left them and sat at the counter next to Larry Norwood. "He's still optimistic that we're going to find Brittany alive and well," Caleb said. "But with each day that passes my hope of that happening is disappearing."

"I hope you're wrong and Tom is right," Portia said and shocked him by reaching across the table and taking Caleb's hand in hers.

Her fingers entwined with his and he couldn't help but think it was a perfect fit. He'd always loved to hold hands with her because her hand fit so neatly into his.

"You can't lose hope, Caleb," she said and her fingers tightened around his. "You have to believe that everything is going to be okay, that eventually we're all going to get a happy ending."

He pulled his hand from hers. "I don't believe in happy endings," he said curtly and got up from the booth. "You ready to go?"

She scooted out of the booth and together they went to the counter to pay. He'd just received his change when he heard her gasp his name.

He whirled around as she grabbed his arm in a death grip. "Dale Stemple," she managed to sputter. "He just went by driving a car. It was him, Caleb. I swear it was him."

Adrenaline pumped through him as he grabbed Portia by the arm and the two of them raced out of the café. This was the break he'd been waiting for, the break they had needed—proof positive that Dale Stemple was here in town.

Now all he had to do was find the man before he accomplished his goal of killing Portia.

Portia's heart pumped a million miles a minute as she jumped into Caleb's car. "Which way?" he asked and she pointed up the street to their right. "What kind of car?"

"It was a black sedan," she replied as she fumbled with her seat belt. The vision of Dale filled her head and created cold chills to creep up her spine. "It has to be him, Caleb. He's the only one who makes sense. None of this happened until he got out of prison."

Caleb started the car with a roar, and with its tires squealing out of the parking lot, they headed in the direction she'd indicated.

"You watch and see if you see the car parked

anywhere," Caleb instructed as he kept his gaze focused on the road ahead.

Portia scanned both sides of the road, seeking the car containing the man who at the moment she feared more than anyone else on the face of the earth. Shops whizzed by and she checked the parking spaces in front of them, but she didn't see the car anywhere.

Had he looked into the café window and seen her with Caleb? Had he followed them here from Caleb's after realizing she wasn't staying in her house anymore?

She clutched the seat on either side of her with her hands, an explosive tension ready to detonate at any moment.

Caleb drove to the edge of the town limits, where the highway cut in and it was impossible to discern which direction the car might have gone. He muttered a curse, slammed his palm down on the dashboard and then looked at her. "Are you sure it was him?"

"Positive." She couldn't fight the shiver that worked through her. "I'll never forget his face. I've thought about him since the moment you mentioned his name to me. It was him. I know it was him."

Caleb pulled a U-turn and went back the way they had come. "I don't know where he was going, but he has to be staying at his parents' house," he said. "I had some of the other deputies check the motel and I know he isn't staying there."

"He must hate me so much. I destroyed his life," Portia said.

Caleb shot her a quick glance as a muscle ticked in his taut jaw. "He destroyed his own life by beating his children and selling illegal guns. You saved those two kids from any more abuse. You should have gotten a damned medal for turning him in."

As he turned a corner the tension inside her rose again. "Where are we going?"

"To the Stemples.'" He held the steering wheel so tight his knuckles were white. "We're going to find out once and for all if Dale is there."

Although that was the very last place Portia wanted to go, she bit her tongue and kept silent. Caleb's hard expression forbade her from speaking any protest. She saw his determination in the slight thrust of his square chin, knew that look well enough to know that nothing was going to stop him from doing what he felt he needed to do.

"Don't be scared," he said as his hands loosened on the wheel.

"What makes you think I'm scared?"

He shot her a quicksilver grin. "Because you're about to claw your way through the seat."

She pulled her hands from the sides of the seat and into her lap. "Shouldn't you call for backup or something?"

"I've got it under control," he replied.

She hoped he did. The only thing that made her

relax slightly was the fact that Dale had been driving in the opposite direction.

When they pulled up in front of the Stemple house, there was no dark sedan parked in the driveway. "Come with me," Caleb said as he cut the engine. "I don't want you sitting in the car all alone."

The two of them got out of the car and she was grateful when he threw an arm around her shoulders as if to shield her from any danger that might suddenly appear.

When they reached the door Caleb gave it a three-knuckle rapid series of taps. He waited only a moment and then knocked again.

"All right, all right, hold your horses," a deep voice came from inside. The door opened and Dale's father, Art Stemple, frowned as he saw the two of them on his porch. "Caleb, Ms. Perez, what can I do for you folks?"

Portia had seen Dale's parents around town since Dale's arrest, but Art Stemple looked as if he'd aged ten years since the last time she'd seen him. Deep lines cut through his face and he looked old and frail.

"Art, we need to talk to Dale," Caleb said. "We know he's in town and I know he's been staying here."

Caleb's words were a lie. They didn't know any such thing. Although Portia was certain that Dale was in town, for all they knew he could be staying

at a friend's place, living in his car or using an alias and staying in a nearby town.

Art's cheeks reddened. "I already told you he wasn't here and that we haven't heard from him since he got out of prison. I don't know why you keep bothering me about this."

"So you wouldn't mind if we came inside and took a look around," Caleb said.

Art's frown deepened as he drew himself up straighter. "I've never had problems with you or any of your brothers, Caleb. I've been a law-abiding citizen all my life, but if you want to come inside and look around then you're going to have to bring me a search warrant and that's all I've got to say on the matter."

Before Caleb could speak again, Art closed the door and Portia heard the distinct click of a lock turning. Caleb once again threw his arm around her shoulders as they walked back to his car.

"There's no doubt in my mind that he's staying here," he said as they pulled out of the Stemple driveway and headed back to Caleb's house.

"How can you be sure?"

He frowned. "I can't be, but I swear when Art opened his door I smelled the faint odor of cigarette smoke. I know Art and his wife don't smoke, but if I remember right, Dale did."

"Like a chimney," she agreed.

"Unfortunately, there's no way I can get a search

warrant without any evidence that he's committed a crime. As far as the law is concerned he served his time and is a free man."

"So what do we do now?" she asked.

"We go back to my place and I make some phone calls. I want to see if I can get Tom to agree to putting some men on surveillance at the Stemple place. Dale might not have been there now, but eventually he'll come back and we can at least bring him in for questioning. We can't lose sight of the fact that it's still possible that somebody else is behind all this."

"I don't think so," she replied. "He's the only one who makes sense. He has a reason to hate me and I wasn't having any problems before he got released from prison."

"Trust me, Dale is at the top of my suspect list."

She could tell that he was far away from her, deep in thoughts of how best to find resolution for her problems.

She'd been disappointed that he'd halted the conversation she'd wanted to have with him about their past. She suspected that with all that had happened since then he probably thought she'd forgotten about it, but she hadn't. Sooner or later she was going to have that conversation with him and admit to him that she might have made a mistake.

I think Caleb has been angry since the two of you broke up. Benjamin's words came back to her. If what he'd said was true, then Caleb's anger implied a lack

of closure and perhaps a depth of emotion where she was concerned that she hadn't known he was capable of feeling.

She glanced at him now, noting the strong line of his jaw, the sensual lips that had always driven her half-insane. She'd compared every man she'd ever dated to Caleb and each and every one of them had come up short.

Within minutes they were back in the house. Caleb immediately excused himself and disappeared with his cell phone into his bedroom.

Portia went into the guest bedroom and sat on the edge of the bed. Even though she'd slept late, the events of the previous night, coupled with the trauma of seeing Dale again, shot a weighty weariness through her.

Maybe she'd feel better if she took a little nap. She stretched out on the bed and closed her eyes, but a million visions danced in her brain.

Memories of prom night and making love to Caleb whispered through her, bringing with them a heat of desire. She wanted him. She thought she might always want him, but he'd made it fairly clear that if they did make love again it would just be sex, not anything meaningful for him.

Could she live with that? One more time in Caleb's arms, one more time feeling his body moving with hers, and not want more from him? She didn't know.

She closed her eyes and a vision of Dale leaped into her brain. Tension coiled tight inside her as she thought of the man she believed wanted her dead.

Dale wasn't a big man. Rather he had the wiry build of a street scrapper. Some women would find him attractive, with his black hair and piercing blue eyes. The few times she'd seen him, what she'd noticed was the sense of imminent explosion that clung to him, an aura that whispered of hidden danger.

She thought of the person who had attacked her in her bedroom. Had it been Dale? It was definitely possible. The person hadn't been huge, although in the dark of night and with the weight of her fear, the person had been as big as a monster.

Where would this all end? Would Caleb and the rest of the team of deputies be able to keep her safe, to get Dale arrested and back in prison where he belonged?

And how long would she have to live her life in limbo? How long before she could get back to her own home, back to her work and the children that she loved?

As she thought of the kids a raw emotion crawled up the back of her throat and no matter how hard she swallowed against it she couldn't dislodge it.

Tears stung her eyes as she thought of the babies who were such an integral part of her life. When was she going to see them all again? When would she be

able to hug and kiss them, tell stories and watch their little faces light up with joy?

A sob welled up inside her, impossible to contain. She rolled over on her tummy and buried her head into her pillow as the tears began to flow in earnest.

Deep, wrenching sobs overwhelmed her. She cried because she missed her kids, because somebody hated her enough to kill her and finally her tears were for the love that had been lost so many years ago.

A soft knock on the door couldn't stop her weeping. "Portia?" The door opened and she was aware of Caleb entering the room.

"Go away," she said, the words choking out of her on a new sob.

"What's wrong?" The bed depressed with his weight. "Why are you crying?"

"Because I feel like it," she said, knowing she sounded childish but unable to help it.

He laid a hand on her shoulder. "Don't. We'll get this all sorted out. Please stop, you know I could never stand it when you cried." His hand moved in a circular motion on her shoulder blade. "What brought all this on?"

"I miss my kids. I miss my life," she said as the tears began to ebb.

"You'll get it back," he assured her as his hand moved lower, stroking from her shoulder blade to the center of her back. "You just have to be strong a little while longer."

"I don't feel very strong right now." As she turned over he pulled his hand away. She sat up and shoved her hair away from her face. "I'm feeling very weak right now."

For a moment his gaze locked with hers and a new tension twisted inside her. He opened his arms and pulled her against his chest. "Then I'll be strong for you," he murmured against her hair.

She melted against his strong chest, for the first time in days feeling one hundred percent safe. His hands smoothed up and down her back and she burrowed closer against him, wishing she could remain in his arms until Dale Stemple was behind bars.

She had no idea how long they remained like that, and nothing else would have happened if he hadn't pressed his lips against her temple, if he hadn't stroked his hand down to her hip.

A fire lit inside her, one that she knew only he could put out. She didn't care about consequences or promises. She just wanted him right now in this very moment.

She leaned back from him just enough to capture his mouth with hers. He met the kiss with eager greed, their tongues meeting and swirling together as fire torched through her.

The kiss lingered until they were both breathless and when he finally pulled away from her, his eyes

glowed with a heat that threatened to melt her into a puddle.

He didn't say a word. He stood from the bed and held his hand out to her. She knew he intended to take her into his bedroom and make love to her. She saw his intention in the depths of his eyes, in the tension that held him rigidly in place.

She had only a moment in which she knew she could halt things before they flared out of control, a single second to decide if she wanted to listen to her head or her heart.

There was really no decision to be made, she thought. With a sweet anticipation winging through her, she stood and took his hand.

Chapter 10

Caleb's heart thundered as he led her down the hallway to his bedroom. He knew what they were about to do was stupid, but he felt drunk and reckless with his need for her.

Somebody's hand trembled but he wasn't sure if it was hers or his own. He felt a tremor through his entire body, a tremor of anticipation.

They reached his bedroom, where the sun shimmered in through the window filtered by the thick leaves of a maple tree just outside. He dropped her hand when they were next to his bed.

For a long moment he just drank in her beauty. Dappled by shadow and sunlight, her eyes shone

with desire and her breasts rose and fell with her quickened breaths.

He was afraid to speak, almost afraid to move, worried that the moment would be shattered and she'd change her mind and walk away.

He held his breath as she stepped closer to him and her fingers went to the buttons on his shirt. She caught her lower lip between her teeth as she began to unfasten the buttons, her gaze focused on the task rather than looking up at him.

Remaining perfectly still, he felt his arousal start in the crash of his heartbeat, the fever that seemed to sweep over him and the uncomfortable tightening of his khaki slacks.

As she reached the last of the buttons, she finally looked up at him as she pulled the shirt from his shoulders and allowed it to fall to the floor.

He couldn't remain still another minute. He pulled her roughly against him and once again took her mouth with his. She tasted like half-remembered sin, like youth and desire. It was a taste he'd never forgotten, would never forget.

As the kiss continued he began to unfasten the buttons that ran down the front of her blouse. He began slowly but by the time he reached the last button his fingers were clumsy with haste.

The blouse fell away, leaving her in her bra. With her gaze still locked with his, she unzipped her white shorts and slid them down the length of her legs.

Both her panties and her bra were plain, no lace or frills, just sturdy white cotton that Caleb found sexier than anything he'd ever seen in his life.

"You're so beautiful. You take my breath away," he whispered.

A blush swept into her cheeks and she shook her head as if to negate his words. That had always been part of Portia's charm, that she didn't recognize just how beautiful she was.

As she got into the bed he took off his shoes, socks and slacks and then joined her. He took her into his arms, relishing his bare skin against her, but impatient with the underwear that kept them from being completely naked with each other.

No old memories of prom night intruded into his mind. He was firmly in the here and now and making love to Portia the woman, not Portia the inexperienced teenager.

As he kissed her again he wound his arms around her and unfastened her bra, eager to feel the weight of her breasts in his palms, taste her nipples as they pebbled with pleasure in his mouth.

He pulled the bra from her and slid his lips down the length of her neck. Her hands wound in his hair, fastening there and pulling slightly in anticipation of his mouth sliding down her body.

She whispered his name as his hands cupped her breasts and his tongue flicked at one of the erect nipples. She moved beneath him, twining her slender

legs with his as he continued to tease and kiss first one nipple and then the other.

Her hands untangled from his hair and smoothed down the length of his back, sparking electric sizzles with each touch.

He was ready to take her, swollen and half-mindless with the need to plunge into her, but in the part of his mind that still worked rationally he knew he'd be cheating her by moving too fast.

"Caleb," she whispered and he raised his head to look at her. "I want us naked," she said, as if she'd read his mind, as if she knew his need.

"Me, too," he said. He rolled away from her and tore off his briefs at the same time she removed her panties. When they came back together his body ached with the feel of her nakedness against his.

He slid his hand up her inner thigh, heard the slight gasp of pleasure that she released as his fingers found her heat.

She arched her hips up to meet him and, at the same time, wound her fingers around the hard length of him. Intense pleasure crashed through him as she moved her hand up and down. She seemed to know just how much pressure to use, what kind of touch evoked the sharpest response.

He wanted, needed to take her over the edge before he found his own release. He gently pushed her hand away from him so he focused completely on bringing her as much pleasure as possible.

As he continued to stroke her intimately, he felt the rising tension in her. Her breathing grew more rapid and she began to moan, the deep, throaty sound increasing his desire. Her legs tensed and she cried out his name as he brought her to climax.

Almost immediately he rolled away from her and fumbled in his nightstand drawer for a condom. He ripped the foil package with more force than necessary and rolled the protection into place.

She was ready for him as he eased between her thighs and entered her. She welcomed him by clutching his buttocks and pulling him deep within.

He closed his eyes and refused to move, afraid that if he did it would be over before it began. They fit together as perfectly as they had years ago and the scent of her, the familiar contours of her body against his, caused a wealth of emotions to crash through him, emotions that had nothing to do with the physical act itself.

He opened his eyes and looked down at her, surprised that her features swam as tears filled his eyes. She, too, had tears glittering in her eyes. He quickly closed his again and began to move his hips against her.

She moaned again and it was a sound that stole all thought from his mind. He stroked into her faster and faster and felt her tightening around him as she once again reached her peak.

As she cried out and shuddered, he climaxed, the force of it stealing every breath from his body. For a long moment they remained unmoving, gasping for breath, then he crashed to his back next to her, the only sound in the room their efforts to find a normal beat of their hearts.

"Wow," she finally said.

"My sentiments exactly," he replied. He closed his eyes for a moment, willing the emotions that had momentarily gripped him away.

He got out of the bed and padded into the bathroom and almost immediately was struck with a thousand kinds of regret.

He washed up and then stood in front of the mirror over the sink and stared at his reflection. "What the hell are you doing?" he asked the man in the mirror.

This was going to end badly. The emotions he felt for Portia scared the hell out of him. Portia was everything he desired and everything he refused to have in his life. Making love to her now had been one of the biggest mistakes of his life.

As always a knot of anger twisted in his gut. Twice he'd put his heart on the line for a woman and both times it had been trampled into the ground. He'd be a fool to put his heart out there again.

Caleb was a man meant to be alone and even though making love to Portia had been beyond wonderful, it didn't change his mind.

He returned to the bedroom and was slightly disappointed that she hadn't gotten dressed but rather remained naked in his bed. He grabbed his slacks from the floor as she sat up and clutched the sheet to her breasts.

"Caleb, we need to talk."

"Why? Portia, what we just did was pretty stupid." He pulled on his pants and refused to look at her, afraid that he would do something even more stupid.

"Funny, I don't feel stupid," she replied.

A wave of shame swept over him as he heard the faint tinge of hurt in her voice. He sat on the edge of the bed and looked at her. She looked incredibly hot even with the faint bruising around her throat and the red area on her jaw. "Sorry, I'm being a jerk."

She smiled. "Yes, you are, but you get points for recognizing it."

"I just don't want you to make this into something bigger than it is," he said and reached down to grab his shirt.

"Don't worry, I'm not planning my wedding announcements. I don't even know if I'll be alive tomorrow. I don't want to talk about the future, Caleb. I want to talk about the past."

"Why? We can't go back and change anything." He tensed, wishing she would just leave it alone.

"You're right, I can't change anything, but I can tell you that I was wrong not to believe you. I was

wrong not to trust you. I allowed gossip and innuendo to screw up my head."

He hadn't realized how much he'd wanted, needed to hear that from her until now. It was as if he'd carried a weight with him for the past ten years and her words finally banished it.

"That night that you were out of town for your grandfather's funeral I went to the café to hang out with a bunch of kids. Jayme Cordell was there alone and I sat in a booth with her. It wasn't a big deal. In fact, I spent the whole night telling her all about you, about how much I missed you and how I knew you were the right girl for me."

He looked toward the window where the sun had disappeared. The forecast that morning had been for hot and humid and with a chance of late-afternoon thunderstorms, but the weather was the last thing on his mind as he gazed back at the woman he'd once loved with all his heart, with all his soul.

"It was nothing but innocent conversation and to tell the truth I think I bored her to death with all my talk about you. When I decided to head home she left the café, too. I walked her to her car and I guess enough people saw us leaving together that they got the wrong impression."

"And I heard the gossip and thought the worst." She frowned, the gesture doing nothing to detract from her loveliness. "It didn't help that I had my mother pounding it into my brain that all men were

alike, that all of them were cheaters. I heard the rumors and instantly believed them."

She left the bed, magnificent in her nakedness, and crouched down in front of him. "I'm sorry, Caleb. I'm sorry that I hurt you, that I screwed things up between us. That's what I wanted to tell you."

He wanted to kiss her again. He wanted to take her back into his bed and make love to her all over again, with the weight of anger gone from his chest. But his head refused to allow him what his heart desired.

"Thank you for telling me that," he said. "And now I need to go make some phone calls and see what we can do to catch the man who wants you dead."

He didn't know what she expected from him, but he could tell by her expression that this wasn't it. She gracefully rose to her feet and moved away from him.

He left the room without a backward glance.

A rumble of thunder accompanied Portia as she left the guest room after she'd showered and dressed. Caleb was on the phone in the kitchen and she curled up on the sofa with only her thoughts as company and her cell phone in her hand.

She needed to call her mother. It was possible that the story of the break-in at Portia's house had made its way around the town. Doris would be worried if she couldn't get hold of her daughter.

She punched in the number that would connect

her to her mother and steeled herself for the conversation to come. "Hi, Mom," she said when Doris answered.

"I was wondering when I was going to hear from you," Doris said. "I heard there was trouble at your place last night. Where are you now?"

"I'm staying with Caleb. He'll keep me safe from whoever is after me."

There was a long pause. "And who is keeping you safe from that womanizing man?"

With her heart still filled with the lovemaking she and Caleb had just shared, with her head still reeling from the brief discussion they'd had, Doris's words aggravated Portia to the breaking point.

"Stop it, Mom," she exclaimed with a harsh tone. "If you can't say anything nice, then just don't talk. I'm sorry Dad left you years ago and I'm sorry you never got over it, but that doesn't mean that all men are bad. Your bitterness has driven everyone out of your life except me, and if you continue, you'll end up driving me away, too."

"I didn't raise you to talk to me that way," Doris said, but her voice was filled with more hurt than anger.

Portia drew a deep, steadying breath. "I love you, Mom, but I won't let you beat up on Caleb or any other man I might date. I won't let you ruin what happiness I might find with your bitterness."

"I love you, too, Portia. I just don't want you to get hurt. I don't want you to go through what I did."

"I won't, Mom. Oh, I might get hurt, but I'll never allow any heartbreak to keep me from seeking happiness again." She softened her voice. "You have to let it go. You have to let your bitterness go, Mom."

There was another long silence. "I'll think about what you said," Doris said grudgingly. "Although after all these years I'm not sure I know how to begin to do that."

"I just wanted to let you know that I'm all right, that I love you and I'll talk to you later." Portia hung up as Caleb came into the room.

"Everything all right?" he asked.

"Yes, I was just checking in with my mother. I knew she'd be worried."

Caleb sat on the opposite end of the sofa from her. "I checked in with Sam McCain. He's been sitting on the Stemple place since we left earlier but there's been no sign of Dale. When Sam's shift is over Dan Walker is going to take over and continue surveillance."

"Maybe he's staying someplace else around town," she said. "Maybe he has a friend or a relative we don't know about."

"It's possible, but I still think he's been staying at his parents' place. Art acted shady, like a man who was hiding something, and I know I smelled cigarette smoke."

"But we still can't be a hundred percent sure it's Dale who is after me," she said.

"True, but it doesn't matter who it is, I just want them under arrest." A rumble of thunder sounded overhead and the room got increasingly darker. Caleb got up from the sofa and went to the window. "Going to storm," he said.

"We could use some rain." She watched him as he remained staring outside. His shoulders were rigidly straight with tension and when he'd come out of the kitchen his eyes had held a guarded expression that brooked no intrusion.

Her heart expanded with an emotion she'd tried to deny, but in that moment she was faced with the truth. She was still as deeply, as profoundly in love with him as she had been years ago.

The knowledge didn't surprise her; it only sent a small edge of pain through her.

She'd hoped that by making love with him again, by telling him that she'd made a mistake before, that somehow he'd profess his love for her, but that hadn't happened. The only thing it had managed to do was broaden the distance between them.

There were moments she felt his love, saw it shining from his unguarded eyes, felt it in his simplest touch, but there was also an inexplicable darkness, an anger in him that she didn't understand.

"Tell me about Laura," she said.

He turned from the window and looked at her, the

dark shutters in his eyes firmly in place. "Why do you want to know about her?"

"Because she's a part of your past. Because I'm curious."

"We dated, we broke up, end of story." He shrugged as if to dismiss the issue, but there was something raw and unbridled in his voice that let her know there was far more to the story.

"She hurt you," Portia said softly. His jaw tensed as his mouth compressed into a thin slash. "You must have loved her very much," Portia added.

A burst of laughter left him, the sound bitter and harsh. "I'm not sure love had anything to do with it." He sighed and moved away from the window at the same time thunder rumbled once again.

He sat in the chair opposite the sofa and gazed at her for a long moment as if deciding whether to say more or not.

"It was nothing but lust that Laura and I initially shared," he finally said. "She told me she wasn't looking for anything permanent and neither was I, so we started dating with no expectations of it going any further than that."

He paused and broke his eye contact with her, instead focusing on the wall over the sofa as the room darkened with the storm overhead. "We'd been dating about four months when she came to me and told me she was pregnant. We'd gotten careless one night and apparently it hadn't been without consequence."

Portia's heart twisted in her chest. Laura had been pregnant? Did Caleb have a son someplace? Maybe a daughter whom Laura had taken away from him? Certainly that would explain the anger Caleb seemed to carry.

"Even though I didn't love Laura, I cared about her and I thought love would come so I asked her to marry me. The idea of being a father blew me away. I wanted that more than anything I've ever wanted in my life." His hands clenched into fists at his sides. "I had it all figured out. I knew I'd be an awesome dad and I could make myself be a good husband."

"So you and Laura got engaged," Portia said.

He nodded. "And as we planned the wedding I committed myself and my heart to Laura and the baby. It was going to be a quick, simple wedding. I wanted it to happen before the baby arrived. Family has always been important to me and I was determined that we'd be a happy family. The wedding was all set for a Sunday afternoon a month away when she came to me and told me she couldn't go through with it."

A flash of lightning lit the room, followed closely by a thunderclap that shook the windows in their frames. Portia jumped but stayed focused on Caleb, whose features were tortured by incredible pain.

"She left and you don't know where your child is?" Portia asked, guessing that's what had happened.

Again that bitter laughter burst from him, shooting

an arrow of sympathy for him through her heart. "No. I wish that's what had happened. She not only didn't want to marry me. She didn't want to have my baby. She aborted it without telling me."

"Oh." The single word leaped to Portia's lips as tears blurred her vision. She couldn't stay on the sofa with him across the room, his heartache so big it filled the entire house.

As she got up and walked toward him, her tears spilled down her cheeks. His grief burned hot and painful in her throat as he stood, his body vibrating with emotion.

She wrapped her arms around his neck, vaguely surprised when he didn't push her away but rather gathered her close to him.

As she began to cry harder he held her by her shoulders and looked at her. "Why are you crying?" he asked.

"For you, Caleb. I'm crying for what you lost and because I wish it would have been me who was carrying your baby. I'm crying because I would have cherished your child."

He pulled her against him once again and outside the storm unleashed itself, pelting rain against the windows as they grieved for what might have been.

Chapter 11

He had to get her out of his house, Caleb thought three days later as he stood at the kitchen window to drink his morning coffee. Portia was still asleep and he relished this moment that held no tension.

Every since he'd told Portia about Laura's betrayal he'd felt vulnerable and had compensated by keeping his distance, which had created a nearly impossible, uncomfortable tension between himself and Portia.

For the past three days they had been in a wait-and-see pattern, waiting for Dale or whoever was after Portia to make his next move, wondering if and when another attack might come.

It was time to take the game to the next level. He knew the person who wanted to harm her was just

waiting for the right opportunity to strike, and tonight Caleb intended to present that opportunity.

It was a dangerous gamble, but he couldn't allow things to go on as they had any longer. She'd touched him too deeply with her tears for him. She'd floored him with her statement that she'd wished she'd been pregnant with his child. She was getting beneath his defenses and he couldn't allow that to happen.

It was time for action, but the risk he was going to take made him feel slightly sick to his stomach. If anything went wrong, if anything happened to Portia, he didn't know how he would ever be able to live with himself.

"Good morning."

He whirled around from the window at the sound of her voice. "Good morning," he replied. "Coffee's made."

She was already dressed for the day in a turquoise sundress that made her eyes more blue than green. She poured herself a cup of coffee and sat at the table. "I think it's time I find another place to stay," she said.

He looked at her in surprise. "And where would that be? Who could keep you as safe as me?"

"I don't know, but we can't go on like this. I can't handle the tension anymore. Besides, I can't stay here forever and it doesn't look like anything is going to happen while I'm here."

"I know, and that's why I think it's time to up the

stakes." He joined her at the table and his heart beat just a little bit faster as he thought of the plan he'd spent half the night going over in his mind.

"Up the stakes how?" She curled her fingers around her coffee cup, as if his words had created a chill she needed to banish.

"I think probably our potential killer has been watching the house. By now everyone in town knows you're staying here, so he knows that, as well. My car has been parked in front the whole time so he knows I've been with you every minute of the day and night. I think whoever is after you is nearby. It's just my gut instinct, but my gut is rarely wrong," Caleb said.

"So, what's your plan?" she asked.

She was so beautiful with the morning light splashing on her features, and a new fear clutched his guts as he leaned back in the chair and eyed her intently.

"After dark tonight I'm going to drive away. Benjamin will sneak into the backyard and hide. He can move like a shadow in the dark and hopefully the perp won't see him taking his place. I'll park and come back to hide in the front yard. We'll keep the house under surveillance and see if Dale or whoever shows up, and if he does we'll have him arrested before he can do anything to hurt you."

"What if he isn't watching the house tonight?" she asked.

"Then we'll do the same thing tomorrow night

and the night after that. Eventually he'll be here to see my car gone and he'll assume that you're here by yourself."

"And if this doesn't work? What if he's too smart to take the bait?" she asked.

"Then we come up with another plan." He leaned forward. "But I think he hates you more than he has sense."

"Gosh, that makes me feel warm and fuzzy," she said dryly.

"Portia, we won't go through with this if you don't want to. I want you to understand that with any plan there's risk, but I believe the risk in this case is minimal." God, at least he hoped the risk was minimal. He'd worked and reworked it around in his head, afraid to go through with it and yet afraid not to try.

She frowned thoughtfully and turned her head to gaze out the window. "I'm so tired of being afraid. I'm tired of my life being on hold." She raised her chin and looked at him once again. "Let's do it. I want this ended and if that can happen tonight, then let's get it over and done."

He nodded and hoped that he wasn't making a mistake. They ate a silent breakfast, each lost in their own thoughts, and then Caleb took the phone back to his bedroom and called Benjamin to set up the plans for the night.

The afternoon stretched into evening with first

Portia pacing the living room and then Caleb restlessly walking from room to room.

At six-thirty they sat down to a dinner of baked chicken and rice that Portia had prepared. Although Caleb's stomach was twisted into too many knots for him to feel hungry, he forced himself to eat.

Portia picked at the food on her plate, as if she had no appetite, as well. He wished he could tell her that everything was going to be all right, that by this time tomorrow night she'd be back home with her world once again as it should be, but he couldn't.

He had no idea what the night might bring. It was possible that whoever was after her wouldn't show up, wouldn't take the bait. Caleb would give it three nights and if nothing happened then maybe it was time they considered other arrangements for Portia.

If she continued to stay in his house he was afraid they'd make love again, he was terrified that he'd forget his own commitment to remain alone. Ultimately he was afraid that he'd be hurt again and he couldn't allow that to happen.

She released a sigh and shoved her plate away. "I can't eat. I have too many things on my mind."

He didn't ask her what things, afraid of what she might say. Since the night they'd made love he'd felt emotions coming off her that he didn't want to feel, knew that it was possible she had fallen for him again.

"Caleb, whatever happens tonight I want you to know that I'm thankful for everything you've done for me," she said.

"You can thank me after we have our bad guy behind bars," he replied.

"I'm almost grateful we had this time together. We needed a healing between us." Her eyes shone bright as she gazed at him. "I hope there has been a healing, that you forgive me for being young and foolish and easily influenced years ago."

A lump crawled into the back of his throat. "It was a long time ago, Portia." He pushed his plate to the side and thought about how devastated, how angry he'd been when she'd cast him out of her life.

He tried to summon that anger now, to use it as a shield against her, but no matter how hard he tried he couldn't get it back. All he felt was a profound sadness and the acceptance that it had never been in the cards that they would be together.

"I don't hold a grudge," he finally said. "I always knew how your mother was and that she had to have influenced your decision to break up with me."

"I can't put all the blame on my mother," she replied. "I should have trusted my heart where you were concerned instead of letting other people get inside my head."

"And maybe I should have fought harder to make you believe me," he replied. "I'm glad we talked about it, but it's just a part of my past now." These last

words were said as a reminder to her and to himself that she had no place in his future.

She got up from the table and carried her plate to the sink and then she turned back to face him. "I'm going to go get my things packed up. If this goes the way we want it to, then I'll be ready to go back home immediately." She hesitated a moment, as if waiting for him to say something, but he merely nodded and she left the kitchen.

He stared out the window where the first edges of dusk were beginning to appear. The shadows at the base of the trees deepened with each passing moment and his heartbeat stirred a little faster as he realized it would soon be time to put his plan into action.

He grabbed his cell phone from his pocket and called Benjamin to double-check things. When he ended the call he once again looked out the window. There were plenty of places for Benjamin to hide in the backyard and still keep an eye on the house. The same was true of the front yard.

There was a full moon that night and the sky had been cloudless all day. The moonlight would aid them but make it more difficult for them to stay hidden to whoever might approach the house. But he was confident they would manage to cling to the shadows and stay out of sight.

It was a remarkably easy plan and no matter how Caleb twisted and turned it he couldn't find any weaknesses that might lead to disaster. If somebody

wanted to harm Portia tonight there was no question in his mind that either he or Benjamin could take him down before he even got close to her.

By eight-thirty, dusk had begun to transform to darkness. Caleb stood at the window and Brittany filled his mind.

An aching emptiness seeped into him at thoughts of his missing sister. Caleb and his brothers and the rest of the town of Black Rock had done everything they could to find her. The case had gone cold and the Grayson men were left wondering what they might have missed, what they could have done differently.

Knots of tension formed in the pit of his stomach. At the moment he felt as if they had already lost Brittany. He couldn't lose Portia, as well. He was aware that this plan had risks, but he believed they were minimal. Dammit, it had to work. It had to flush out the bad guy and give Portia back her life. And then he could get back to his own life, whatever it might be.

Darkness had fallen completely when he sensed Portia behind him. "It's almost time, isn't it?" she asked.

He turned to look at her. "Changed your mind?"

"No, I'm just ready to get this night over with. I want this person in jail and if taking a chance like this accomplishes it, then let's get on with it."

He fought the impulse to pull her against him,

to whisk her back into the bedroom and make love to her one last time. Instead he looked at his watch. "I'm going to move the car down the street about a block. Benjamin should be in position in the backyard by now. I'll park the car and then double back here. Benjamin will watch the back of the house and I'll watch the front and hopefully with my car gone, our perp will believe you're here all alone."

"Okay," she said, her voice reedy with nerves. Her eyes were huge and her lower lip trembled with anxiety.

"Don't be afraid," he said.

She offered him a forced, brave smile. "What makes you think I'm afraid?"

"I can hear your knees knocking together," he said.

She laughed and in that moment she looked more beautiful than he'd ever seen her and a sweet, haunting desire filled him.

Without thought, he grabbed her to him and captured her trembling lips with his own. He knew it was a stupid move, but he wanted one last embrace, one final kiss before he finally told her goodbye.

She wound her arms around his neck and clung to him as if he were her lifeline and for just a moment she felt like his.

He wanted to lose himself in her arms, kiss her forever, but, aware that it was time to go, he reluctantly stepped away from her.

"Lock the door behind me and I'll see you around dawn," he said as he opened the door. "Or earlier if our plan works."

He left the house and heard her lock the door behind him. He'd just pulled his keys from his pocket and unlocked the car door when his cell phone vibrated in his pocket.

He grabbed it and saw from the lighted caller ID that it was Benjamin. "Yeah?" he answered in a hushed tone as he stepped off the front porch.

"Tom called me to a car accident out on the highway. I'm just leaving now, but I wanted you to know I'll be about ten or fifteen minutes late," Benjamin said.

Caleb frowned. He'd assumed his brother was already in place. "I was just going to move my car in front of the Johnsons' place," he whispered in case an intruder was within earshot. "We get called there so often I figured it wouldn't look too suspicious parked there, but now I'll go back inside and wait for you to get into place. Call me back when you're in the backyard."

"Got it," Benjamin replied and then clicked off.

The Johnson family had two teenage boys that were often in trouble and at least once a month they responded to neighbor complaints about loud music or parties. Nobody would think it odd that two patrol cars were parked in front of that house.

Caleb would miss her. The thought stunned him.

In the time Portia had spent in his home she'd filled it with color and meaning. She'd made it feel like more than a place to sleep. She'd made it feel like a home.

He'd liked seeing her first thing in the morning and that she had been the last person he'd see before going to sleep at night. He liked the small talk he'd shared with her, the way her eyes lit up when she was tickled about something.

Yes, he'd liked having her with him—too much. And now he needed her away from him, back to her own life so that he could get back to his.

He'd give this plan three nights and then he'd have to figure out something else. Maybe he could move Portia into the cabin with Jacob. That way she'd be out of his house and still protected.

He couldn't help the small smile that crossed his lips as he thought of how irritated Jacob would be to have his isolation broken by Portia's presence.

His smile lingered only a minute and then fell as he pocketed his cell phone. He was just about to head back into the house when he heard a scrape behind him…the sound of a footstep on the concrete drive.

He started to whirl around but something hard smashed into the side of his head. Pain exploded in a cascade of pinpoint stars as he staggered back from the car.

As he fell, he had a moment of panic, of knowledge that Portia was in danger. He caught a glimpse of

who had struck him, shocked that it hadn't been Dale Stemple or any of the people on their short list of suspects. Then darkness roared out and grabbed him.

The minute Caleb left, Portia headed for the kitchen to make herself a cup of hot tea. She was chilled to the bone and achingly aware of the fact for the next five minutes or so she was here alone and potentially vulnerable.

Before reaching the kitchen she walked over to the bookcase and looked at the photos on the shelves and her gaze lingered on Caleb's picture.

Love filled her, along with sadness. How long would it take her to get over this round with Caleb? It had taken her a long time to get over him when they'd broken up long ago. The truth was she'd never really gotten over him.

She sighed and went into the kitchen to fix herself the tea, hoping that would keep her awake until dawn and Caleb's eventual return into the house.

Caleb. As she filled the teakettle with water she continued thinking about him. She'd spent the last three days fighting the need to tell him how she felt about him. She wanted a second chance with him, an opportunity to get it right, but she was afraid that he didn't want the same thing.

There was no question that he wanted her on a physical level and she didn't doubt that he cared about

her. There were moments when she felt his gaze on her that she thought she saw love in his eyes, but wondered if it was just her wishful thinking.

As she waited for the water to boil she glanced at the clock. It had only been minutes since he'd walked out the door. Was he already in place, hiding in the shrubs in the front of her yard or maybe across the street in her neighbor's yard?

Was Benjamin watching the back of her house, waiting for a potential killer to appear? This night would be endless. And what if it didn't yield the desired results?

She couldn't stay here much longer. Each and every minute she stayed in this house, each and every moment she remained in Caleb's life, would only make it more painful when it was time to say goodbye.

The problem was she didn't know where else to go. She supposed she could stay at her mother's, but she'd never be able to live with herself if she brought danger to her doorstep. There was no way she could battle her allergies to Mr. Whiskers and stay with Layla.

There was no question that she felt the safest right where she was, that she trusted Caleb more than anyone else on the face of the earth to keep her safe. But there was no way to keep her heart safe if she continued to stay here with him.

Her suitcase was packed, but she didn't know

where she would be taking it when she left here. Would she be going home, with Dale or whomever behind bars and the rest of her life stretching before her? Or would she be carrying it someplace else, someplace where Caleb thought she would be safe until this matter was resolved?

Portia jumped as the teakettle began to whistle and moved it off the hot burner. It took her only moments to make her tea and as she carried it into the living room there was a frantic knock on her front door. What the heck? She quickly set the cup on one of the end tables next to the sofa as her heart beat unnaturally fast.

Whoever was at the door couldn't be a threat. Caleb would have never allowed the person to get close enough to knock on the door.

With a horrible sense of foreboding prickling through her she went to the door and turned on the porch light. A woman stood at the door, her features twisted in alarm. "There's a man in your driveway," she yelled through the door. "I think he's hurt." She disappeared from Portia's view.

Was it a trick? Where was Caleb? Her heart beat even faster as she left the door and went to the front window where she could see the driveway.

The beat of her heart felt like it stopped as she saw Caleb's car still in the driveway and his body crumpled next to it. But before she could do anything

else, her front door opened and the woman walked inside.

For a moment Portia didn't recognize the woman who held a knife in one hand and Caleb's set of keys in the other. Her pale blue eyes shone with rage. Then recognition struck and she gasped.

Rita Stemple had gained weight and her light brown hair was now a glossy black. Gone was the browbeaten aura that had always clung to her. Instead she looked like an avenging warrior with murder on her mind.

"Hello, Portia. I'm afraid your deputy boyfriend is a bit under the weather. He had an unfortunate encounter with a baseball bat." Rita took a step into the room.

Caleb! Portia's heart crunched in her chest and she fought an overwhelming sense of despair. Was he dead? Had she killed him? She couldn't think about that now, she thought as she focused on the woman in front of her.

"Rita, what's going on? What are you doing here?" A scream was trapped deep inside Portia as terror spiked through her veins but she tried to keep her voice cool and calm.

"Surely you know why I'm here." Rita's fingers tightened on the knife handle as she took another step into the room and dropped the set of keys to the floor. "You ruined my life, Portia, and now it's payback time."

"Rita, I was obligated to report signs of abuse to the authorities," Portia said desperately. "I could have lost my license if I hadn't reported it."

Rita slashed the knife through the air and Portia's fear was so great it felt as if her heart stopped beating for a moment.

"I'm not talking about those damned kids. I never wanted them in the first place. They were Dale's idea. He's the one who wanted them. They needed discipline to keep them in line."

Portia stared at her, stunned as she realized the truth. It hadn't been Dale who had been abusing the Stemple children. It had been Rita. Wrong. They had all gotten it so wrong.

"It's Dale I care about and you screwed it all up for me and him," Rita exclaimed.

"I don't understand. What are you talking about?" Portia asked. *Keep her talking,* she thought to herself. As long as she was talking she wasn't using that wicked-looking knife.

"I was a good wife while Dale was in prison. I visited him when I could. I wrote him every day and never cheated on him. I got a job and sent him money to make his time easier and I waited for him to get out so we could be together again." Rita's voice was raw with emotion. "On the day he was released I went to his parents' house so we could plan our life together and he told me he didn't want me anymore." Angry

tears filled her eyes but she didn't loosen her hold on the knife.

"If you hadn't turned us in nobody would have known that he was selling illegal guns, he wouldn't have gone to prison and we would still be together. Now he wants to divorce me and move on with his life without me and it's all your fault."

Without warning she lunged toward Portia. Portia did the only thing she could think of. She grabbed her cup of tea off the end table and threw it in the woman's face.

Rita screeched in outrage as the hot liquid splashed her. She started to raise her hands to wipe her eyes and Portia took the opportunity to kick the knife out of her hand, then Portia shoved past her and tried to get out the front door.

She got halfway there when she was tackled from behind. She sprawled to the floor and quickly turned on her back in an effort to defend herself.

Rita had the knife back in her hand and Portia drew her legs up and kicked in a frenzy, trying to keep the blade from hurting her. One of the kicks connected with Rita's stomach and her breath whooshed out of her on a strangled sob of rage.

She slashed the knife downward and Portia rolled to evade the killing stab. She managed to get to her feet and backed away from Rita, who stood and advanced with a murderous intent.

"There's nobody to save you, Portia. You should

have been dead the night I crawled through your window and tried to strangle you." Rita's chest rose and fell with her labored breathing. "You took away the only thing that mattered to me. It's your fault he doesn't love me anymore. You and your meddling ruined my life. And for that you deserve to die!"

Once again she leaped forward and this time she connected with Portia, the knife ripping across Portia's shoulder even though she stumbled backward to get away.

The pain rippled through her and she released the scream that had been trapped inside her since the moment Rita had appeared in the house.

Reeling with the agony, Portia fell to one knee, but quickly got up as blood poured from the wound and a wave of dizziness cast her sideways on unsteady feet.

This was it, she thought as a sob wrenched from her throat and an overwhelming weariness seeped through her.

She knew Caleb had done his best to protect her, but neither of them had ever considered that they were looking for a woman. None of them had thought about Rita. And now Caleb was dead and Benjamin apparently hadn't heard her scream and there was nobody left to save her.

She pressed her hand to her wound in an attempt to staunch the flow of blood and fell to her knees, unable to summon any more strength to fight back.

Fear mingled with grief, not for her own death, but for Caleb's.

"Please," she whispered and she wasn't sure if it was a plea to let her live or one for death to come quickly.

Rita grinned and the coldness in her eyes intensified. "It's time for revenge," she said.

At that moment the front door burst open and Caleb entered like a raging bull. The side of his head was bloody but his expression was cold and determined. He didn't say a word but rather raised his gun and fired. The bullet hit Rita in the knee and she screamed with agony as she fell to the floor.

Caleb rushed to Portia's side as Benjamin came through the door. "Portia." Caleb gathered her into his arms. "Stay with me," he said.

"I thought you were dead," she said as tears filled her eyes. She reached a hand up and touched the side of his head where blood was still wet and sticky.

"You've always known I have a hard head," he replied.

She closed her eyes, knowing she was safe, that the danger had passed. She was vaguely aware of him calling for an ambulance and then she knew nothing.

Chapter 12

"Maybe you can get a big permanent tattoo to cover the scar," Layla said the next afternoon. She'd arrived at the hospital just a few minutes earlier with a huge bouquet of flowers and a package of temporary tattoos.

Portia had received twelve stitches and was going to be released from the hospital in the next few minutes. "Trust me, after all I've been through a scar is the last thing I'm worried about. Besides, I'm not really the tattoo type of woman."

"I can't believe it was Rita. I can't believe she was the one who was abusing those poor kids." Layla shook her head. "It just goes to show you that you can't know what goes on behind closed doors."

"I'm not sure I want to know what goes on behind closed doors in this town," Portia replied.

"Where's your hero? I figured he'd be here with you," Layla said.

"He was here until about an hour ago and then he got a call from Tom and had to leave. I think Tom needed an official report about what went down last night." Caleb had been right at her side when the doctor had stitched her up, and when he'd insisted that Portia remain hospitalized for blood loss and trauma, Caleb had slept in the chair next to her hospital bed.

They hadn't spoken much except to replay the events that had happened while Caleb was unconscious and Portia had been fighting for her life.

It had felt like the fight with Rita had taken hours, but in reality it had all gone down in a matter of minutes. Benjamin had arrived on the scene to find Caleb getting up, having regained consciousness, and together the two men had burst into the house, praying they weren't too late to save Portia.

"He's supposed to be back here to take me home in an hour or so," she said.

"So what happens now between the two of you?" Layla asked.

"Nothing. I go back to my life and he goes back to his." Portia ignored the pain that sliced through her with her words.

Layla released a dry laugh. “The way I see it neither of you have much of a life going for you. I’d kind of hoped you two would have realized you belong together and there would have been a happily-ever-after kind of ending for you two. It would have given me hope that there might be that kind of an ending for me.”

Portia sighed. “To be honest, I’d kind of hoped for that kind of an ending for me and Caleb.”

“I knew it!” Layla sat up straighter in her chair. “I knew you were still in love with him,” Layla exclaimed triumphantly.

“It doesn’t really matter. He’s made it clear a million times that he doesn’t want a relationship and so it’s finished.”

“Well, that sucks,” Layla said with her usual aplomb.

They both turned as Benjamin came through the door. “I was in the area taking a missing person’s report and thought I’d stop in and see how the patient is doing,” he said.

“Who’s missing?” Layla asked.

“Jennifer Hightower. You know her?” Benjamin asked and both Layla and Portia shook their heads. “She’s a twenty-two-year-old and works at the convenience store out on the highway. She didn’t come home last night and her roommate hasn’t heard from her since she went to work at the store last night.”

"She's probably holed up with a boyfriend somewhere," Layla said.

"I hope that's the case," Benjamin replied and then smiled at Portia. "So, how are you doing?"

"I'm fine, ready to get out of here and get back to my house," she said.

"I just thought you'd want to know that Rita had surgery on her knee and is doing fine. She'll be in good shape to spend the rest of her life behind bars." Benjamin stuck his hands in his pockets and rocked back on his heels.

"All's well that ends well," Layla said.

Benjamin nodded. "I had a long talk with Dale Stemple this morning. He wanted me to pass along his sympathies to you. He had no idea Rita was so crazy and he was afraid of letting anyone know he was back in town." Benjamin pulled his hands from his pockets and shrugged. "He seems like a changed man. He told me all he wants to do is get his life back together again and hopefully someday get back custody of his children."

"But wasn't he convicted of child abuse?" Layla asked.

Benjamin shook his head. "No. He agreed to a plea bargain on the illegal weapons charges, but he's always proclaimed his innocence in the abuse of his children."

"But surely he knew it was going on," Portia said.

"The marks that I saw on those kids were evidence of abuse."

"Dale maintains that he was working or out of the house most of the time. He had no idea what was going on with the kids. The only marks he saw on them could be chalked up to regular childhood bruises and bumps."

"And you believe him?" Layla asked dubiously.

Benjamin hesitated a moment and then nodded. "Yeah, I do. Anyway, Portia, I'm glad you're doing okay. It looks like you finally get to return to your life."

"Thank you for everything, Benjamin," she replied.

"I'll just get out of here," he said. "I've got to see if I can figure out where Jennifer Hightower might be." He nodded to both Layla and Portia and then left the room.

"I should get going, too," Layla said as she got up from the chair next to Portia's hospital bed.

"Thanks, Layla. The flowers are beautiful, although I think I'll pass on the tattoos."

Layla walked toward the door and then turned back to her. "Portia, if you really love Caleb, then don't be afraid to fight for him. Tell him how you feel, make him realize the two of you belong together. Love is really the only thing worth fighting for." She turned and left the room.

Portia eased herself out of the bed and went to the

window to look outside as she thought about Layla's parting words.

With her nightmare behind her there was nothing to confuse her feelings where Caleb was concerned. She loved him. It was as simple and as complicated as that. She'd always loved him and she had a feeling she would go to her grave still loving him.

There was no question in her mind now that she had misjudged him years ago, that she'd made the biggest mistake of her life when she'd broken up with him.

And she believed with all her heart, all her soul, that he loved her, too. But could she get beneath the defenses he'd erected around his heart? Could she make him see that they deserved a second chance to find happiness together?

Love is really the only thing worth fighting for. Layla's words were still playing in her head a few minutes later when Caleb walked into the room.

"Hey, how are you doing?"

She turned from the window and smiled at him. "Pretty good. I'm ready to get out of here, that's for sure."

"I just spoke to the doctor and he said you've been released." He walked over and stood in front of her and he took her chin between his fingers and tilted her head upward. "Yes, you definitely look better than you did last night. Your color is back and your eyes are shining bright."

With love, she wanted to say, but she didn't. She didn't want to talk to him about her feelings here in the middle of a hospital room, where anyone could walk in and interrupt what she wanted, what she needed to say.

"I'm just ready to go home," she said as he dropped his hand from her chin.

"Then let's get out of here." He picked up the vase of flowers that Layla had brought and together they left the room.

Thankfully one of the nurses had provided a clean T-shirt for Portia to wear home. The one she'd worn the night before had been ruined, torn by the knife and bloodied by the wound.

They left the hospital and got into Caleb's car. She noticed her suitcase was in the backseat. He'd made sure that she'd have no reason to go back to his house. Her heart sank.

"I talked to Wally this morning down at the garage and he said your car is finished. He'll have it delivered to your house sometime this afternoon so you won't have to go without wheels," Caleb said as he started the engine.

"Great. I think I'll take the next couple of days and finish painting the inside of the day care before I have the children come back. A fresh start sounds like a wonderful idea." She glanced at him, wondering if he had any idea how badly she wanted a fresh start with him.

He kept his gaze focused on the road, apparently completely unaware of the war going on in her heart. Should she tell him how she felt? Or was it smarter just to tell him goodbye and never let him know the depth of her love for him? Could she live with her regrets of what might have been if she didn't say anything at all?

She wouldn't die without him in her life. She'd go on to find happiness eventually, but she would always remember the deputy with the dark eyes and that charming half grin, the boy who'd taken her virginity and the man who had stolen her heart.

By the time they reached her house she knew she had to speak what was in her heart. As she carried the flowers, Caleb grabbed her suitcase from the back and together they walked to her front door.

She unlocked the door and went inside, nervous tension coiling tight in the pit of her stomach. She walked through the living room to the kitchen, aware of him following close behind her.

She placed the vase on the counter and then turned to look at him and in that moment she knew she was going to tell him everything that was inside her. Layla was right, this kind of love was definitely worth fighting for.

"Caleb." Her throat was painfully dry and she wasn't sure where to begin.

"Portia," he replied with a smile. He dropped her suitcase to the floor. "I'm glad this is all over for

you, that your life will return to normal again and you don't have to be afraid anymore. So I guess this is goodbye." His eyes were dark and unreadable.

"It doesn't have to be." She took a step toward him, her legs suddenly feeling wobbly with nerves. "I'm in love with you, Caleb. I want a second chance. I think we belong together."

She paused, watching his features intently. Nothing changed. It was as if he hadn't heard her. She took another step closer to him, now standing close enough to smell his familiar scent, to feel his body heat radiating over her.

"Caleb, say something. I'm baring my heart here." Tears began to burn her eyes. "I love you. I've always loved you and I want to spend my life with you. You're the one, Caleb. The one I want to share my hopes with, the one I want to build dreams with, you're the one I want for the rest of my life."

For just a quicksilver moment a longing flashed in his eyes, but it was gone as quickly as it had appeared. "Portia, I told you all along that I'm not looking for a relationship." His gaze couldn't hold hers and instead he stared down at the floor. "I'm sorry if I somehow led you on."

"You love me, Caleb. I know you do," she exclaimed with fervor. "For God's sake, give us our chance to get it right. Let me into your life like I know I'm already in your heart."

His gaze shot back to her but instead of seeing joy

in the depths of his eyes, she saw despair as he took a step backward. "Don't do this, Portia. Don't make it more difficult than it already is."

"I'm not trying to be difficult," she protested. "I'm trying to make you see that we belong together."

He shook his head and took another step back from her. "We don't belong together. We had our chance and we blew it. I just don't want to put my heart on the line ever again."

She stared at him in stunned surprise. "You know what I think, Caleb? I think I hurt you and I'll always be sorry for that. But I think Laura devastated you."

She paused and fought back her tears. "I was always secretly afraid that I'd become like my mother, afraid to look for happiness, afraid of being hurt again. Caleb, if you embrace your bitterness and keep love out of your life forever then you're going to wind up like her, cold and alone."

He jammed his hands into his pockets. "I did what I promised I'd do. I got you your life back and you aren't in danger anymore. I can't do anything else for you, Portia."

"You mean you won't do anything more for me," she exclaimed as tears fell from her eyes. "Because you're afraid."

"You think what you want. Find a good man, Portia. Get married and have all those babies you

always wanted. I'll see you around." He whirled on his heels and strode out of the room.

A moment later she heard the front door close and knew he was gone. Gone in a way he'd never been gone before. A tight band squeezed her chest in a pain she'd never felt. She recognized it as complete and utter heartbreak and the shattering of dreams never realized.

She sank down at a chair at the table and laid her head in her arms and cried for everything that might have been and now would never be.

"Joey, we don't put our beans up our nose," Portia said as she used a napkin to wipe the baked beans off the four-year-old's nostrils.

"How come?" he asked.

"Because beans don't like noses, beans like mouths," she replied and kissed his forehead before moving to the next child who needed a kiss, a face wipe or help with their lunch.

It had been three days since Caleb had walked out of her kitchen and not looked back. For the first two days Portia had lost herself in finishing the painting of the interior of the day care and getting things ready to welcome back the children.

They had returned yesterday and the last two days had been filled with happy kisses, fierce hugs and enough laughter to keep heartache at bay, at least during the day.

It was only after the kids left and she'd finished eating dinner that the house resounded with a silence that was deafening and the heartbreak became so overwhelming she could scarcely stand it.

It might have been easier if she believed that Caleb didn't love her, if she was certain that he had cast her out of his life because he didn't want her. But she didn't believe that and that was as heartbreaking as anything.

She knew eventually the pain would lessen, that there might come a time when she would think about Caleb and not feel the excruciating arrow of pain through her heart. But she was a long way from that point in time at the moment.

"You okay?" Melody pulled Portia from her thoughts.

"Fine." Portia smiled at the assistant who had been a godsend through the entire ordeal. "I'm just glad to have the kids back."

"They're all thrilled to be back here," Melody replied. "Every day they were at my house they asked when they could come back here and be with Ms. Portia."

Portia's heart expanded with love for all of the children who were in her care. "You need to have some babies of your own, Portia," Melody said.

"Maybe someday," Portia said wistfully. "And now we'd better get the rest of the lunch mess cleaned up

before Joey actually does manage to get a leftover bean up his nose."

The rest of the afternoon passed all too quickly and then it was time for the parents to arrive to pick up their children. As always, when the last child left, Portia felt as if a little piece of her heart had been ripped away.

The silence in the day-care center heralded in thoughts of Caleb. As she straightened books and put toys away, her head filled with thoughts of the man who'd refused to accept her love, who had refused to embrace his own love for her.

Even if he didn't want a future with her, she hoped that someday he could put aside his bitterness and find a life partner, some woman he would love to distraction. The thought of him spending the rest of his life alone made her ache for him.

In the three days that had passed since she'd last seen him, had he thought of her? Did he have any regret in his heart?

She hadn't ventured into town, had been afraid that she might catch a glimpse of him, that she might have to make friendly conversation if they met on the street and she just wasn't ready to do that. Her pain was still too fresh, too raw.

Eventually they would run into each other at a town function or in the grocery store. Eventually she would have to smile and pretend that the mere sight of him didn't break her heart all over again.

She straightened a stack of coloring books and then turned to leave. She gasped as she saw the object of her thoughts standing in the doorway.

"Hi, Portia," he said.

"Caleb." Her heart leaped into her throat at the sight of him. He was clad in a pair of worn jeans that hugged the length of his legs and a white T-shirt that stretched taut across his broad shoulders. He looked strong and sexy and Portia wanted to order him away and throw herself in his arms at same time.

"You're off duty today?" she asked, pleased that her voice sounded normal and not strained with the tension that gripped her.

"On vacation," he replied. He took a step into the room and looked around. "The new paint looks nice, bright and cheerful."

"Thanks. What are you doing here, Caleb? I'm sure you didn't come here just to check out the new paint," she said, a hint of irritation in her voice. If he thought they could be friends now, he was dead wrong. She couldn't be friends with a man she loved, a man who refused to admit he loved her.

He raked a hand through his hair, causing that charming curl to droop across his forehead. He focused his gaze on her and in the depths of his brown eyes she saw a hint of vulnerability.

"I've tried, Portia. For the last three days I've tried hard to convince myself that I did the right thing in walking away from you. I tried to tell myself that

I was the kind of man who could live alone, that I could wrap my bitterness around me and that that was all I needed to keep me warm, but I was wrong."

He made no move toward her and she remained rooted in place, afraid to hope, afraid to believe the reason he might be here. "You're right. You hurt me years ago when you didn't believe me, when you thought I'd cheated on you. And you're right again, Laura made me leery of ever trusting a woman again."

He drew a deep breath and cast his gaze out the nearby window. "I didn't want to love you, Portia. I thought what we had was just a physical attraction. I thought what I felt for you was nothing more than leftover emotions from the past. I thought I was done with love, but I was wrong."

Once again he looked at her and in his eyes was a softness, a deep yearning that made Portia catch her breath. He walked over to where she stood and took her chin between his thumb and finger.

"When we were sophomores in high school I thought you were the cutest girl I'd ever seen. When we were juniors you were not only my best friend, but the girl I wanted to spend all my time with, and when we were seniors I not only wanted you with a man's passion, but I realized how much I loved you, as well. And as a woman you absolutely take my breath away."

He dropped his hand from her face but didn't

move away from her. "I made you a promise a long time ago. I promised to be true to you and love you forever. I didn't break that promise years ago and I don't intend to break that promise in the future."

His words created a song in her heart, a happiness that filled her heart to capacity. "Caleb Grayson, if you don't take me in your arms this minute I'm going to die."

He smiled then, that sexy beautiful grin that never failed to light a fire in her. He pulled her against him and the kiss they shared held all the passion of youth, the joy of forgiveness and a love that she knew would last until the end of time.

When the kiss ended he looked down at her. "You're the one for me, Portia. The only one I want to wake up to in the morning, the only one I want to hold in my arms through the night. I want you to marry me, Portia."

"Yes," she said. "Yes, I want that, too. We'll get it right this time, Caleb."

"It is right," he replied, his eyes shining with promise and the love she'd known burned deep in his heart.

She placed a hand on his cheek. "I want to have your baby, Caleb."

He tightened his arms around her and gazed at her with a hunger that nearly stole her breath away. "I want that. I want you and marriage and babies."

"You already have me. It will take a while to

arrange for a marriage, but we could start working on that baby thing right away," she said.

His eyes lit with a flame that shot fire through Portia's veins. "What are we waiting for?" He took her by the hand and led her out of the day care and toward her house, to the happily-ever-after they were meant to share.

Epilogue

Brittany Grayson awoke with a gasp. She sat up on the cot and an overwhelming despair swept through her. Waking was the worst, when she left happy dreams of family and safety and realized the tiny cell wasn't a nightmare, but rather her reality.

As always when she first awakened she studied her surroundings, looking for any weakness that might provide an escape.

The barn had been transformed into a jail, with five cells complete with strong iron bars. Each cell not only had a bed, but also stainless-steel bathroom fixtures.

The interior of the structure had been soundproofed and in the first couple of days after she'd slept off

whatever drugs she'd been given, she had screamed herself hoarse, but nobody had heard her cries.

She had no idea who her captor was or what he intended to do with her. All she knew was that she'd lost track of the days she'd been here, he wasn't feeding her enough to keep her strong and she was in terrible trouble.

She closed her eyes for a moment and summoned a mental picture of her brothers. Tom with his quiet confidence, Jacob with haunting secrets that darkened his eyes, Benjamin with his easygoing personality and ready smile and finally Caleb with the big heart that he tried to hide. Her heart ached with the need to be with them.

They would be frantic. They would be looking for her, but she didn't even know where she was, didn't know if she was still in the small town of Black Rock. She didn't even know if she was still in the state of Kansas. For all she knew she could be hundreds, thousands of miles away from her home.

Tears burned but she bit them back, refusing to cry. She'd already cried buckets full of tears and crying wasn't going to get her out of here.

The last thing she remembered before awakening in this cell was being in her car and getting ready for a night out at Harley's. She had a little crush on one of the bartenders and had been looking forward to spending the evening in a little harmless flirting.

She'd put the key in the ignition and an arm

had come from the backseat and around her neck, pinning her back to the seat while a hand had pressed a noxious-smelling rag to her face.

Stupid. She'd been so stupid. She'd left her car doors unlocked and when she'd gotten into the car she hadn't thought to check the backseat.

She was a deputy, for God's sake, and she hadn't practiced the first rules of safety. And now she was in trouble, terrible trouble.

She heard the sound of a man's whistling and it shot terror through her. He was coming! Was this the time he would kill her?

She stood from the cot as the whistling grew louder and then the outer door opened and he stepped inside. As always he wore a ski mask to hide his features. What wasn't usual was that he carried an unconscious red-haired girl in his arms.

"Good morning, Brittany." He had a pleasant voice that Brittany thought sounded vaguely familiar but she couldn't place.

He opened the door to the cell next to Brittany's and laid the young woman on the cot. Brittany saw her face and recognized her. Jennifer Hightower. She worked at the convenience store where Brittany often stopped for a cup of coffee on the go.

"What are you doing? Let her go!" Brittany grabbed the steel bars of her enclosure. "You creep! You pervert!"

"Ah, sticks and stones..." He stepped out of

Jennifer's cell and locked the door. "You should be happy. For you, she's company and for me, she's an audience."

"An audience?" Brittany's heart thundered in her chest.

"I do my best work when I have an audience." He pointed to the empty cells. "When I have those full, then the games will begin." He laughed, a horrifying sound of anticipation. "Unfortunately, you probably won't find the game as fun as I will."

He laughed again and then began to whistle as he left the barn and closed the door behind him. A wash of terror swept over Brittany as she sank back down on the cot.

Glancing over at the unconscious woman in the cell next to her, her mind raced. They had to still be close to Black Rock for him to have abducted Jennifer and brought her here.

Impotent anger balled her hands into fists. It was her duty as a deputy to protect and serve the people of Black Rock, but she couldn't help Jennifer. She couldn't even help herself.

She cried out her brothers' names in her head, willing them to find her, to save her. She knew in the very depths of her being that if they didn't find her before those other cells were filled with women, then she would never see them again.

* * * * *

A sneaky peek at next month...

INTRIGUE...

BREATHTAKING ROMANTIC SUSPENSE

My wish list for next month's titles...

In stores from 18th November 2011:

- ❑ Colby Brass & Colby Core – Debra Webb
- ❑ Man with the Muscle – Julie Miller
- & Bear Claw Conspiracy – Jessica Andersen
- ❑ Just a Cowboy – Rachel Lee
- & Her Private Avenger – Elle Kennedy
- ❑ Winchester Christmas Wedding – BJ Daniels

Available at WHSmith, Tesco, Asda, Eason, Amazon and Apple

Just can't wait?

Visit us Online

You can buy our books online a month before they hit the shops! **www.millsandboon.co.uk**

Alana Matthews can't remember a time when she didn't want to be a writer. As a child, she was a permanent fixture in her local library, and soon turned her passion for books into writing short stories and finally novels. A longtime fan of romantic suspense, Alana felt she had no choice but to try her hand at the genre, and she is thrilled to be writing for Intrigue. Alana makes her home in a small town near the coast of Southern California, where she spends her time writing, composing music and watching her favorite movies.

Send a message to Alana at her website, www.AlanaMatthews.com.

For my children

BODY ARMOUR

BY
ALANA MATTHEWS